THE O'FLYNN

LADY BENEDETTA AND THE O'FLYNN

THE O'FLYNN

A Novel

BY

JUSTIN HUNTLY McCARTHY

AUTHOR OF

"THE GORGEOUS BORGIA" "SERAPHICA"
"IF I WERE KING" ETC.

WILDSIDE PRESS

TO

SIR HERBERT BEERBOHM TREE

IN MEMORY OF A PLEASANT JEST

CONTENTS

CONTENTS

THE O'FLYNN

THE O'FLYNN

I

COMING HOME

A MAN leaned on the bulwark of a ship and stared across a squabble of waves at a coast rising from the horizon. The water about the bows was a troubled green, for the sea still churned from the late bad weather. The land that he could now see distinctly without aid of spyglass was green too, with a warmer, kinder color than the hue of the querulous ocean. The man at gaze was indifferent to the bickering of the billows; his sturdy stomach had defied them when they were leaping their loftiest in the past days of angry weather and it now disdained their faded brawlings. The sea might wear what color it pleased for him; it was the color of that distant coast which concerned him, thrilled him, almost troubled him out of his soldierly serenity. Though no mist of tears dimmed the lightness and brightness of his wide blue eyes he knew himself—and was not in the least ashamed of the knowledge—that a very deluge of moisture would drench his cheeks if he allowed the Moses of his imagination to strike the rock of his fortitude.

He had often thought of that home-coming, had thought of it by camp-fires and in trenches, in squalid inn garrets and dreary barracks, on damnable marches and wind-bitten bivouacs, in the houses of princes and the hovels of peasants, in theatres and inns and churches, in brothels and canteens. He had seen it in the gallery of his imagination by many lights according to his moment's mood and his moment's surroundings. Here was the way he had liked best to picture it. He saw himself coming back bulging with booty, his fingers glittering with jewels, his waistcoat pockets ticking with watches and plump snuff-boxes, his breeches pockets overflowing with gold pieces, his bosom stuffed with letters of credit drawn on every bank in Dublin, to make a brave show in his native land. He remembered these dreams now as he looked down with a smile and a sigh at the dingy white coat, ragged, patched, and stained with travel that was flapping about his thighs in the sea-wind, at the boots that would have been the better for a cobbler's helpfulness, at the less than dubious linen visible at his wrists, and at the tarnished lace of the shabby hat he held in his hand to let the sea-wind cool him.

The dingy white coat—plus the boots and the hat and the rest—was the uniform of a captain of Austrian dragoons, of a regiment of dragoons that might indeed be described as in the highest degree irregular and that had ceased to exist almost as suddenly as it had come into existence. It had been a regiment of merry devils while it had endured, a levy of desperate adventurers recruited from every country in Europe. They were gallant gallow-birds, all, that agreed in little else, maybe, but at least agreed in this that it was well to pay heed to the orders of the Irishman who had rallied them and who had so prompt an eye for mutiny and so prompt a pistol for a mutineer. The Turks had known them and hated them and killed them whenever they could, but the score at the end was at least ten Turks to each Christian—let them be called Christians in Heaven's name—ere the last battle before Belgrade reduced the regiment to an insufficient rating of some sixteen men and a captain with three bullets in and two swordcuts on his body.

The traveller smiled at such memories as he regarded his ruined uniform. It was at least a proof relative of past valor; a proof positive of present penury. Perhaps it did not matter much after all. He was coming back to his own again, to what promised at least to mean affluence to a battered soldier of fortune. He would be master of the old castle that had cradled his boyhood, that had cradled his race; he would be the O'Flynn, the latest of so many O'Flynns able to support that dignity with something like splendor in the eyes of an adoring peasantry. He could buy himself a new coat, new hat, and new boots soon enough; the rest of the magnificence should follow rapidly. Such were the thoughts that had tickled him since he got the letter from O'Rourke, the letter addressed to his old quarters in Paris; the letter that found him in Vienna recovered from his wound, and already beating up for a new following; the letter that told him that his father was no more, and that he had the right to style himself the O'Flynn.

Such had been his journeying thoughts. But now—as the ship pitched in the wallowing seas and the sails were strained with the soldier's wind that whistled her to Erin, as the green hills came nearer and nearer under that sky of broken sunlight—he found that he was thinking very

3

little, indeed, of his home-coming, or of his ancestral castle, or his ancient title, or of the country that he had not seen for more than twenty years. His thought kept harking back to one subject and one object alone, and that object was no other than his fellow-passenger, the dainty, daring girl who came on board the *Roi-Soleil* at Brest, who had the captain's cabin as betokened a traveller of importance, and who had kept her room for the better part of that squally voyage, small blame to her.

He had only seen her twice: first, on the day when she came aboard, which she did with a mixture of state and secrecy which amused him that was, happily, easily amused; and secondly, in an hour of calm, when she climbed to the deck and stood for a while against the rail drinking in the sweet cleanness of the sea air. Then he had made bold to speak to her as one passenger may speak to another passenger, especially if one passenger happen to be an Irish soldier of fortune and the other a pretty girl, and had found her courteous and frank and kindly, though she quitted him almost instantly after he addressed her. Now he saw her for the third time, for she had come on deck since his ascent, and was standing but a little way from him, looking, as he looked, at the nearing green hills over the pitching waters that still whispered of last night's storm. There was a bright color on her cheeks, and a bright color on her lips, and a bright color in her eyes, and the O'Flynn was quite convinced that he had never in all his life seen a woman so beautiful, so desirable, so adorable.

He was ruefully aware that he cut but a poor figure in his dingy Austrian uniform, its white coat all smudged and smeared and worn and tattered. But the O'Flynn was never a man to be abashed by such unimportant trifles as a shabby suit, and he turned from where he stood to address the girl with as jaunty a carriage as if he bore the best coat in Versailles upon his back, and were moving among the gallants of the court of the Sun-King. The girl looked at him with a smile that did not deny conversation, and while she smiled the O'Flynn was enabled to get a steadier look at her than the chances of their travelling companionship had yet permitted. She was a tall lass of her hands; even the O'Flynn, who over-topped by a little six feet of humanity, found that there was no need for him to stoop in order to look in other eyes. She carried her fine height courageously; she was exquisitely slim without seeming in any way meagre; her face was as fair and as brave as the day, and the hair that crowned it and framed it was of a pale gold. As for her eyes, they were of that blue which tinges certain skies over certain seas, or certain seas under certain skies—at least that is what the O'Flynn told himself their tender hue suggested; and as far as he was concerned the description was apt and satisfactory. He turned the epithets on his tongue in the Gaelic speech that was native to him: even as he had neared the lady his nimble wit had twisted a couple of verses in her beauty's praise. But he kept his rhymes to himself, being a wiser man than many poets, and when he spoke it was in plain prose.

"It's the dirty weather we've been having," he asserted, with that cheerful acquiescence in a cheerless fact characteristic of a race sustained against adversity by patience and by hope.

The girl nodded, her fair hair flowing in a fine disorder before the audacity of the sea-wind that stung her cheeks to the ruddiness of an autumn apple. "I am no great sailor," she admitted, "but I grew weary of being cribbed below, and the sweet air renews my spirits."

The O'Flynn admired his fellow-traveller mightily. The glimpses he had got of her since she came aboard had fired his fancy, and, now standing face to face with her, he rejoiced to read the patent of a beauty greater than such fleeting vision had permitted him to appreciate. But she was so very beautiful, and so seeming careless of her beauty, that for the moment even the O'Flynn's composure failed and his loquacity flagged.

"Yonder's Ireland," he said, resolved to say something, and thinking of nothing better to say. As he spoke he gave a jerk of his shoulder in the direction of the nearing shore.

The girl's eyes brightened at his words, and she extended her hands prettily toward the horizon. "Yonder's Ireland," she echoed, and her voice was full of joy.

The O'Flynn eyed her meditatively. "Is it your first visit, maybe?" he questioned.

The girl vehemently shook her head, and her blown tresses swayed with her action. "I know Ireland well," she replied. "Ireland is very dear to me; dearer than ever now—" She paused suddenly, as if she felt conscious that for some reason she was saying too much; but she smiled very pleasantly upon her companion in compensation for the unfinished sentence.

The O'Flynn was not to be so put off, however. "Why is the dear land dearer to you now than ever?" he questioned, and even as he questioned there came a change over the girl.

She still smiled, but her smile was less careless than it had been; her manner was still gracious, but her manner was more alert; she looked at the man by her side with wary eyes. "I suppose it's because I am seeing it again," she answered, quietly. "The places we are fond of, like the people we are fond of, grow dearer to us after absence."

O'Flynn noticed something of her change of bearing without understanding it. "And is it long since you've been away from the old land?" he asked, and even with that asking the girl's carriage grew more cautious and her smile more cold.

"Perhaps it seems longer than it is," she said, thoughtfully, and drew a little away from her fellow-voyager.

O'Flynn did not notice the movement, for he had turned away and was leaning over the rail staring steadily at the distant land. "It's twenty years," he said, meditatively, "since I saw Ireland last—twenty good years and more. Sure, I wonder what it will be like after all this age of days. Maybe it's not knowing the old place at all I'll be finding myself." He laughed loud at his conceit, and turned on his elbows to see if his companion shared his hilarity. To his chagrin he discovered that he was alone upon the deck. The pretty lady had taken advantage of his momentary mood of isolated reflection to vanish from his side. O'Flynn swore softly to himself with much intensity of phrase and a Macaronic variety of idiom.

"Now, why is she after disappearing like that?" he asked himself, sourly, and even on the interrogation a survey of his appearance seemed to supply the inevitable answer. A man in such a mean coat, in such ancient

2

boots, a man that carried such a battered hat upon his unkempt head was plainly no very favorable apparition in the sight of a young lady of quality that travelled fine and commanded the use of the captain's cabin. The O'Flynn's ready smile assumed an unfrequent grimness as he surveyed his tatterdemalion habiliments. "I've known many great ladies and many fair ladies look worse clad than this in a taken town," he thought, and then was angry with himself for so thinking, angry at the thought of this fair girl of the ship being in such peril and shame and pain as he had seen women brought to often enough. He gave a whisk of his hand across his forehead as if to banish disagreeable images, and to cheer himself whistled a jigging tune. He lingered on the deck, too, in the hope that the fair girl might appear again. But he waited in vain. For whatever reason, she seemed to have had enough of the open air, enough of his society.

O'Flynn paced the deck; O'Flynn hung over the bulwark to survey the frothing water below and the growing greenness beyond; at every ship's sound he turned toward the doorway that led below. But for all his longing and all his impatience he was gratified with no further speech with the pretty lady, and with no further sight of her until the *Roi-Soleil* had made its way across its measure of waters, until the spires and roofs and chimneys of the Cove had long been countable and recognizable, until the faces of them that thronged the quay were plainly visible, until the vessel ran alongside the landing-place and coiled ropes whizzed through the air, skilfully directed, and the *Roi-Soleil* was made fast to the soil of Ireland. Then, but not till then, did the young lady appear again upon the deck. This time she was quite unapproachable

COMING HOME

for the O'Flynn. She was in the captain's care, and kept
close to his side; and she was muffled up in a hooded
cloak that seemed to envelope her person like an im-
penetrable cloud. He got, indeed, a glimpse of her face
as she crossed the gangway hanging on the captain's arm,
and she vouchsafed him the slightest of slight salutations
that seemed to mark the end of that short sea-chapter in
the life of the O'Flynn. It was with a heavy heart that
he carried himself over the gangway in his turn and set
foot on Irish land.

II

IN MY LORD'S CLOSET

AT about the time when the *Roi-Soleil* was sailing from Brest, my Lord Shrewsbury received a visitor in his official apartments at Whitehall. My Lord Shrewsbury was in his private life a fastidious gentleman that professed to be very choice in his friendships and acquaintanceships. Although those that did not love him qualified him by the name of traitor, he always carried himself as if he not only believed himself to be but was generally admitted to be one of the noblest as well as the stateliest of men. In his political life, however, my Lord Shrewsbury made many strange acquaintances, and it was one of these strange acquaintances that he was waiting to receive and was anxious to receive on the day in question. My Lord Shrewsbury had given instructions that the moment a certain man came to his doors with a certain word on his lips he was instantly to be admitted to my lord's private apartment. He expected the man, so he told his confidential servant, at or about noon, and as the gilded clock in my lord's closet struck the first stroke of twelve the man he was expecting made his appearance.

Lord Shrewsbury's visitor was a man to whom at a first glance an ordinary observer would never think of devoting a second glance. Probably, however, any one devoting such a second glance might be tempted to give a third and thereafter even a fourth. The man was commonplace enough, of middle height, with a countenance that seemed largely devoid of expression; his coloring, his habit, and his carriage were all nondescript; he might edge his way through a crowd and scarcely attract the notice of any one, and yet there was no man in England, with the exception of his Majesty King William III., whom Lord Shrewsbury was not more pleased to see that morning. As soon as the man came he was shown into the private apartment of his lordship and he waited there for a few seconds alone. In those few seconds he stood before the fireplace looking at the clock with an air of listless indifference, the indifference of a man who thought little of life and expected little of life. The indifference remained upon him even when he was perfectly well aware that my Lord Shrewsbury had lifted the curtains that separated the closet from the adjoining room and was standing close behind him. He did not turn or show any sign of knowledge of my lord's entrance until my lord spoke.

"Well, Hendrigg," Shrewsbury said, "you are punctual."

The man turned slowly round with no more than the faintest suggestion of an ironical smile upon his face, as he faced the great nobleman whom his admirers were pleased to call the King of Hearts.

"I am always punctual, my lord," he said, quietly, "that is how I manage to get so much work done."

My Lord Shrewsbury nodded approval. "You are a good worker, Hendrigg," he said, "a better never served the King."

The King of Hearts was silent for a moment looking at

the man before him. Perhaps he was thinking of how often he had spoken of a king and a king's service with no thought in his mind of the monarch from Holland that was now busy in his state apartments but a little way removed from the room in which they stood. Whatever the reason for his silence, that silence seemed to be disapproved by Hendrigg, who, without any pretence of deference, interrupted his lordship's reflections.

".I take it," he said, "that your lordship has business for me now. The sooner your lordship lets me know what this business is the sooner I can put it in hand and, therefore, the sooner it will be finished."

My Lord Shrewsbury smiled good-humoredly at the man's brusqueness. He knew what Roger Hendrigg was, and he knew his worth and was willing to humor him. He bade him to be seated and, seating himself near him at the little table which seemed so large in the small chamber, leaned over the smooth surface and began to give him his instructions in the rapid tones of one that has prepared what he has to say and is able to say it as quickly as possible.

"I have information," Shrewsbury said, "that the wife of James Stuart is striving to do her husband a good turn by sending him over her jewels to replenish his emptied exchequer. Mary of Modena"—Shrewsbury's loyalty prevented him, apparently, from according the titles of Queen and King to his abandoned sovereigns—"Mary of Modena has few jewels left, but those few are rare enough. One is the blue Mogul diamond, another is the great Turkish ruby, and the third is the famous necklace of pearls which she owes to Dick Talbot. Any one of these jewels is valuable enough to raise a small army for James Stuart; the three together, if they come into his hands, could keep him in funds for another six months at least. You will readily understand that it is my wish and the wish of all those who serve his Majesty"—and, as he spoke, he glanced deferentially at the portrait of William of Orange which adorned the wall—"that these jewels should not come into the hands of James Stuart."

He paused for a moment as if expecting Hendrigg to say something, but Hendrigg, having come to listen and not to speak, said nothing. He merely nodded his head, and Shrewsbury, as one that took as well as gave command, went on.

"We are given to understand that Mary of Modena has entrusted each of these jewels to a different lady of her court to be conveyed to Ireland by a different route. The Mogul diamond and the ruby go by ports for which we have already taken precautions. The pearls, we believe, are to travel by way of Brest, and the pearls we leave in your hands."

Hendrigg looked at the speaker with a shade more interest than he had hitherto accorded to his narrative.

"Am I to go to Brest?" he questioned.

My Lord Shrewsbury shook his head, "No," he answered. "We believe they will be conveyed from Brest to Cork by a young lady, the Lady Benedetta Mountmichael, who will be travelling ostensibly to visit her father, my Lord Mountmichael, who has taken advantage of the situation in Ireland to reside for the time being on his Munster estates. It is your task to see that the pearls do not arrive at Mountmichael."

Hendrigg nodded. "Is that all?" he said. "That is easy enough."

13

"Not quite," Shrewsbury continued. "You are then to proceed to Dublin where you are to obtain, under conditions of absolute secrecy and security, an interview with my Lord Sedgemouth."

Here again Shrewsbury paused and scrutinized the face of Hendrigg, evidently expecting to read some surprise on the man's countenance on the naming of that name. His expectation was disappointed. Hendrigg's face showed no surprise, only tranquil acquiescence. Hendrigg uttered no word: he waited, plainly, for further instructions.

"You have heard," Shrewsbury went on, "of my Lord Sedgemouth as a devoted champion of the Stuart cause, as the most outspoken adherent of the misguided dynasty that has happily been dethroned."

"I have heard all that," Hendrigg quietly observed, "but my knowledge of mankind has not convinced me that those that have much loyalty on their lips have necessarily any loyalty in their hearts."

Shrewsbury shot a sharp glance at the speaker, but there was no satirical expression on the man's pale, patient face, whatever satirical thought may have lingered in his mind. Hendrigg had a way of saying what he pleased, but it was not always given to his hearers to be sure of the precise significance of his speech.

"Then," Shrewsbury went on, "it will not surprise you to learn that my Lord Sedgemouth is, in fact, devoted to the service of his Majesty King William."

"It does not surprise me in the least," Hendrigg remarked, dryly. "I have known so many men profess devotion to James Stuart one day that were stanch servants of King William on the morrow that I think my surprise would be to find a voluble Jacobite that was not orange at heart."

Before the plainness of the man's speech, the bluntness of the man's manner, Lord Shrewsbury's lips tightened a little, but he showed no further sign of heeding Hendrigg's remark, and he went on in his usual somewhat labored voice that aimed to give, not merely the meaning, but more than the meaning of each ample sentence.

"My Lord Sedgemouth remains in Dublin waiting for a message from me. You shall be the bearer of that message, good Hendrigg, and thus kill two birds with one stone. When you have managed the matter of the jewels you will go to the Irish capital and put yourself in communication with his lordship. There is, I understand, a tavern in the town, within a stone's-throw of the castle, that carries the sign of the Isle of Cyprus. My Lord Sedgemouth, as advised by me in a secret interview I had with him before he went to Dublin, makes it his habit to frequent this tavern nightly waiting for the message that I have not yet sent him—the message that you are now going to carry."

He paused at the end of this sentence, surveying Hendrigg intently—paused, indeed, so long that Hendrigg, who was essentially a man of action, grew impatient at the delay, and made bold to press his lordship.

"What message do I carry, may it please your lordship?" he asked, with the easy tone of a man who knew himself to be important enough to take liberties with great statesmen. Lord Shrewsbury condescended to smile at the peremptory questioning of the man who was, nominally at least, his servant.

"We live, my good Hendrigg," he said, "in troubled times."

Hendrigg grunted unsympathetically. He knew from long experience that when Lord Shrewsbury began in this fashion he was inclined to be lengthy and also inclined to be dull. My Lord Shrewsbury disregarded the grunt, and continued his harangue.

"We have had the misfortune to be for a time like a rudderless ship upon a troublous sea. The pilot in whom we had trusted"—and here my Lord Shrewsbury heaved a heavy sigh—"that pilot, I say, had deserted us, and we were left, as it seemed, to the mercy of winds and waters. But happily, as you know, we were rescued in our hour of distress by one who now commands the noble vessel that carries the name of England"—here again my Lord Shrewsbury cocked a deferential eye in the direction of the portrait of William of Orange—"and under whom we have every reason to hope that we may reach a favorable haven and ride awhile in safety. But, my good Hendrigg, that pilot of whom I speak, that false, pernicious pilot who abandoned us in our hour of danger, has now turned pirate, and menaces this at present happy realm with all the devices that tyranny can command and treason can assist."

His lordship paused to take breath, and Hendrigg grunted again still more disapprovingly, but my Lord Shrewsbury was too full of his fancy to heed his subordinate's protest, and my Lord Shrewsbury persisted.

"To quit metaphor, my friend," he said, and Hendrigg heaved a sigh of relief as he said it, "by the pilot turned pirate I mean, as no doubt you have already guessed, our late master, James Stuart. That malignant and unscrupulous despot has enthroned himself in Ireland, an island that, unfortunately, is always oblivious of the benefits it has received from the Government of England, and in the capital of that distracted country he continues to levy war against our beloved sovereign and to menace the peace of his loyal subjects. I wish I could say to you, my good Hendrigg, that the efforts of James Stuart are unavailing, are but a beating of the winds, a sowing of the sands, a ploughing of the seas, but, alas! I cannot truthfully and confidently say as much. There is in politics always a chance that the wrong cause may prosper at least for a season, and it is within the limits of human conception that Heaven, for some inscrutable purpose of its own, may allow James Stuart to return for a time to the scene of his former iniquities. That possibility I hope, with your aid and that of my Lord Sedgemouth, successfully to checkmate."

He showed signs of continuing his oration, but by this time Hendrigg's patience was exhausted, and he showed the fact in speech.

"If your lordship," he said, "will kindly tell me what I am to do and what Lord Sedgemouth is to do, in as few words as possible, we shall be nearer to the fulfilment of your wishes."

Lord Shrewsbury winced a little at the directness of the man, but he was too well aware of Hendrigg's value to resent his frankness, so, with a slight shrug of his shoulders, he condescended to be unfamiliarly brief.

"The thing is simple enough," he said, with a faint note of testiness in his voice. "If James Stuart is allowed to continue his career of crime in Ireland his final overthrow is daily rendered more difficult and more costly both in the money of our exchequer and the blood of our brave soldiers. It has occurred, therefore, to certain advisers of

his Majesty"—and here my Lord Shrewsbury smirked
complacently with the wish to make it plain to Hendrigg
that he was the intelligence referred to—"though not indeed with his Majesty's cognizance, because his Majesty's
spirit of mercy and tolerance is familiar to all, that it
would be well for this distracted kingdom if the turbulent
element which is, as it were, centred in the person of James
Stuart, could be removed from the political field."

My Lord Shrewsbury paused again and eyed Hendrigg
sagaciously, and again Hendrigg, surlily resentful of my
lord's eloquence, pushed directly at a purpose.

"Do you mean assassination?" he questioned, sharply,
and frowned slightly as my Lord Shrewsbury threw up his
hands in horrified protest.

"Assassination, my good Hendrigg! Certainly not. The
idea that has occurred to me"—he coughed hastily—
"that has occurred to certain advisers of his Majesty, is
that it might be perfectly feasible to remove James Stuart
from his quasi-regal position in Dublin, to put him, as it
were, out of the way temporarily, to secure from him, by
a little firm if gentle pressure, some form of abdication
which would paralyze his supporters and annihilate his
hopes. I suggested the idea to my Lord Sedgemouth when
he did me the honor to visit me incognito in London a
little while ago, and my Lord Sedgemouth appeared to be
taken with the notion. My Lord Sedgemouth has a cool
head and a cool heart, and I think he is safely to be relied
upon in this adventure. But to carry out our purpose it is
essential that my Lord Sedgemouth should obtain some
appointment very near to the person of the late usurper,
and, as I gather from the communications which I have
received in cipher from his lordship, James Stuart is for

some reason unwilling to grant my Lord Sedgemouth the post he covets. It seems that James Stuart regards my Lord Sedgemouth as too untried a servant for any signal mark of courtly favor, and has bade him prove himself worthy of reward."

My lord paused for an instant. Hendrigg yawned ever so slightly, but the yawn was visible—a distinct hint to the Minister that his hearer was getting fatigued. My Lord Shrewsbury, albeit irritated, took the hint, and gave the course of his narrative the spur.

"It seems," he went on, "that James Stuart has an almost childish desire to bring about the capture of Knockmore Castle, in Wicklow, which is at present held for his gracious Majesty"—and again the eye sought the picture—"by his gracious Majesty's trusted and valuable servant, General Luitprand van Dronk. The place is perfectly safe, the forces that James Stuart has been able to spare are hopelessly insufficient; Van Dronk could hold out for another twelve months with ease. But if James Stuart is wholly incapable of taking Knockmore, on the other hand Knockmore, considered strategically, is of little or no importance to us. It would not matter to us, so far as our campaign in Ireland is concerned, if Knockmore were captured or if General Van Dronk chose to abandon it to the enemy to-morrow. Under these peculiar circumstances it has occurred to my Lord Sedgemouth, and I must admit that his suggestion seems to me not unhappy, that if he could insure the capture of Knockmore by himself he would so ingratiate himself with the Pretender that James Stuart would be bound to accord him his confidence and the post he covets."

Once again my lord paused, and now Hendrigg nodded

approval. Here at least was something tangible, something that might be done, something that perhaps was going to be done.

My Lord Shrewsbury, pleased in spite of himself by the approval of his agent, continued.

"Unfortunately, however, for Lord Sedgemouth's scheme, his undoubted courage is not fortified by military gifts, and even if it were, James Stuart's forces are in no condition to take Knockmore under any generalship. His Majesty's advisers have, therefore, decided to insure my Lord Sedgemouth's success. I have here"—and as he spoke he drew from his pocket a folded paper—"a document signed by his Majesty, commanding General Van Dronk to surrender Knockmore to the bearer on the sole condition, and this is to save the reputation of his Majesty's brave soldiers, that he is permitted to march out with all the honors of war. This paper you are to deliver to Lord Sedgemouth in Dublin, and he will find the occasion to present it to General Van Dronk."

"How," questioned Hendrigg, "am I to make myself known to my Lord Sedgemouth? How am I to insure his confidence in me?"

Shrewsbury nodded approval of the question of the man whom he trusted so deeply.

"That is arranged for," he said. He drew from his finger a heavy gold signet ring and placed it on the table in front of Hendrigg. "This," he said, "is one of the signs agreed upon between my Lord Sedgemouth and myself. Here is another," and he drew from his waistcoat pocket a gold piece that had a hole punched through the middle of it. "This is a guinea of James Stuart," he said, "that we show to be no longer current. The third will

be the paper I have given you. Do you thoroughly understand what you have to do?"

"Thoroughly," Hendrigg answered, simply. For his
own purposes a nod would have been enough answer, but
he saw that Lord Shrewsbury wished him to speak.

"Then I think," said Lord Shrewsbury, "there is nothing more to be said."

"Nothing whatever," Hendrigg agreed, with something
like a show of cheerfulness on his impassive countenance.
Then he rose, collected the ring, the coin, and the paper,
concealed them about his person, and, wishing my Lord
Shrewsbury a brief good-day, passed calmly away from
that august presence. Had he known that he was never
to enter it again he would have passed away as calmly.

III

ALL ON THE IRISH SHORE

IT was whimsical, and he saw its whimsicality at the time, but Flynn's first thought on setting foot on his native shore after a generation of absence was not so much joy at a meeting as a regret at a parting. For he was going to lose his fellow-passenger, and for the first time in his life, a life that was familiar with many meetings and many partings, he felt a queer ache at the heart at the thought that he might never see her again. He could have wished to trace some faint reflection of his own condition on the face of the girl, but any such hope met with no results. She was frankly blithe and cheerful to be done with the sea and the ship, and to walk the earth again and to be going where she was going, though where that was O'Flynn had no idea. She had not volunteered to tell him, and any cunning suggestions he had thrown out were left politely unanswered. A carriage, with a coachman and a pair of footmen, was waiting for the lady on the quay. These, he learned, were to convey her, for temporary rest and refreshment, to the best inn that Cork could offer—after which she was to set upon her journey. With a pleasant smile she gave her hand and he stooped and kissed it with the exaggerated courtesy of the old soldier who essays to play the gallant. Then she got into her coach and the coach rumbled away, and O'Flynn found himself feeling very dismal indeed.

However, he had to be jogging. For him, as his hands fumbled in the empty pockets of his breeches, for him there was no lingering in best inn or worst inn in Cork, neither for him was there any hiring of coach or taking of post. For all that he was going back to claim an inheritance and assume the airs and the position of a country-gentleman, he was for the moment scarcely better off than any beggar by the roadside. The few coins he had that were sewn into the flap of his waistcoat were a sort of sacred depository not to be lightly drawn upon. However, O'Flynn had good spirits; he had breakfasted on board the ship, he had a stout pair of legs and he told himself that Shank's mare made ever the best riding. He knew the way well enough, and it was, therefore, at once with the wish to get to his journey's end as soon as possible — and the wish to forget how sorry he was for the departure of the fair lady—that he set out on his road.

He had soon crossed the city, which, as he noted, had changed little, if at all, during the years of his absence, and found himself in the open country. The day was bright, with a brisk and pleasant wind that had been strong enough to dry the night's rain and leave the road neither muddy nor dusty. It was not a good road—there were no good roads —but O'Flynn had tramped worse in Silesia and Poland and the low countries, and birds were calling to birds in the hedges and the sky was of a dappled blue and O'Flynn's spirits tempted him to whistle as he trod sturdily along the causeway. He occupied himself as he walked for a while with thoughts of what he would do with his inheritance; then, having arranged these matters fairly to his satisfaction and having decided upon the mode and color of his necessary new clothes, he fell to the making of songs in the Gaelic, a pastime he had always delighted in and had indulged often enough in less congenial conditions.

It was just noon and he had covered something like a third of his journey when his stomach suggested to him that it was time to dine. For this suggestion he was not unprepared, as he had consigned to the huge pockets of his white coat a small store of provisions from the ship's table made in a skilful moment of forage during the temporary absence of the captain. He sat down by the roadside under a blackthorn hedge and prepared to enjoy himself. It was not a very sumptuous meal—a thick slice of ham, a chunk of cheese, and a corner of bread—but it served the turn, and he made merry over it; and it had not to be eaten dry, for he produced from the other pocket of his coat a handsome, if sadly battered, old silver flask from which he assisted himself to several libations of a ripe old brandy. Then, the rage of thirst and hunger satisfied—so he quoted Homer to himself as he sat—he produced a clay pipe from an inner pocket and tobacco from his waistcoat and filled and smoked and assured himself that he was as happy as a king. Yet all the time he knew he wasn't; all the time he knew that he was really thinking of the girl, and her dark hair seemed ever to be fluttering across the sunlight.

He was disturbed in his meditations by the sound of wheels, and, looking up, from his lazy ease, he saw a coach approaching him and in another second realized that it was the coach, the coach that carried the lovely lady. It came by him slowly enough, rumbling along the road with its great heavy wheels, and the two footmen hanging on behind jolting about like puppets over the nodosities of the road. But the fairy princess was inside it and she looked out as he scrambled to his feet and nodded in reply to his military salute, and so the coach went on and turned the road and was out of sight, and there stood O'Flynn staring after it with his heart in his mouth. So she was going his road. Where was she going? If he only knew. For a moment he thought of keeping the coach in view. Then he reflected this would be like spying upon a woman who had plainly shown no intention of letting him know either her name or her whereabouts, and he resisted temptation sturdily. The more sturdily, perhaps, because for all his length of leg and quickness of motion he could not hope to overtake a coach drawn by such good horses on a road so viable.

He did not resume his seat by the roadside, but strolled leisurely along the winding road, busy with his thoughts. The pretty lady — would she be more interested in him, he wondered, if she knew who he was, the O'Flynn of O'Flynn, returning after twenty-odd years of foreign service to the castle of his ancestors—to dwell there in ease and plenty and splendor? He wished he had been able to tell her this; this was what he had meant to tell her, but then the pretty lady had given him no fitting occasion to unbosom himself. His reflections drifted into the past, to his earliest memories. He thought of his grandfather, a grim, old gentleman in rusty black whose only pleasure was to talk of the days when he had served King Charles against his rebels, and whose reputation among the countryside people of being a miser had filled his childish mind with awe and horror. He thought of his parent, Phelim O'Flynn, the flagrant opposite of his grandsire, always gorgeous in tawdry raiment, always noisy with drink, always riotous, quarrelsome, truculent. O'Flynn remembered with a sigh that if he had feared his grandfather he had undoubtedly hated his father.

To Flynn O'Flynn the year 1623, which numbered among its less important incidents the whimsical Spanish escapade of Baby Charles and Steenie and the publication of the works of Mr. William Shakespeare, dramatist, in folio form, was chiefly remarkable for the fact that it was the birth-year of Phelim O'Flynn, who was destined by providence to become, thirty years later, the parent of Flynn O'Flynn. Phelim O'Flynn, unlike his parent, was no cheese-parer, no skinflint, no putter-by. He never cast a prophetic eye upon the financial heavens and weighed the possibility of a rainy day. It was ever light come and light go with him, and Desmond O'Flynn, his father, saw with a sour eye the waxing prodigalities of his son. Desmond O'Flynn had always been a near man—the only one of his race of whom such a characteristic could be recorded —and the fact caused no little comment, satiric and pathetic, among a peasantry who had come through generations to regard the O'Flynn as a kind of symbol of all the lavish instincts of man. They accounted for his misfortune in various ways, attributing it for the most part to some whimsical vengeance of offended fairies, and they rejoiced with simple sincerity when they saw that Patrick O'Flynn differed from his thrifty sire and returned to the honorable traditions of the stock. Desmond O'Flynn in no wise shared their rejoicings over his son.

When Desmond O'Flynn came to his death it was found that he had left to Patrick the estate, together with such a sum of money as, according to the calculations of the prudent man, would maintain the castle in decency and comfort for a careful heir. The hopes of vast wealth which had been entertained by Phelim were gravely dashed when the Dublin lawyers explained to him the position of affairs. The common belief of the peasantry in Desmond O'Flynn's great wealth was rudely shaken by this revelation, and in order to justify a former credulity a present imagination set itself to work to establish a legend. It was whispered about the countryside that Desmond O'Flynn, being a miser and having a miser's mania, had hidden the treasures he was reputed to possess in some obscure nook of the castle. This belief troubled Phelim O'Flynn little enough in the beginning. He had money enough and to spare, for it never occurred to him to carry out the old man's suggestions and attempt to live upon the interest of the money left to him. He squandered his capital with a prodigal excess, entertaining boon companions of both sexes from Dublin, and seeming to take as much pleasure in making his money spin as his father had in making his lie quiet.

Flynn O'Flynn was a bit of a boy when his father came into the inheritance he seemed so determined to get out of. Between him and his father there had never been much love lost. The father had loved but little the wife that was Flynn's mother, the mother that Flynn never knew, and his distaste for the woman that gave him an heir he carried on with undiminished vigor to that heir.

Flynn passed an unhappy youth in Castle O'Flynn, the victim of his brutal father's tyranny, the butt of his father's coarse friends, his only pleasures the wild life of the countryside, and his only companions the peasants, who saw in him an honorable descendant of the O'Flynns of old time. Flynn learned to fish and ride and climb and fight. He grew tall and broad and strong, and with his growing strength there grew a hatred for his surroundings and a resolve to have done with them. This resolve came to a head on one wild day when the taunts and bullyings of a drunken friend of his drunken father ended in a brawl in which Flynn handled his tormentor so roughly that he lay on the floor like a dead man, and even Phelim O'Flynn, drunken and ruffianly though he was, was sober enough and wise enough to keep his hands off his angry offspring.

That evening Flynn O'Flynn said good-bye to the only man in the castle for whom he cared at all, to Conachor O'Rourke, that had been his grandfather's servant, and was now his father's servant, and that always had loved Flynn well. A little later Flynn had left Ireland and thereafter came twenty-odd troubled years of wars in this country and that, of the wearing of one uniform after another, and the following of flag after flag, of tramping across Europe and tasting all changes of luck as is the way of the vagabond soldier of fortune, now with a pocketful of money gratifying every taste, now with empty purse and empty belly grinning cheerfully in the face of adversity. As Flynn tramped the Cork highroad and recalled the life that lay between his leaving his native land and this, his return to it, he smiled as he thought to himself that there lay the material ready to his hands for as good a volume of memoirs as another. He pictured himself seated at ease in Castle O'Flynn, eating of the best and drinking of the best, and employing his leisure in the compilation of his biography. Absorbed in the agreeable fancies thus stimulated, the briskness of his footsteps began to flag and his pace on the roadway had diminished to a mere leisurely walk, when that occurred which dissipated his dreams and quickened his speed.

IV

ROGER HENDRIGG came out of the hot air of my Lord Shrewsbury's closet in Whitehall into the cooler air of the street with a sense of physical relief. He was naturally impatient of the slow processes of men like the great nobleman he had just quitted, who, from long force of habit in the affairs of state, took ten times the time needful for the conception of a plan and twenty times the time needful for its execution. Yet he felt no resentment at the fact that it was his place in life to serve masters of slower wits and lamer resolution than himself.

He knew very well that he was one of the men that help to make history; and he knew, equally well, that history would never take any notice of his pains. He was well content, however, as men of his kind have been content through all the ages and will be content so long as the ages endure, to know that he did the things that were of moment, and to rejoice in the doing of them for the mere sake of the doing. Certain men are sent into the world from time to time with the special aptitude for secret service, for employing the arts of the spy, for playing the part of the mysterious and malignant busybody who causes plots and counterplots and who is ever the treacherous instrument ready at the hand of unscrupulous governments.

29

Roger Hendrigg had been the active hand and the active brain in many plots in the course of his mysterious life. He had served under many ministers and had always served his employers with fidelity. He had no principles, no politics, no creed; his only impulse was the joy of the creature that, working in the darkness, accomplishes facts for which he will never be given credit, but which are often potent enough to upset a government or to change a dynasty. There were very few people in the world who knew Roger Hendrigg as Roger Hendrigg; there were certainly hundreds who knew him in some one or other of the many impersonations under which it had been pleasant as well as profitable to him to play his part in the capping and mining of the politics of his time. His career, which had begun not very long after the Restoration, had originally been passed in the service of a Stuart sovereign, but as time went on and that sovereign and all that that sovereign represented began to grow unpopular, Hendrigg's intelligence as well as Hendrigg's interest drifted in the direction of the hostile party. It seemed to him, judging as he did of things about him from the level of a burgess, but with an intelligence vastly above the understanding of the average burgess, that the Stuart cause had run its course in England. He calculated that those that represented change and protest and revolution were likely to be winners in the struggle that he, scarcely less acute in his perceptions than the strongest thinker of his time, foresaw to be inevitable.

With the first dawnings of conspiracy against the supremacy of James II., Roger Hendrigg gravitated naturally toward the new impulses and the new forces, and those that were directing those impulses and those forces found in him an instrument rarely adapted for their purpose.

HOW ROGER BECAME SOME ONE ELSE

What Roger Hendrigg's past was no one knew except Roger Hendrigg, but at least it had served to equip him with a substantial education, with a remarkable experience of men and things, and with a knowledge little less than extraordinary of the workings of the middle-class mind of his time. Those that knew him and trusted him declared that he could gauge to a nicety the exact effect of any political movement upon the common thought of the hour, and predict to a nicety what effect would be produced upon the average man of the average city by any particular act of Parliament, proposition of a minister, or hinted usurpation of a kingdom.

It may well be understood that such a servant found great favor in the eyes of the masters who used him; and the favor was never misplaced. If, indeed, Roger Hendrigg had no political principles or beliefs, he was invariably faithful to those that employed him for so long a time as the particular job upon which he was engaged might take, whether that job were the assassination of a statesman, the fomenting of a conspiracy, or the furtherance of a parliamentary election.

Master Hendrigg was one of those politic persons who from a long experience of the world's affairs was a firm believer in the possibilities of chance. He knew well enough that the best-planned scheme, ably thought out by able men and wisely entrusted to able fingers, might be blown into no more than a little handful of dust by some trifling accident too trivial to be other than unexpected. No less was he confident, being as he was a fatalist, that in the carrying out of well-planned strategies, fortune or fate or chance or luck, or whatever it may please the player of the game to call the whimsical goddess who pre-

sides over such desperate adventures, was often likely, out
of kindness or malignancy, which ever it might be, to give
the enterprise a friendly jog with the elbow when that
friendly jog was least expected. When, therefore, Master
Hendrigg quitted the presence of my Lord Shrewsbury,
though he was well aware that what he had to do was simple
and straightforward and well devised, and it scarcely taxed
his cool head, heart, and hand to carry the thing through
to a befitting conclusion, he yet had at the back of his
brain a kind of feeling, which he would have disdained to
call superstition but which was superstition none the less,
that something, anything, might happen, would happen to
assist him toward his end.

As he snuffed the kindly May air that came blowing toward Whitehall from the green spaces beyond, a feeling
stole over him vaguely akin to that which the poet ex-
periences on a May morning, a feeling of hopefulness hard
to translate into words. After all, in his own way, Master
Hendrigg was a poet if he had ever chosen to argue the
point and to insist that the word, in its modest Greek sense
of maker, might justify him in claiming at least the simu-
lacrum of a laurel wreath. At least let this be recorded of
him as so much honor to his memory, that he loved his
work as much as any rhymer of rhymes that ever serenaded
the muses and dreamed of a forehead whose baldness was
obscured by the bays.

As it happened Master Hendrigg's feelings or premoni-
tions or fancies, whatever you may please to call them, did
meet with what, at least, seemed to him to be a justification. For when he was making his arrangements for his
journey to the port from which he was to take ship for
Ireland, he found at the post-house that another person

was no less anxious than he to proceed with all convenient speed to Ireland. This person pleased Master Hendrigg mightily, for Master Hendrigg's point of view was that of a man to whom all human beings were either more or less endurable masters or more or less serviceable tools. This person was a plump, middle-heighted, smooth-faced, smooth-haired, foolish, self-satisfied individual who seemed to consider himself of an infinite importance, and made as mighty a bustle about the furtherance of his journey as if he were going to take command of his Majesty's forces. Such a man was a natural delight to a philosopher of Master Hendrigg's grim disposition, but his natural delight was soon changed to the liveliest interest, though he showed no sign of it, when he learned what the fussy individual's purpose was and his point of journey.

The fussy individual made no secret of himself, of his business, or of the many little matters that concerned him. His name, it appeared, was Peter Morford. He had been for some time drawer in the service of a vintner in the Minories that kept a tavern by the name of the Bishop's Head, and he was now journeying to Ireland and to Dublin on a special purpose. That purpose was to serve a kinsman of mine host of the Bishop's Head, one Master Bandy, of the Isle of Cyprus inn in Dublin, hard by Dublin Castle. Master Bandy was an Englishman that, for this reason and that, had adventured his career as a publican in Dublin, being lured thereto by the tales he had heard tell of the drinking capacities of the nobility and gentry of the island. The Isle of Cyprus inn was a tavern that had once been a great nobleman's house. When that great nobleman came to evil days at the end of a dissipated fortune and a dissipated life the great house had been, in the fulness of time, bought up by Master Bandy, who had converted the stately mansion into an amazingly stately tavern.

This mansion tavern, or tavern mansion as you please to regard it, boasted a cellar as unexplored as a virgin forest of the Amazon. Master Bandy, wisely anxious to set his cellar in order, had written to his kinsman to send him a competent assistant to perform the necessary task, and Master Bandy's kinsman without hesitation had laid his hand upon the shoulder of Master Peter Morford and bade him go forth and do the good work with a light heart. Such was the simple tale this Master Peter Morford told in far less simple language to the secretly amused but outwardly impassive Hendrigg on the early stages of their journey together.

To many a listener the narrative would have seemed tame and unattractive enough, but to Master Hendrigg it was fuller of fascination than the mystical murmurings of the sibyl. Already he recognized that the strange divinity of chance had again unexpectedly come to his assistance. He felt the sudden exultation that an unarmed man might feel, so far as it was ever possible for Master Hendrigg to feel unarmed against occasion, if when face to face with some desperate and well-accoutred enemy, an unseen friend had thrust a trenchant weapon into his hand. Already, as Master Morford babbled, fat and garrulous, the gray face of Master Hendrigg softened into a kind of enthusiasm, and his voice, on the few occasions on which he spoke in approval of what Master Morford had to say, had something in it of a whimsical, if sinister, tenderness. Master Hendrigg might almost be said to caress his companion with his looks, while in his mind a scheme was swiftly shaping, a scheme of transmutation protean in its simplicity.

HOW ROGER BECAME SOME ONE ELSE

Never did strange sea god shift himself more swiftly into shape of bird, or beast, or fish, than Master Hendrigg in his mind's eye saw himself metamorphosed into the personality and credibility of Master Peter Morford. While, with unmoved face, he waited upon the garrulity of the Londoner, his inner man was chuckling grimly over the tragic comedy that he was rehearsing at all points. The first act of that tragic comedy ended in his complete ingratiation into the good graces of the travelling drawer. The second began at the midway break in their journey. Here they had to seek lodging for the night, and here Master Hendrigg, professing very truly an intimate acquaintance with the place, as indeed there were few towns in England with which Master Hendrigg could not boast intimate acquaintance, advised the somewhat bewildered citizen to seek shelter, not in the more recognized hostelry of the place whose charges, so Master Hendrigg averred, were intolerably high, but in a place dear to his own heart where good fare was to be obtained at little cost.

Master Morford, already delighted by the interest shown in him by the intelligent stranger, was further delighted by a suggestion that promised to spare the purse in his pocket, and he readily agreed to follow. Master Hendrigg led the way from the main street of the place through highways and byways to an obscure inn in an obscure quarter of the town. Though this inn had an unattractive outside it showed pleasant enough within; a word or two from Master Hendrigg was sufficient to insure the privacy of a room, a clean cloth, a commendable supper, and some wine of a quality sufficient to content even such an authority as Master Morford. If the landlord of the inn had any previous acquaintance with Master Hendrigg he was at least at pains to betray no sign of familiarity. He took Master Hendrigg's orders with the deference due from a host to a traveller who knows his way, and in a little while the two newly-made friends were seated opposite a well-spread table sharing a sound meal and sound wine.

Under the influence of food and drink the little Londoner expanded. He babbled on with red cheeks that increased their color as he named over with loving alacrity vintage after vintage. His eyes shone with a benign brightness as he enumerated and extolled this year and that year with its crudescence of Burgundy and its plentitude of Bordeaux, while his tongue seemed to trip with ecstasy over the vine-grown slopes of the Neckar and the meadows of the Moselle. He talked of champagne and he chuckled as he talked, he rolled in his mouth the rotund name of opulent Hungarian liquors—the special drinkings of popes and emperors. One would think that the cellar in the Minories had been packed with all the barrels and all the bottles of all the wines that had ever run since Noah so unfortunately forgot himself, so eloquently did the little man dilate with waving hands and eager jerkings upon the wealth of liquors that could be commanded by the patrons of the Bishop's Head.

While he spoke, spinning his words till the very air seemed to take to itself a kind of vinous heaviness and the cloudy smoke to wreath itself into the imagery of a Bacchic procession, all the while the hard, set, expressionless face opposite watched him with a watchfulness that was not betrayed by any hint of intelligence in the closely lidded eyes or the tightly set mouth. Anacreon would have rejoiced over the babble of Master Morford unless, indeed, the tragical tale be true which Athenæus hints at, that the poet whose name is most linked with the worship of the grape was, in point of fact, a water-drinker. If ever Master Morford talked to the clients of the Bishop's Head with so eloquent a praising of his master's wares it might well be hard to understand why that master could be persuaded to part with him. The little man babbled, the little man gabbled, his companion plied him home and hard. The smoke wreaths thickened, the glasses emptied and filled as if by magic, and Master Morford grew more voluble and Master Hendrigg more taciturn as the evening wore its way. Spurred by his own eloquence Master Morford passed from praises of his master's cellars to praises of his master; and, by a not illogical transition, from praises of his master to praises of himself. He began to expatiate, as is the way of a certain kind of sot, upon his own gifts and ambitions. He sketched for himself a golden future in Dublin—how he would ingratiate himself with Master Bandy; how he would in time supplant that worthy in the command of the Isle of Cyprus; how he would even, in the fulness of time, marry Master Bandy's daughter, albeit he had no knowledge whatever either that Master Bandy was blessed with a wife or blessed with a family.

So he rattled on till his rattling fell into stammers and stutters and the more voluble he sought to be the more incoherent his utterance became, and all the while the changeless face opposite showed itself fitfully through drifting volumes of smoke, quiet, watchful, seemingly wholly uninterested, wholly unamused. At last Master Morford's feeble wits surrendered wholly to the fumes within him and without him and he was for dropping on to the table in a sodden stupor. But he had with him a careful companion that would permit of no such folly. He

37

was firmly lifted from the table, firmly supported on his feet, firmly propelled toward an opened door. Nothing in the world, so the voice of his guardian assured him, would be better for his condition than a couple of gulps of night air.

Master Morford, with those words drumming in his ears, staggered out into the quiet of the night, staggered a little way down the quiet of the street, staggered a little further into the loneliness of the country lane all sweet almost to sickliness with the dew-drenched perfume of the June flowers, and there, as Master Morford, a little sobered by the coolness of the sweet air, began to find his speech again and to renew to his quiet companion his confidences of the glorious future before him, an unseen hand was lifted. There was a gleam of something bright across the night and in that instant Master Morford's intoxication and Master Morford's ambition came forever to an end.

Many days after a hedger and ditcher plying his trade came across a body lying in a deserted field and imperfectly covered by hastily gathered branches from the adjoining trees. The body was already in a state of decomposition; nobody in the neighborhood was missing; the times were wild and inquiries seemed superfluous. When the unknown corpse was buried with such hasty rites as the local parson found leisure to administrate, a traveller, that called himself by the name of Peter Morford and that carried letters of introduction from the landlord of the Bishop's Head, in the Minories, was already many days advanced on his journey to Dublin.

V

AN ADVENTURE ON THE ROAD

THE O'Flynn's meditations and reflections were suddenly disturbed like the pleasant stillness of the morning by the sharp report of a pistol-shot. The sound seemed to come from no great distance and it instantly stimulated Flynn to an alacrity that was curiously in contrast with his previous manner of indifferent strolling. Although he was somewhat cumberously equipped for running with his high boots and his long and flapping coat, he made his way along the road at a pace that many a younger and less heavily accoutred man might have envied, and as he ran he was spurred to new efforts by the faint sound of voices in altercation carried to him by the breeze.

The road he followed turned off, perhaps a quarter of a mile ahead, sharply to the left. On turning this corner, Flynn saw what had happened, saw, perhaps, in some degree what he had expected to see. The coach that had passed him but a little while ago was partially in the ditch, behind it one servant, with a very pale face and with very uncertain fingers, was doing his best to bind up the wounded arm of his fellow. On the box the coachman, as pale as his crimson jowl permitted, was, or affected to be, doing his utmost to restrain the startled and struggling horses. By the open carriage door stood the young lady

of Flynn's dreams, looking a little angry but not at all
alarmed, holding a pistol in her hand. Opposite to her on
a big horse sat a man whose face was hidden by a half
mask and who was in the act, when Flynn arrived within
seeing distance, of returning his discharged pistol to the
holster. The man was saying something to which the
woman replied. What the words were Flynn was unable
to hear. Coming as he came, neither man nor woman
saw nor heard him, and before Flynn could call out the
girl had lifted her pistol and fired steadily enough at her
opponent. Flynn was not, perhaps, altogether surprised
to find that she missed her mark, and in another moment
the fellow had swung himself off his horse and had got the
girl by the wrists, squeezing them till she was compelled to
drop her weapon. As he did so he called to the girl in a
voice which now Flynn could hear very well, and which
he knew to carry an English accent, that he would do her
no hurt if she were quiet, but that he must have what she
carried. But even as the man spoke thus, and even as the
pistol fell from the girl's fingers Flynn had joined the battle
and flung himself upon the assailant, who immediately released the girl to deal with his new adversary. The grip
of Flynn's right hand was upon the fellow's throat, slowly
squeezing the breath out of him, and Flynn's left hand was
busy in preventing his enemy from getting at the pistol he
sought for from his belt. So they struggled for a few
seconds, and while they struggled the young lady, with
admirable composure, picked up the fallen pistol and, going to the carriage, proceeded to load and prime it again
as coolly as if such things as these were of daily occurrence
with her.

Flynn's antagonist was a powerful man and he struggled

hard, but there were few men as powerful as Flynn and none that Flynn had ever encountered with anything like the gripping power of Flynn's fingers. In a few seconds all that was visible of the man's countenance under the mask was of a disagreeable blue color. Then Flynn, taking the pistol from the relaxing fingers, fetched him a tap under the left ear which knocked all consciousness out of him. Flynn left him a huddled heap in the roadway and turned to salute the lady, whose composure in rearming herself he vastly admired.

"Madame," he said, raising his ragged hat with the gallantry of an Amadis, "I fear I owe you some apology for interfering in a business which you were evidently perfectly capable of managing for yourself."

The young lady laughed. "I am not so sure of that," she said, "as I was five minutes ago. I thought I was all right with that pistol in my hand and him an easy mark on horseback, for I am a good shot, I would have you know, and you must not take this day's blunder as a test of my skill. But there, I don't know how I missed him, and I think it might have gone badly with me but for your appearance, for the most of my men were of little service."

By this time the two footmen had come forward; he that was wounded, he that had made the only attempt to defend his mistress, dangled an arm that could be of little further immediate use. Flynn saw that his wound was bandaged in proper military fashion and then, with the aid of the other footman and the coachman, he got the carriage out of the ditch and squarely planted on the highroad again.

Now, while they were thus engaged the highwayman, that had lain for a while very quiet on the road and wholly unheeded by Flynn, came of a sudden to his senses again, and, seeing how busy his enemies were, took advantage of their business to make his escape. His horse, that had shown no alarm at the recent scrimmage, was peacefully nibbling grass at a little distance off. The highwayman rapidly scrambled to his feet, ran to his steed, sprang into the saddle and was off before Flynn could make any attempt to delay him. As he vaulted into his seat his mask swung loose for a moment and gave Flynn the barest glimpse of a smooth, expressionless face. But in an instant the highwayman had adjusted his vizard again; in another instant he was thundering along the road as fast as his horse could carry him and was soon out of sight.

Flynn, careless of the fellow's fate, took advantage of his resuscitation to insist on escorting the young lady to her destination. At first she protested, assuring him that there was no further cause for alarm, but Flynn was persistent and carried his point. He was permitted to ride by the young lady's side in the coach; he was permitted to learn the young lady's name. She was Benedetta, daughter of Lord Mountmichael, the English Irishman who owned the big Norman castle that Flynn remembered so well in his boyhood. To Mountmichael then Flynn journeyed as happy as if he had been promoted to a command of irregular cavalry, rejoicing in himself and the sunlight and the rough country road beneath him, finding everything under the sky delightful because a bright girl's face smiled on him by his side.

What they talked of Flynn could scarcely remember when it was over. It sufficed that they talked, or that she talked, and Flynn would have wished with all his heart that the journey had been, not to Mountmichael, but to Jerusalem at the shortest.

However, they reached the outskirts of Mountmichael soon enough and there the Lady Benedetta was all for having O'Flynn to come in and meet her father and partake of their hospitality. But Flynn, with an eye to his dirty coat and his shabby boots, was resolute in refusal. He would pay his respects later, he promised; for the moment he had pressing business which compelled him to push on. He was thinking to himself as he spoke thus of the visit he would pay to Mountmichael and the fine clothes he would wear, and the dashing appearance he would cut, which would, he hoped, obliterate the recollection of his present ragged appearance. So he saluted the lady very profoundly and the coach rumbled through the gates of the park and Flynn watched it out of sight, and then turned on his heel and made his way briskly by roads unchanged from their old familiarity in the direction of the dwelling of his sires.

That dwelling he would behold in a few minutes; when he had topped that little crest of hill he would see before him the old place. He pictured it to himself as he had seen it last, comfortable and solid and populous, a human hive of guests and servants, a place where a rude plenty was always dispensed and the air was genially heavy with the odors of wines and meats and the fumes of perpetual punch. That was what he thought to see again as he forced his pace to the top of the incline. What he saw was a strangely desolate and dilapidated building, hideously unlike the picture he had been forming in his mind. The walls were blackened in places by the ravages of a fire that had done much to throw the northern part of the building

43

into ruin, but save for these marks on the blackened masonry no other sign of the existence of fire came from the apparently abandoned pile. No spirals of kindly smoke hinted to the returned traveller that the habitation, if habitation it could still be called, contained a hearth and was prepared to afford any kind of welcome.

With a strange amazement and despair in his heart, Flynn hurried forward and shouted as he sped in the hope of attracting the attention of the occupants of the castle, for even in that instant of bitter disillusion he could not quite banish his long fond belief in the presence of the jovial troop of servants he remembered in his youth. For a while no answer was given to his vehement "hulloa!" but at length when he was within a few yards of the main door, which lay open, a whimsical figure appeared upon the threshold. This was an old man wretchedly clad in an ancient suit of faded homespun, who stared for a moment stupidly at the advancing figure. Then, as Flynn halted in front of him, the old man lifted up a pair of grimy hands to heaven and exclaimed in a trembling voice: "Lord be praised! It's the young master."

The gentleman in the *Arabian Nights*, that on a memorable occasion shattered the day dream of magnificent voluptuousness by overturning his basket of glass, was scarcely more astounded by the contrast between the kingdom he had builded in his dreams and the shattered fragments of that kingdom which lay about his feet, than was the O'Flynn when, standing before the ruined walls of his ancestral home, he learned from the lips of his ancient retainer the tragedy of its fall. In lieu of the comfortable inheritance he had looked forward to, of the habitable mansion in which he was to dispense a generous, if not too lavish, hospitality, stern necessity offered him nothing more than a huddle of stone walls very imperfectly proof against the inclemencies of the weather—a larder so lean that it might almost be regarded as non-existent, vacant wardrobes, and an absolutely empty cellar.

How these misfortunes had come to pass for the moment failed to touch Flynn's imagination. The hard, abiding, and inexorable fact remained, that he, in his ragged uniform and shabby boots, was almost too well dressed and well endowed a gentleman for the lordship of the squalid castle which his approaching fancy had gilded with all the gold and the jewels of Aladdin's palace. He whistled a marching air thoughtfully as he looked at his ragged domestic, who eyed him furtively through a shock of russet hair with a look in which love and admiration and awe were whimsically blended. It was plain that to this poor creature the dingy Austrian uniform was a fairly magnificent garment and that a man who came to the doors of Castle Famine, for so it seemed the place was called in the neighborhood, in so handsome a habit was a gentleman to be regarded with reverence, even if he did not carry the almost sacred title of O'Flynn.

While Flynn was thus musing bitterly on the jests of the jade Fortune who had brought him across the breadth of Europe in pursuit of the glittering bubble that had now burst before him, two other figures came slowly onto the scene from round the corner of the dismantled keep. One was a tallish fellow in a bottle-green coat of respectable antiquity that needed more care than its owner bestowed upon it. The other was a shortish, thick-set fellow in a rusty-brown surtout. The two men, who were both smoking pipes, came to a halt and stared with astonishment at the stranger who stood by the doorway, then, hastily laying down their pipes upon a convenient window-ledge, they hurried forward with peremptory demands to O'Flynn to name himself and his business.

O'Flynn turned to his henchman. "Who are these gentlemen?" he asked.

The old man threw up his hands with a wail of despair. "Heaven forgive us," he cried, "it is no fault of mine. Sure these are the bailiffs."

At the utterance of a word always ominous in the ears of an Irish country - gentleman, O'Flynn turned to the two men who were now standing quite close to him and very sternly demanded their business. The men, flushed with the insolence of their little office, replied in a manner that was vastly displeasing to Flynn. They flourished a writ in his face and informed him in a kind of chorus that he was no longer the master in his own house. For the moment Flynn forgot what that house and the master of it meant. His old affection for the place, his old memories of it rekindled in a rage, and in another instant he had taken the pair of bailiffs by the scruffs of their necks, a bailiff to each hand, and was hammering their heads together with a vehemence and a vigor that afforded him a temporary satisfaction it was far from giving to his astonished victims. Then suddenly Flynn's sense of humor prevailed over Flynn's sense of indignation and, releasing the two men as vehemently as he had seized them, he gave each of them a push which sent them squatting on the stones of the court-yard, and, resting his palms on his hips, he laughed loud and long at the situation in which he found himself.

VI

CASTLE FAMINE

THAT gaunt portion of the habitable earth which
was known as the banqueting - hall of O'Flynn
castle was perhaps as cheerless a place of human residence as was known, even in the desolated Ireland of the
time. It had been once, undoubtedly, a spacious and
well-furnished apartment, but time, neglect, and indifference alike had worked their ways upon it until it became
its present hideous mockery of former splendor. When
Desmond O'Flynn was young, his native penuriousness
denied to an already dilapidated mansion those cares
and sustentations which would have kept its youth green.
Phelim O'Flynn, when the place passed at last under the
command of his itching fingers, cared not a curse for the
way he was housed, so long as he had enough to eat and
enough to drink, and a drunkard and a Bona Roba to
keep him company. When toward the end of his ill-
spent life all means of raising the wind seemed denied him,
his sodden fancy was stirred to a last flicker of vitality
by a sudden belief, or half belief, in the country-side
legend of the buried treasure of his father. His efforts,
crude, clumsy, and stupid, to discover the whereabouts
of this fairy gold only added to the tragic degradation of
the dwelling which had been the house and the pride of

47

THE O'FLYNN

so many generations of O'Flynns. With crowbar and pickaxe in hand the degenerate O'Flynn would stagger from room to room of his ancient mansion, boring a hole here, and breaking through a partition there, and rooting up a stone elsewhere, till the traces of his vandalism were apparent in every room of the insulted dwelling-place. On one occasion, in the course of his drunken investigations, he contrived to set fire to the castle and the conflagration was with difficulty stopped after lasting injury had been done to the old place.

Since Phelim's death, and the descent from Dublin of the brace of bailiffs upon the ruined residence, the old man, Conachor O'Rourke, that was left the sole guardian of the ancient pile, had not the heart—even if he had possessed the power—to arrest the march of destiny. Perhaps, because it was the largest room in the castle, the banqueting - hall seemed most to show the injuries of Fate. The great door, through which generations of O'Flynns had passed to the outer world, and through which the outer world had advanced to taste the hospitality of generations of O'Flynns, creaked boltless and lockless upon its uneasy hinges. The huge fireplace, that had so often been the centre for gatherings of the wit and chivalry of Munster, yawned now, an empty mouth, long denied through the severest pinch of winter the consolation of a leaping flame. The windows that had once been splendid with stained-glass carrying the escutcheons of the ancient Milesian families that had been privileged to inter-marry with the O'Flynns, were now for the most part dismally lacking in glass, and the ragged wisps of the lead settings swayed lugubriously in the abandoned spaces. One window had not merely lost all the glazing and framing that had served to make it a shelter against rough weather, but had been, besides, so damaged by the fire that was Phelim's handiwork that it grinned, a huge fissure, in the side of the wall, and the young trees from without thrust their branches through the aperture and adorned with the tender green of their leafage a room that sadly needed adornment. Where costly curtains once had been suspended, now filthy conglomerations of cobweb hung. From their blackened frames the few family portraits, that still disgraced the walls, drooped ominously to their doom. The hangings, that had been meant to hide the masonry of the walls, swung dismally in tattered strips that made the nakedness, they pretended to conceal, more flagrant and more shameful. A lusty struggle of grass competed successfully with the attenuated fibres of a rotting carpet to conceal the stonework of the floor, and everywhere dust and dirt displayed themselves in triumphant assertion of the progress of decay.

The only cheerful thing in the cheerless apartment was a rude whiskey-still that had been installed on the spot where the semi-regal chair of the head of the house had been wont to stand, and the only occupant of the desolate room was the attendant spirit upon this still. This was a man who, if his figure was suddenly viewed from behind, might almost have passed for a boy, so slender was his form and so erect his carriage; but when observed from the front might, to judge by the wrinkles that lined his face and the elf locks that fringed his forehead, be of a greater age than the Judaic patriarchs. This strange creature, who seemed to be half gnome, half leprechaun, was seated by the strange engine of his distillations watching with an intent eye the process, while at the same time he scraped an ancient fiddle and teased it into utterance of a plaintive Irish air. It was one of those strange Celtic tunes to whose intense suggestion of pathos the irony of mankind has been pleased to associate words of a grotesque good-humor.

As the elfin creature continued his fiddling, muttering the while to himself the words of his ditty beneath his breath, the echo of his song was caught up outside by two dissimilar voices, and in another moment the peace of the distiller was disturbed by the entry of a pair of men. The new-comers, similar only in the fact that each carried a fishing-rod, were whimsically dissimilar in all beside. One was tall and gaunt with something of the air of a weather-beaten seaman, and this one was habited in a faded blue coat incompletely sprinkled with brass buttons that gave him something of the appearance of a fairly successful ostler or an unsuccessful highwayman. The other, that was as unusually short as his companion was unusually tall, carried a cinnamon-colored coat that covered him almost from his ears to his heels, and this, with the quaint sharpness of the features that peered out of the monstrous collar of the garment, gave him a curious appearance of some strange and misshapen bird. As they came into the room the old man, that was busy distilling, looked up from his work and questioned the intruders.

"Have you got anything?" he asked.

The one in the blue coat shook his head lugubriously. "Devil a thing," he said, and deposited his fishing-rod in the corner with the air of a man that, having tried for greatness and failed to achieve it, is content to repose on his own sense of small superiority.

CASTLE FAMINE

The little bird-like man in the brown habit was less philosophical. He stood in the centre of the hall and attempted to explain in a thin, high, chirpy voice, that would more than ever have suggested a bird-like association to any intelligent ornithologist. "You see," he said, "you see, Mr. O'Rourke, it's this way. If you happen to be a city-bred bailiff you're liker than not to make a poor sportsman when first you try your hand with a line and fly."

The blue-coated gentleman, whose name was Gosling, seemed now to consider that his companion had occupied the rostrum of eloquence long enough. He interposed, and his interposition was quite in the grand manner. As he spoke, he extended a condescending hand in the direction of his dwarfish colleague, as if he intended thereby to convey a sympathy with his friend's excuses and, at the same time, a justification of himself.

"There never was, if I may say so, a genteeler service of a writ in all Dublin than mine. I tell you it's hard to say which was the more pleased with my gentlemanly carriage, my employers or my victims—but there, to nab a debtor is one thing, to land a salmon another."

The little distiller turned round upon his stool and faced the bailiffs with a snarl upon his face that recalled an angry cat. "All very true, gentlemen," he snapped, "all very true. But unless such truths can fill your empty bellies, you are likely to go fasting the day."

The brown bird of a bailiff piped dismally. "Is there nothing in the damned place at all ?" he asked.

O'Rourke shook his head. "Whist! don't be using bad names to the ould place. Sure there's some bread I made myself—and there's whiskey I made myself, and there's many a saint now in heaven that had no better fare for his daily supper."

For a moment silence fell upon the dejected company, then the little man in the brown coat looked at the big man in the blue coat and chirped an interrogation that was meant to be jocular and that seemed to fail dismally in the effort. "I don't think I was meant to be a saint, was I, Gosling?" he asked.

The man in the blue coat shook his weather-beaten head. "Our trade was never framed for the shaping of saints, bedad!" he asserted, and the brown bird nodded wisely to his words.

But their conversation was rudely interrupted by the fury of O'Rourke. Rising on his thin legs he screamed shrilly at them: "What should the likes of you know about saints, you murdering, yellow-bellied Protestants. Heaven forbids us to think of your ugly skulls with halos on them."

Something in the vehemence of the passion of the little man seemed to impress the Dublin bailiffs; that so small a body could contain so great a rage, had in it something of the surprise that is suggested by the cataclysms of Nature—an earthquake, a water-spout, or a tornado.

The little man of the brown coat protested. "Easy, now, Mr. O'Rourke, easy— Remember we're your guests." He meant to be conciliatory, but his conciliation was wasted upon the angry O'Rourke.

"No guests of mine, by the Holy," he protested, "nor of my poor master, neither. You can go back to Dublin this instant minute and never a tear from either of us over the dirty backs of ye."

Bailiff Gosling of the blue coat waved large red hands of deprecation. "You know very well," he pleaded, "we can't go back to Dublin. Here we have got to stick till our little claim on the estate is paid."

Coin put in his word to enforce his comrade. "When we know who they are to be paid to, Scotch James or Dutch William," he said.

The old man shook his head aggressively. "Then, God help you," he growled, "you'll be sitting here till the Doom-Bell rings, if you are allowed to live so long. Who is going to pay the debt I ask you, for all it's only ten pounds? Is it the young master?"

The legal gentleman in the blue coat waggled a solemn forefinger at O'Rourke and uttered a pronouncement with a judicial gravity founded upon the manner of a distinguished Dublin judge. "He that inherits property, inherits the responsibility thereof. That's sound law, my lad."

O'Rourke shrugged his shoulders and plied the bellows industriously, bringing the pale glow of the brazier to a lively blaze.

"It may be sound law in the Four Courts," he said, "but it's the devil's own nonsense in Castle Famine. Sure, the young master hasn't a sixpence, nor a shilling neither. Poor gossoon, to come back here all the way from them foreign parts with the smell of an inheritance in his nose, and only to find these four empty walls and you two blackguards in possession."

The little man in the brown coat chuckled softly. "I'm not likely to forget our first meeting," he said, with a grin in the direction of his brother bailiff, and his brother bailiff answered with a nod.

"That's true for you," O'Rourke observed sarcastically.

Gosling took up the tale that Coin's remark suggested.

53

"Why, he took the pair of us by the two scruffs of us and rattled our heads together. Sure, here is a bad end to a good bailiff, says I to myself, as well as I could for his fingers on my throttle—and then of a sudden he let me go, and began to laugh at his own anger; and he gave me a push and I squatted on the floor."

Coin tapped his chest. "Same here," he agreed. "Then he began to talk. Lord, how he talked."

O'Rourke abandoned the bellows and rubbed his grimy hands together approvingly. "The master has got the gift of the gab, as good as another, or better, maybe, please the Lord."

He turned to busy himself about some process of distillation, but was arrested by a sudden question from Gosling.

"Where is he now, anyhow?"

O'Rourke turned upon his questioner with the snap of an angry dog. "Sure, it's no business for a pair of mangy process-servers to be asking how the O'Flynn is passing his time. Ah, poor boy, sure a turn of fortune may come any day."

Gosling eyed the little man curiously. "What's that?" he asked; and Coin questioned, "How?"

Pleased by the interest he had aroused, O'Rourke condescended to explain. "Did you never hear of the buried treasure of the O'Flynns?"

Gosling shook his head, so did Coin.

"Never," Gosling said emphatically, and Coin echoed him, "Never."

O'Rourke held up his grimy hands in protesting indignation. "Musha, the likes of you for ignoramuses. Sure, it's known and believed, and fancied by half the countryside that the ould lord, that was the young master's grandfather, hid away a fortune somewhere snugly within these same four walls."

The bailiffs looked at each other. Gosling rubbed his stubbly chin, thoughtfully. Coin questioned, "Why did he so?"

O'Rourke deigned to explain. "He was always the fanciful man and I think he took a kind of dislike to his son, my young master's father no less, and small blame to him, maybe, for that same. Anyways, he left word in his will that there was a treasure hidden in the castle for him to have that should find it, and that was about all he left, barring the ould place and the few acres."

This time it was Gosling's turn to question. "And did no one find the treasure?"

O'Rourke shook his head sadly. "Sorra a one. My late master lived upon credit, as a gentleman should, and the young master quarrelled with him when he was no more than a gossoon and went off to the wars abroad, and that was the last I saw of him for twenty long years."

There was a moment's silence. The bailiffs were evidently estimating, with minds trained in the forms and processes of law, the credibility of O'Rourke's story.

Then Coin inquired thoughtfully, "Why did he come back?"

O'Rourke sighed. "When the ould man died last year, mad drunk, as he had lived, I wrote a line to the poor boy to an address he had left me in Paris, telling him that he was now the O'Flynn and the heir to the estate. And the letter found him after a while, somewhere in the low countries, and back he travelled to find himself the lord of this ruin.   Sure he was a bit down in the mouth at first, but then he remembered the ould talk about this treasure, and ever since he's been prowling about and looking for it in the most unlikely places.   Holy Virgin, what's that ?"

VII

THE KING OF THE CASTLE

EVEN as the old man was speaking, a strange rumbling noise in the great chimney had distracted the attention of his listeners and now attracted his own. Suddenly a shower of bricks accompanied by a cloud of dust came rattling down the chimney on to the vacant hearth, and were immediately followed by the figure of a man. He lay for a moment sprawling among the rubbish and then rapidly raised himself to a sitting posture, and faced the astonished company. The new-comer, who had chosen so singular a method of entering the apartment, was a broad-shouldered, well-built man of some six feet high, and of perhaps some five or six and thirty years of age. Long exposure to weather had given to his countenance something of that settled aspect which tends to defy the lapse of time, and leave the spectator uncertain whether he is beholding a young man or an elder. The man was clad in what might once have been a smart uniform, but now the white coat, with its blue facings, was so worn and shabby that even a fall down a chimney could scarcely accentuate its degradation; and the boots and breeches were as dilapidated as the coat. But the wearer of these ancient garments seemed either to be unaware of, or indifferent to, their condition; and no less unaware of, or indifferent to, the eccentricity of his manner of entrance.

He surveyed the amazed trio for a while with the smile that was characteristic of his features intensified to an emphatic grin, and his bright, blue eyes danced with amusement. After a second or so, however, he assumed an air of gravity and, scrambling away from the canopy of the chimney, got to his feet with as much dignity as he could muster.

"Good-morning," he said, cheerfully.

O'Rourke rushed forward to attend upon his master. "Lord have mercy! Is it yourself?" he cried, as he busied himself in dusting with his hands the lappets of his master's coat.

Flynn nodded. "It is. Who else? What are you staring at? Mayn't a man enter his own house by his own chimney if it pleases him, without unnecessary comment?"

O'Rourke's curiosity defied etiquette. "But what were you doing in the chimney at all at all?" he asked.

But for a moment the O'Flynn left his curiosity unsatisfied. He pointed to where his hat lay on the floor with an air as stately as if that ragged head-covering had been the helmet of a hero or the crown of a king. "My hat," he observed, dryly, and Coin and Gosling, pushing forward at the same time in competition for the honor to secure it, knocked their heads together in the attempt. Coin, recovering the sooner from the shock of the collision, presented the hat to its owner, who flung it on to his head with a swaggering air:

"Thank you," he said, splendidly, and then condescended to answer O'Rourke's inquiries.

"Why, I was making a tour of inspection of the premises,

looking for that same treasure they talk of. In the room beyond I found a mighty big hole in the wall, and, as I was peering into it, I'm damned if what I was standing on didn't give way beneath me. I thought I was killed entirely, but, heaven be praised, there was only a floor to fall. What is there for breakfast ?"

O'Rourke shrugged his shoulders. "The usual."

"What's that ?" Flynn asked.

"Nothing," O'Rourke answered, laconically.

Flynn turned reproachfully to the two bailiffs who stood watching him with unconcealed admiration. "Didn't I bid you go fishing ?" he asked.

Coin hastened to answer him apologetically. "You did, and we obeyed you, but never a fish could we tickle."

Flynn sighed heavily and stretched his arms. "It's beginning to wish I hadn't come back I'd be — if it wasn't for one thing."

"What's that, O'Flynn ?" the eternally curious O'Rourke questioned.

"Never you mind," Flynn reproved him. Then, turning, he addressed the bailiffs. "Lord save us, gentlemen, it's twenty years since I saw the ould place, when I was no more than a lanky-leggy bit of a lad. I didn't like my father, heaven forgive me—and my father didn't like me, heaven forgive him—so I took French leave to France and I've followed the wars ever since. But when I heard my father was dead I came back to claim my inheritance and live like a gentleman for the rest of my life. Lord! Castle Famine!"

He called attention with a magnificent sweep of his right arm to the squalid environment in which the company

59

stood. Marius among the ruins of Carthage was never more nobly heroic.

Gosling, practical bailiff that he was, put a pertinent query. "Why do you stop here if you like the place so little?"

O'Rourke turned upon the bailiff in a fury of indignation. "Whist! Is it for the likes of you to question the young master?"

With another splendid gesture Flynn restrained the wrath of his dependent and condescended to satisfy the servant of the law. "Faith, it's a question I'd find it hard to answer with any show of reason. I hunger and I thirst and I go ill-clad, while it is but crossing the seas again to find service and a full belly and a new coat. And yet I don't want to be crossing the seas again, just yet."

Coin gave a little dry, cackling laugh and rubbed his hands together with the air of a man that knows more of the world than most others. "So help me," he said, "I am a town-man and know the bloods. I'll stake my reputation as a fashionable bailiff that there is a lady in the case."

O'Rourke turned upon him now as he had turned upon Gosling a moment before with the same vehement show of irritation. "Sure, it's crazy nonsense you're talking."

And once again the O'Flynn sought to modify his servant's wrath with a gesture. "It's crazy nonsense enough," he admitted, "but it happens to be true."

Again O'Rourke's hands were uplifted in the pathetic gesture of astonishment and despair which was habitual to him when brought face to face with the whimsicalities of his master. "Heaven help us! Who is it?"

The O'Flynn seated himself comfortably at the table

after having first made sure, by careful examination, that the chair in which he proposed to seat himself was of a solidity worthy of the confidence to be reposed in it. Then he stretched his legs with the air of a man who likes to tell a story and believes that he can tell it well, and began to talk:

"There was a young lady aboard the boat with me. Sure she travelled grand, the captain's cabin and all that, and she kept her cabin for a bit because of the dirty weather. But she came on deck in a flap of calm, and I saw her, and, oh! she was good to see, and I spoke with her as fellow-passengers may—and, oh! but she was good to hear."

He paused for a moment absorbed in rapturous recollections and Gosling took advantage of the pause to punctuate it with a question. "Who was she, maybe— ?"

Flynn waved a large hand at him. "That's neither here nor there. She landed at Cork as I did, and there was a fine coach to whisk her away, like Cinderella's in the story, with coachman and footmen and all. Away she went, and I gaping after her with my heart in my mouth it was so crazy to go with her."

He sighed deeply and allowed his chin for a moment to rest in depression upon the dingy piece of linen which sought to pass muster for a cravat.

Coin, who was interested in the story, shook his memory. "What did you do then?" he asked.

With another sigh Flynn raised his head and resumed his narrative. "For obvious reasons it was not convenient for me to linger in the city of Cork where the inns cost money even to an Irishman returning from foreign parts. For obvious reasons it was not convenient for me to take

61

coach or post to my ancestral domain. Shanks' mare was a good-enough mount for an old soldier that has tramped all over Europe. I had nothing to carry but my clothes on my back and the sword by my side, so I travelled light."

While Flynn had been talking his henchman had been busy in the concoction of a bowl of punch. Having completed the process to his satisfaction, as he made sure by taking a sip of the brew, he now ladled out a steaming mug of the mixture and carried it to his master. "Take a drink, O'Flynn," he suggested.

Flynn met the suggestion cheerfully. "I will," he said.

His large hand closed upon the cup, lifted it to his lips, and tossed its contents down his throat. He smacked his lips approvingly and handed back the empty vessel to O'Rourke. O'Rourke replenished it and placed it on the table hard by his master's elbow. He then filled a mug apiece for the two bailiffs and himself, and the three men sat sipping together and waiting for the O'Flynn to resume his story. This the O'Flynn, cheered by his drink, proceeded to do.

"Well, it was none such a bad day for walking. There had been rain, but the rain was over, leaving the road none too muddy and the leaves clean. The sun was bright and my spirits were high, for I thought, sirs, I was coming home to peace and plenty at last. Peace and plenty—Castle Famine!"

He sighed again and seemed inclined to drop into a despondent reverie, but O'Rourke, who loved a story like all his kind and who resented these interruptions, spurred him from his silence. "Never mind that now. Get on with your story."

"Well," Flynn resumed, "after I had left the city it was

a lonely land I was walking through—as bare of folk as a piece of Poland after a Russian raid. I had tramped about ten miles Irish and was beginning to yearn for the hunk of bread in my pocket, when I was called from carnal passions and appetites by the sound of brawling voices beyond the turn of the road. There was a woman's shrill voice in the quarrel, so I swung my legs to the arena."

"What did you find?" O'Rourke asked, eagerly, his fingers twitching and his eyes dancing with sympathetic excitement.

Flynn went on. "Why, there was a coach on one side in a ditch and a servant beneath nursing a broken arm. My pretty lady stood in the roadway with a pistol in her hand, and opposite to her on a big horse was a fellow in a laced coat whose face was hidden by a half mask. As I came up, and before they saw me, Miss Pretty fired and missed, and then my boy on the horse was off it and had her by the wrists. Not for long, though—I think you may have noticed that I have a kind of grip in my fingers."

He had addressed his last remark especially to the bailiffs, and the big man in the blue coat took it upon himself to answer it. "I have that same," he admitted, and rubbed his neck pensively.

The O'Flynn continued. "Lord! How surprised my friend was when he felt my thumb upon his windpipe. He let go of my lady at once and he made a good fight for it, I will say that for him, trying to get me off and trying to get at his pistols. Miss Pretty, as cool as you please, took advantage of our little altercation to load and prime again, in readiness for the worst, bless her heart! But nothing worse happened."

"What did happen?" Coin asked.

Flynn explained. "Well, I choked my land-pirate with the one hand till he was quite blue and nigh silly, and, with the other, I took his pistol from him and fetched him a clip under the ear that did his business."

He gave a dramatic pause which showed that his belief in his powers as a narrator were not unjustified.

"Were you after killing him?" O'Rourke asked in a thrilling whisper.

Flynn laughed. "Devil a bit. He lay on the road like a log, and I impounded his pistols and troubled no more about him, having other things to think about."

Coin looked sly and spoke slyly. "The young lady, for instance?" and the least suggestion of a wink disturbed the legal gravity of his countenance.

A noble enthusiasm came into Flynn's voice as he continued: "Ah, the young lady, the dear young lady. She thanked me as if I had been a paladin, and between us we shook the coachman into courage and did our best for the servant's damaged arm. And while we were thus busy, my rogue in the road came to his senses and crawled to his horse that had stood quite patient near him, the faithful beast, and nipped into the saddle and was off before we could wink. Then Miss Pretty got into the carriage again and I made bold to ask leave to join her and rode at her side for the rest of the journey. I wish we had been journeying to Jerusalem, but it was no farther than Mountmichael yonder."

O'Rourke snapped his fingers for joy. "Was it the Lady Benedetta, then?" he said, triumphantly asserting rather than questioning.

Flynn made a gesture of comic despair. "There, I have let the cat out of the bag, and the prettiest, most whimsical, skittishest kitten it is. She wanted me to go into the castle and know her father, but I was in neither trim nor temper for meeting with English gentility. But she made me promise to visit her one day."

"And will you?" Gosling asked.

Flynn nodded. "For sure I will, if only I can find that treasure. Maybe I will whether I find it or not. In the mean time I've been writing the most elegant verses in her honor. Well, well, I'll be troubling you for a little more punch."

Coin nimbly took charge of Flynn's cup, nimbly replenished it, nimbly restored it to Flynn's extended fingers. "It's a pleasure," he said.

Gosling took a deep pull at his own mug and observed meditatively, "Punch is a fine thing."

O'Flynn caught him up at the word in a flame of enthusiasm. "Punch is a grand thing," he declared. "Do you lose your temper? A bowl of punch will set you right again. Do you lose a fortune? A bowl of punch will console you. Do you lose a battle? A bowl of punch will give you the wit to win another. Do you lose a kingdom? A bowl of punch will make you the equal of a king. Oh, honest usquebaugh, mellow sugar, and yellow lemon, what a heaven-sent medley you make! Between you and me and the doorstep, I think when the ould gods were tossing their nectar it was hot whiskey punch they were drinking."

Gosling clapped his hands. "Nobly thought," he declared.

Coin agreed with him. "And nobly spoken," he added.

Flynn seemed pleased at the approval of his companions. "Fill up again," he cried; "if we can't eat, let us thank the powers that we can drink. Here's a health to the pretty lady."

65

VIII

THE PRETTY LADY

NOW even as the O'Flynn lifted his glass he saw and wondered at an expression of sudden surprise and sudden admiration that conquered the faces of the three men who stood before him, each with a mug of punch in his lifted hand. O'Flynn was standing with his back to the gap in the wall of the ruined hall, and so standing he was unaware that a figure had come for a moment into the frame of its open space, shutting out something of the sunlight that flooded from the smiling country outside, but giving, in exchange, the gift of a gracious presence that was better than sunlight. Stirred by the expression on the faces of his companions O'Flynn, with the lifted glass still in his hand, swung on his heels—with military swiftness and military precision—and saw standing in the opening, parting the leaves that shaded it, a rare and gracious figure —the figure of a girl of perhaps twenty, clad in a green riding-dress, a girl whose fair face was framed with golden curls, a girl who smiled at him frankly with the smile of old acquaintanceship as she asked with a dainty mixture of audacity and temerity, "May I come in?"

O'Rourke clawed eagerly in the direction of his master. "Sure, it's Lady Benedetta herself," he whispered, telling his master what that master already knew with a sense of joy which even his nimble wit was barely capable of translating into instant speech.

All he could find to say was the lady's name, "Lady Benedetta!" And he said it with a kind of gasp which was far from heroic or romantic, but was certainly as joyous and reverential as any inarticulate sound could conveniently be.

Lady Benedetta seemed neither surprised nor amused by the commotion she caused among the occupants of the hall. Addressing herself with grave serenity to the master of the castle, she said: "I gave you a good week's grace, Chevalier. And then as you wouldn't come to see me, I took my maidenly modesty a-horseback and rode over to see you. Well, aren't you glad to see me?"

Just for once the O'Flynn's presence of mind, a presence of mind which he had hitherto relied upon as being imperturbable, deserted him. He stared, gasped, and at last stammered some disconnected words in which, "Of course, glad, delighted," might perhaps have been heard and appreciated by the lady to whom they were addressed. She at least seemed wholly self-possessed, very sweetly mistress of the situation and not in the least degree embarrassed by the embarrassment of her host or the broadly expressed admiration on the faces of the rest of the company.

"Well," she said, gaily, "you have got to entertain me, for my horse must have a rest. I stabled her before I came in. Pray present your friends."

As she said this she turned a pleasant smile in the direction of each of the two whimsical limbs of the law who were standing side by side and eying her with flagrant approbation.

The lady's suggestion added to the unusual embarrassment of the O'Flynn. He glared angrily from the big man in the blue coat to the little man in the brown coat, wished them both at the devil, and then with a desperate rallying of his senses resolved to make the best of a bad situation. He tweaked Gosling by the shoulder and jerked him forward.

"Certainly!" he said, "this is my friend, Sir George Gosling."

The blue-coated bailiff made an exaggerated bow. "Your health and song, ma'am," he said, and would have said more but that O'Flynn interrupted him by taking little Coin by his brown collar and bringing him in front of his companion.

"This," he said, gravely, "is my Lord Coin."

Coin, delighted at the nobility thus fantastically accorded him, gave a funny little duck of his funny little head, lifted an erect forefinger to the level of his eyebrows and murmured, "Delighted."

He was evidently seeking further utterance, laboring phrases, but his efforts at social intercourse with the great were rudely interrupted by the O'Flynn, who, standing in front of the pair, began to shepherd them out of the room with a savageness suggestive rather of the wolf, than of the sheep-dog. "Well," he said aloud, "I am sorry you must be leaving, but I know what inveterate sportsmen you are."

But while Coin protested, "Oh, we are not so inveterate as all that," and Gosling insisted, "There's no hurry," the voice of the O'Flynn rumbled thunderously in their ears heavy with menace, "Yes, there is. I wouldn't keep you from your pleasures for the world. If you don't clear out I'll wring your necks."

THE PRETTY LADY

There was such a look of menace on the countenance of the O'Flynn that the pair of bailiffs, in whose memory his rough handling still lived very vividly, hastened to take the hint. With many awkward gestures of salutation, Coin and Gosling shambled from the room and Benedetta and Flynn were left together with O'Rourke.

For a moment neither spoke. Benedetta's quick glances had swiftly taken in the strange condition of her surroundings, the ruined hall, the ragged hangings, the broken windows, the dominant air of squalor and poverty. Now they rested with an expression of kindly curiosity upon her host, who for his part had never ceased to regard her since her entrance with an expression of frank adoration. Benedetta laughed.

"What odd creatures your friends seem to be," she said, and she laughed again as she spoke, and Flynn joined in her laughter with a great show of enthusiasm.

"You have got the right word of it," he said, and hastened to invent explanations. "They are odd, devilish odd. That's their great charm, to my mind. Now, you would never believe it to look at them, that those two fellows are noted bloods in Dublin, famous lady-killers."

Benedetta laughed again. "Indeed I never should. But I am not sorry they have gone, for my visit is to you, Chevalier. And if you will give me something to eat I shall be grateful for I am as hungry as a hunter."

If his beautiful visitor had asked the O'Flynn for the roc's egg, or the Holy Grail, she could hardly have caused him more embarrassment.

And he echoed her words, "Something to eat," with an air of pathos that something amazed the lady.

"Something to eat," echoed O'Rourke, standing by the

fireplace. He sadly clasped his hands together and murmured, "Oh, Lord!"

Unaware of the agitation she was causing, Benedetta
went on: "I said to myself this morning, if the Chevalier
is so distant it is my part to be forward. I will ride over
to visit him and make him invite me to dinner."

By this time Flynn had recovered a little from the staggering effect of his pretty lady's request. He took himself,
as it were, by the collar of his coat and shook himself into
an air of cheerful satisfaction as he made Benedetta an extravagant bow. "Madam, I am more than honored," he
said, "and more than fortunate in having my larder excellently plenished."

He turned to his faithful dependent, who stood a diminutive image of despair by the hearth, and addressed him
with the air of one that has troops of servants at command.
"Conachor, what shall we offer Lady Benedetta—what
about that haunch of venison?"

Something in the glance of the O'Flynn's eye seemed
to inspire a lively intelligence in his henchman. The little
man moved forward, rubbing his hands together briskly
while his brain hummed with subterfuges. "Ah, sure,"
he began in a voice of good-humored protest, "ah, sure your
honor has forgotten that you gave that same haunch to his
Riverence, to make his Sunday dinner."

Flynn slapped his forehead with a well-feigned air of
surprise. "True, true, so I did. Well, well, let us make
the best of it, and bring in the game pasty."

Again O'Rourke caught, as it were, the ball his master
tossed him and flung it back again. "Is it the game pasty
you're after?" he asked, querulously. "Sure, we finished
it last night at supper."

Flynn gave a sigh of regret. "Devil fly away with my memory, so we did," he declared. He turned to his visitor in his grandest manner. "The best game pasty, Lady Benedetta—but there, there, if it's gone there's no use in praising it. I am afraid we must fall back upon the baron of beef."

"If your honor does," O'Rourke said, dryly, "there'll be nothing to break your fall. Sure, the hounds got into the larder this morning and made a meal of it before I could scare them."

By this time Benedetta began to understand something of the spirit of the little comedy that was being played out for her benefit, and it was with a perfectly staid face of entire belief in the protestations of master and servant that she now listened as Flynn said to her:

"Really, Lady Benedetta, you find our hospitality at a positive loss." He turned with a rallying glance to his servant. "Come, Conachor, come—what can we set before her ladyship?"

O'Rourke scratched his head thoughtfully and answered after a moment's meditation: "Sure, we've had no fish since Friday, and I distributed, in charity, the remains of the sheep that we had roasted whole on Sunday. There was a fine knuckle of ham, to be sure, but more by token it was so fine that I and the other servants finished it in the servants' hall."

Benedetta's face betrayed no suspicion of the reality of O'Rourke's statement. "Anything will do for me," she protested, blithely. "I have a simple stomach."

By this time O'Rourke was standing between the pair and glancing from one to the other cunningly. "But I'll tell you what I can do," he said; "there's an honorable corner of a cheese and the better half of a decent loaf—"

Benedetta clapped her hands together pleasantly. "Excellent, excellent," she cried. "Nothing better than bread and cheese."

Flynn eyed her dubiously, glad to think she was deceived by the devices of O'Rourke, but wondering if she really could be. He made one last effort to sustain the dignity of the host. "Bread and cheese," he said. "Good! With a glass of wine to help it. Shall we say a bottle of the ould Burgundy, Conachor?"

O'Rourke emitted a little creaking laughter. "Sure," he said, "your honor may say what he pleases, being the O'Flynn, but your honor must be funning when you talk of the ould Burgundy. Sure, 'tis myself that forgot to turn the tap in the barrel the last time of drawing, and now we must wait till the new pipes come over from France, which won't be till next week or later. But if her ladyship wouldn't be above tasting a thimbleful of punch, made as only myself knows how to make it—"

Flynn turned to Benedetta with sudden enthusiasm. "I must confess that Conachor brews a most formidable punch."

"Punch let it be," Benedetta agreed. "Why, spring water would serve my turn—and bread and cheese make the best of eating to a mortal so sharp set as I be."

Flynn made her a profound reverence. "Your ladyship is most amiable to condone our shortcomings." He turned to O'Rourke. "Dispatch, Conachor, dispatch," he ordered, and his ingenious vassal vanished from the room. He turned again to Benedetta. "Will your ladyship be seated?"

THE PRETTY LADY

Benedetta made him a pretty courtesy. "I thank you, Chevalier," she said, and seated herself in the chair of whose solidity O'Flynn was confident.

O'Flynn produced another from a corner of the room, and after testing it cautiously, trusted himself to its capacity for its task, and seated himself in front of his visitor.

For a moment again man and maid looked at each other in silence and then Benedetta began, "And now, Chevalier, tell me why you have never come over to pay your respects."

"Your ladyship must excuse me," Flynn replied, with a royal air of occupation. "The cares of a great estate, the multiplicity of duties, the world of importunate tasks—"

Benedetta shook her head at him reproachfully. "Chevalier, Chevalier, why do you sit here in ease and plenty, while your king waits for you in Dublin ?"

Flynn's smiling face lost its smile. "I beg your ladyship's pardon," he said coldly.

Benedetta went on, "Are you not aware that King James, God bless him, has come to Dublin to make war upon the usurper William ?"

Flynn shrugged his shoulders. "I have heard that James Stuart is in Dublin. What's that to me ? The Stuarts only remember Ireland when they are in trouble." He spoke with animation.

Benedetta looked at him reproachfully. "James Stuart is your king, Chevalier," she said.

O'Flynn protested. "I crave your ladyship's patience. James Stuart may be King of Scotland, might be King of England, but by your favor, he is not King of Ireland. We had our own kings in the old days and may have them again in the new, please God."

Benedetta stared at him with wide, astonished eyes. "What kings are you talking of?" she asked.

O'Flynn's air of slightly ruffled patriotism now gave place to a rather roguish smile as of one that enjoyed beforehand a surprise for his companion. He leaned across the table and spoke to the Lady Benedetta in a confidential voice, "Did you mark the bit of a boy that was here but now?"

Benedetta showed the surprise that Flynn expected. "The old man, your servant?" she asked, looking at her host with the same wonder.

O'Flynn nodded solemnly: "The old man, my servant," he echoed, "that should be my master by rights. That old man, Lady Benedetta, is the direct descendant of a King of Munster, one of the victims of your country and your country's greed."

Lady Benedetta lifted her eyebrows ever so little. "You are pleased to be merry with me, Chevalier," she said.

O'Flynn looked steadfastly at her for a moment and then rose to his feet.

"Conachor, Conachor," he called; "I say, come here."

Even as he called, his little wisp of a body-servant entered the gaunt hall with a tray in his hands, on which bread and cheese and a big jug of punch were carefully placed. He looked at his master wonderingly.

"What is it?" he asked, as he set down the tray upon the table.

The O'Flynn tapped him lightly on the shoulder. "Sure, the young lady wants to have a look at you, not that you are much to look at, I'm thinking—" As he spoke the O'Flynn gave his diminutive retainer a little spin with his finger and thumb that suggested oscillation, and, obediently enough, the little man revolved in a circle for a couple of twirls until O'Flynn again tapped him and arrested his gyrations.

Benedetta leaned across the table and addressed the little man kindly. "The Chevalier tells me you are a king, Mr. O'Rourke."

O'Rourke lifted a finger to his forehead. "I am that same," he said with a comic air of dignity that nearly compelled Benedetta to laugh.

O'Flynn made himself the spokesman for his royal servant. With a stately sweep of his uplifted arm he harangued Benedetta.

"Descended in the direct, unbroken line—as Father Pat can prove to you—from Conachor O'Rourke, King of Munster, called Conachor of the Red Nose, because, saving your presence, he had the way with him of lifting his little finger."

Benedetta laughed gayly. She thought the whole thing was a jest of a somewhat exaggerated humor, but O'Rourke took up his master's statement and accentuated it very gravely: "He was a grand man though I say it that shouldn't—maybe—seeing he was my ancestor. It's his royal tastes I inherit."

Flynn patted the little man on the back. "And mighty little else, my poor boy," he said.

Then he turned to his guest, "But there you are, Lady Benedetta; this poor old gossoon by rights should be king here, with a crown of gold always on his head, and a jug of punch always in his hands."

O'Rourke chuckled. "'Tis I would be liking the same finely," he agreed, "but I'd rather have the punch than the crown any day of the week, for the crown I'd most likely be pawning, while the punch I could always be drinking."

Benedetta laughed again. She was finding these wild islanders very diverting company.

O'Flynn seemed to think that the diversion had gone far enough. He gave O'Rourke a little push. "Well, now," he said, "run away with you for all you are a king."

And O'Rourke trotted obediently out of the hall. When he was gone Flynn turned to Benedetta.

"There, pretty lady," he said, "there is the king I ought to be serving, and instead he is serving me, after a manner of speaking."

Benedetta, who had restrained her laughter in the presence of the little serving man for fear of causing a dependant pain, now allowed herself to laugh gallantly enough. "But of course you aren't in earnest, Chevalier," she protested, "when you talk in this way."

O'Flynn pretended to frown at her, but he spoke seriously enough: "Not in earnest, is it? And why not? What are you doing your own self but worshipping a king without a kingdom, a king without a crown, a king that lives on the munificence of French Louis? Isn't my king as good as that—crownless, too, and landless—and my servant—Heaven help him—to boot?"

As he spoke he handed the Lady Benedetta a slice of bread and a piece of cheese, and filled the mug which O'Rourke had set for her with the punch of O'Rourke's making. Benedetta nibbled thoughtfully at the bread.

"What a strange people you are," she murmured.

O'Flynn protested. "Not so strange as all that. The English, God bless them and mend them, don't understand us. They think we always mean what we say, or they think we never mean what we say, and they are wrong both times."

Lady Benedetta, who had taken a little sip of Conachor's brewage, and made ever so slightly a wry face at the sipping, set down her cup and looked earnestly at the O'Flynn. "I hope," she said, "I am wrong when I think you profess a carelessness for King James. Why do you not go to Dublin to serve his Majesty?"

The O'Flynn slapped his chest with a large hand. "Madam," he said, "I am a soldier of fortune. Will King James pay me well?"

Benedetta raised her gloved left hand in protest. "For shame!" she cried. "His Majesty needs the money of his subjects, the free service of his subjects. For myself I am proud to be able to serve him."

Flynn showed a quick interest. "How so, pretty lady?" he asked.

Benedetta leaned across the table and looked steadily into the face of O'Flynn: "I am going to Dublin to-morrow," she said. "I bring the king money, I bring the king better than money." She paused for a moment, and then suddenly questioned her host. "Chevalier, do you remember that road-thief from whom you saved me?"

O'Flynn put his hand to his forehead with the air of a man seeking to recall some unimportant incident. "I have," he admitted, "a vague recollection of something of the kind."

Benedetta came in quickly upon his attempted reminiscences. "I do not think it was my money he wanted," she said. "No, nor even me. I think he knew of certain jewels I was carrying, and that those jewels were the end of the enterprise."

O'Flynn, seeing that Benedetta was evidently deeply interested in the jewels of which she spoke, felt that he ought to say something, and said it.

"What jewels?" he asked.

Benedetta smiled, with a pretty little air of importance. "The Queen's jewels. The great Turkish ruby, the blue Mogul diamond, and the Pearl Necklace. Each of them is a little fortune and she sacrifices them all to the cause of her husband, as a true wife should. Three of her ladies undertook to carry the treasure to Europe, the Pearl Necklace was my share.

Flynn was determined to have his share in the conversation, but he could think of nothing better to say than, "And 'twas the Pearl Necklace this road-thief was after?"

Benedetta nodded wisely, "So I think, and not as a common thief, but to keep it from poor King James." She rose from her chair as she spoke with the air of one that was about to close an agreeable interview. "Well, Chevalier, are you not coming to Dublin to lend your purse and your sword to the king?"

IX

THE LOVE-MAKER

O'FLYNN, too, had risen to his feet and he faced his guest gravely. "Lady," he said, "I cannot. I am nailed to my estate. And if I wasn't, I belong to no party. What are the Scotchman and the Dutchman to me?"

Lady Benedetta's face showed plainly the indignation she felt at hearing the great cause to which she was devoted spoken of in a fashion so indifferent. "I ask your pardon," she said, rather bitterly, "I thought you were a soldier."

O'Flynn agreed with her cheerfully. "So I am, a soldier of fortune. I have followed the wars since so high. When I first went into action I was no more than sixteen. At first I thought I was frightened, then I found that I wasn't, and I never have been frightened since. But I fight for my living, lady, and not for a king."

Benedetta shook her head sadly, and her blue eyes grew sombre as she regarded her companion. "I am afraid I have been mistaken in you," she said, and there was evident disappointment in the tone of her voice.

But O'Flynn, for all he adored the lady, was not prepared to deny his Irish indifference to the quarrels of two alien kings. "Then mend the error," he said, sadly. "Any man who pays me I will serve faithfully. But there

79

are only two things I will fight for with my own hand, for my own pleasure."

Benedetta raised her eyebrows. "What are these two things?" she said, curiously.

O'Flynn assumed an attitude of dignified resolve, and tapped his chest heroically. "One is my country, my Ireland," he answered.

Benedetta glanced round her with a little shiver. She was used to France; she loved France with its color and its sunshine, and to her the mists and grayness of the Island of Saints had something melancholy in its beauty which depressed her. "Do you call this a country?" she asked, with a faint smile. Then she questioned, "Well, what is the other?"

O'Flynn bowed his head and laid his left hand on his heart. "The woman I might love," he said, earnestly.

Benedetta smiled at his earnestness as she dropped into her chair again. She was willing that the conversation might continue now that it had taken this turn and was presenting her eccentric host to her in a new light. "What a pretty sentiment," she said. "Are you a poet, Chevalier?"

O'Flynn followed Benedetta's example and seated himself before he answered her in the affirmative. "I am, in the Gaelic. If I weren't I should tell you that a man's first business is to fight for himself. As I am I tell you that a man's first business is to fight for the woman he loves, whether she loves him or no, just because he loves her—just because she means to him something that nothing else in all the world could ever mean. There is life, my life, in a nutshell for your pretty teeth to crack."

Lady Benedetta looked at him curiously. He seemed

very much in earnest, and it was strange to hear this shabby man in the ragged habiliments discoursing so eloquently of high passions. "You talk nimbly of love," she said. "Are you a master of love-making?"

O'Flynn leaned back in his chair and laughed jollily, and there was something infectious in the rich sound of his laughter that made Benedetta laugh too, though she could not see any very immediate reason for mirth. "Was there ever an Irishman since Adam," he asked, "that couldn't make love to a pretty girl?"

"You mean you've got the gift of tongues," Benedetta suggested. "A world of words and no soul behind them."

O'Flynn caught at her words and embroidered on them. "The gift of the gab, the gift of the blab," he cried. "Is it stars and roses and angels and wildfire and nightingales and all such nonsense you think I'd be discoursing? Sure, I could be as prodigal of such prettinesses as another, more by token if I was talking the Gaelic. But that isn't the way I'd make love to the girl of my heart."

Benedetta was now decidedly diverted by the drolleries of her host. She had known court lovers and court poets in plenty, but this strange ragamuffin who was patently a gentleman for all his tatters, who could talk of love in so novel a fashion, was a new creature in her experience. "Come, O'Flynn," she protested, "you tease me. What would you say to the girl of your heart?"

O'Flynn accepted the girl's challenge with alacrity. He drew his chair a little nearer to hers, and as he spoke there was a bantering note in his voice that only faintly veiled his earnestness. "I'd say to her, sweeting, sure I know that you're made on the pattern of our grandam in paradise— she that picked the apple—that it's a woman you are and not a saint, and that you eat salt with your porridge like the rest of infirmity."

Benedetta, who had listened to him eagerly, leaned back in her chair with a slightly disappointed expression. "This seems no prosperous prologue," she said, and perhaps would have said more had O'Flynn given her time for speech, but he hurried to the conclusion of his thoughts.

"You're wrong," he declared, "it clears the ground between man and maid; sets them face to face understanding each other, speaking real words, hearing real words."

The big man with the blue eyes was plainly sincere in his speech. Not in this fashion had any of the gallants of France or England paid homage to her. The sweet voice of my Lord Sedgemouth had never been charged with such odd meaning.

"You seem mightily in earnest, O'Flynn," she said. "What would you say next?"

O'Flynn laid one hand lightly on Benedetta's gloved fingers where they rested on the table. "I'd say, you are a woman and a mortal with a mortal's share of faults and naughtiness, and I know that you will grow old and gray in time, if you live to it, and that you'll die anyway, whatever you live to, which is not angelic."

Benedetta withdrew her hand from the gentle pressure of O'Flynn. "Do you call this love-making?" she asked, and there was irony in her voice as she questioned.

O'Flynn did not seem to heed her interruption. He went on eagerly, vehemently, almost fiercely, as if she had not spoken.

"But such as you are, the sight of you sets me crazy. I'd rather hear you talk than another sing; see you walk than another dance; meet you frowning than another smiling; serve you cruel than another kind; woo you hostile than another pliant. Why, I'd follow where you beckoned, though all the queens of Christendom, with their crowns upon their heads, were winking me the other way."

Benedetta clapped her hands together as she might have clapped them in a playhouse after a speech that amused her. "Come, this is better—and yet it leaves me cold," she cried.

O'Flynn went on still borne on the full tide of his enthusiasm, meaning to say his say. "Have you ever taken note, if you're walking of a gray morning and the sun comes whisking out and gilds the causeway, how your spirit leaps? Have you ever heard a blackbird whistle in a tree and begun to think thoughts to his music, thoughts that you never thought before, thoughts that you can't put into words, but that make you wild with delight and wonder and a sadness more marvellous than joy? That is how the thought of you makes me feel."

The suddenness of the personal note at the end of O'Flynn's speech brought a flush of color into Benedetta's cheeks. She lowered her eyelids for a moment, then raising them again looked steadily at him and rose to her feet.

"You mean," she said, quietly, "the thought of the woman you love."

O'Flynn made a gesture of deprecation, his voice was still insistent. "Of course," he said, "that is what I mean."

Benedetta smiled a little at an explanation which was no explanation. She began to understand that she was indeed the mark for this amazing gentleman's strange attentions, and his manner of paying compliments piqued her so keenly that she was unwilling, for the moment at least, to cut him short. So she said softly, "I think in her place I should scarcely believe you."

O'Flynn turned upon her, vehement, voluble, enthusiastic. "Yes, you would," he cried. "I tell you, you would, for you'd know it was truth I was telling with every word of my lips. And when a man wooes a woman so that she can be sure he means what he says, that he is hers, every bit of him, from toe to topknot, the woman can't help being pleased. I defy her not to be pleased."

His admiration blazed so frankly in his eyes, animated so patently his every gesture, that Lady Benedetta, in spite of her amusement at the contrast such wooing afforded with the elaborate phrases and affected suspirations of her admirers in France, seemed to think that it was time to end a situation that threatened to become embarrassing. She rose to her feet with a little laugh.

"Well spoken, Chevalier," she said. "If you will but come to Dublin and serve the king, I am sure some pretty lady will be pleased to receive your addresses."

But by this time O'Flynn had launched the ship of his heart upon the ocean of his eloquence. He was resolved to say what he thought and would not be gainsaid, and he spoke to her with a rush of words that were as ready as they were earnest.

"There is only one pretty lady I want, and that is yourself, no other. Since the first time I saw you, I said to myself, 'that is the woman for me; that's my woman from out of all the world.' And when I saw you this afternoon, standing there in the doorway, debonair as a flower, I thought to myself, 'vagabond soldier though I be, I will win this lady's love.'"

For all the passion in his heart and all the passion in

his speech, there was a faint note of banter in his voice, a slightly ironical smile upon his lips that while it in no sense denied the truth of the words he was pouring forth so swiftly, proved also to the girl's keen wit that he was not unaware of the possible ridicule attached to them, coming as they did, from him in his then condition. He paused for a moment to laugh, and then dropping on one knee as gracefully as any gallant of Saint-Germains could have done, addressed her, looking down on him with wide, astonished eyes, in a spirit of earnestness that appealed very gallantly to her pity without any sense of abjection.

"Why, it might make an ordinary piece of womankind laugh to see me, battered and tattered, poor and spendthrift as I am, kneeling here at the feet of so bright a lady, but not you, Benedetta—not you. You shall see in me not a world-stained soldier of fortune, but a lover worthy even of you, made so by my love for you."

Benedetta was, by this time, not a little perplexed by the result of the conversation. It was all very well to have a sturdy soldier paying her poetic compliments in a ruined hall, but, when these compliments glowed into the fervor of a passionate declaration, the humor of the situation became overstrained. She drew a little away from her proclaimed adorer and her voice was kindly and decided as she spoke.

"O'Flynn, you must not say any more. I'm truly sorry, for I like you finely and you saved my life, but I can never love you."

O'Flynn rose to his feet with a jolly laugh. In the core of his heart he was not disappointed, for he had never, even in the exuberance of his extravagant fancy, believed that he could win the Lady Benedetta thus and so soon.

He had spoken in obedience to those wild impulses that
sway the children of his race just because he wanted to
speak, just because he wanted to tell this fair and gracious
creature that he worshipped her. Now he faced her
smiling and answered her denial with a blithe defiance.

"Why, sweeting," he said, gayly, "how do you know?
Here am I that say you shall and 'tis more likely than not
that I know better than you. You say you don't dislike
me."

Benedetta shook her head emphatically and smiled.
She could not help smiling upon her wild admirer.

"No," she answered, gently.

Flynn made a triumphant gesture. "Why, now, look
there; here's a good start. I tell you, loveliest, that you
are mine, and I will make you love me by-and-by."

Lady Benedetta began to feel a trifle vexed at her wild
wooer's pertinacity. Even as she observed him in his
ragged raiment standing in his ragged house, her mind
called up to her a vision of a very beautiful person, very
suave of speech, very exquisite of carriage, always clothed
very adorably, a man whose sword was feared as much as
his manner was envied. In a word she thought of my
Lord Sedgemouth, and sighed at the thought, for she loved
the exquisite gentleman, and wished him there to woo her
in place of this mad soldier of fortune. So she spoke a
little pettishly.

"You do not understand," she said. "I love another,
and I think he loves me."

O'Flynn had not the grace in her eyes to seem in the
least dashed by this tremendous statement. He only
smiled the more with a provoking air of confidence.
"Well, well," he said, cheerfully, "I'm sorry for it, for

you'll have to give the spark the go-by. But it affects me
not a little. You do not love him so much as I love you,
so mine is the greater claim."

The absolute audacity of his manner, his grotesque
serenity of self-belief were not unattractive to the girl, who
had a sense of humor, and they were certainly amusing.
So instead of answering him seriously she preferred to
treat him in his own spirit of jesting good-humor.

"Do you think," she asked, "I could look at a man who
did not serve my king?"

O'Flynn made a military salute. "Is that all?" he
asked. "He's my king, henceforth, and I am his faithful soldier."

Lady Benedetta puckered her pretty face into an expression of discontent. "How can you serve him here?"
she questioned. "It's in Dublin his soldiers are."

O'Flynn seemed to be in no wise embarrassed by what
the lady said, and it was with a fine air of confidence that
he answered her, "I'll go to Dublin."

Benedetta could not help glancing round at the signs of
penury about her, at the poverty that was so extravagantly
evident in the habit of the man. "How?" she asked.

O'Flynn shrugged his shoulders. "I don't know.
But I'll go. Fair lady, I'll make a bargain with you. I
love you and I mean to win you, and to win you I will do
such deeds as shall make you wonder; and whatever I do,
whatever I accomplish, you and I will know is done for
one lady—and that lady is your angel-self. I will make
you love me, and everything I do I will lay at your
feet."

O'Flynn was now in the full tide of passionate declaration again and Benedetta strove in vain to arrest him.

"Stop! stop!" she pleaded, with lifted finger, but O'Flynn flamed on.

"And I want you to say to yourself every day, 'he loves me better than his soul'—two or three times over—and you'll soon see how used you get to the idea."

He paused as if to view the effect of this suggestion upon his companion, but she only shook her head very decidedly.

"It's useless, O'Flynn. I'm sorry, but it's useless. Now I must bid you farewell, or I shall be late at home and my father will scold me."

O'Flynn smiled at her with bright good-humor. "You may go now, but I shall see you again, never doubt it, and win you, too—or I'm not the man I think I am. Let me bring you to your horse."

He held out his hand to her as he spoke with as gallant a manner as any courtier of the Mall, and he conducted his visitor through the doorway to the dilapidated outhouse that did duty for stables. Here Lady Benedetta's horse waited her, where she had tied it to an empty manger. O'Flynn brought the animal out and mounted the lady. He uttered no further word of love, but gave her God-speed and watched her ride away with a smile upon his face and determination in his eyes.

X

THE COMING OF THE PLAYERS

WHEN O'Flynn saw the last flutter of the Lady Benedetta's green riding-dress and the last gleam of her fair hair disappear behind the distant trees, he turned slowly round and made his way back to his ancestral ruin. Being, as he said of himself, a bit of a poet, the degradation of Castle Famine did not seem more flagrant in contrast with the grace and beauty of the vision that had just quitted it. On the contrary, it seemed to him as if that fair visitation had in a measure blessed and glorified the old place, gilding the gray stones with a wonder greater than sunlight and coloring the bare walls of his hall with lovelier images than the faded hangings had ever shown. When he returned he found Coin and Gosling awaiting him with quizzical looks.

"That's a mighty fine lady of yours," Coin said to him, cheerfully. "Do you know that she is a great heiress?"

O'Flynn hardly heeded what the fellow said. He took from a ledge in the chimneypiece a clay pipe and a battered old earthenware pipkin that contained some strong tobacco he had newly shredded. Slowly he filled the bowl and then going to where Conachor's brazier still glowed, he took up a piece of firewood, thrust it into the flame till it was alight and slowly and deliberately lit his

89

pipe. As the first gray puffs ascended he seemed to recall the bailiff's question, and giving a glance in the direction of the expectant Coin he answered absently, "No."

Gosling rubbed his hands and chuckled over his thoughts.

"She is, no less," he said. "Fifty thousand pounds. Property abroad, France—quite safe whatever happens to England, Ireland or Scotland. Lucky man who weds her."

Flynn seemed to pay him no attention. He seated himself at the table on the same seat where he had faced the Lady Benedetta so short a time ago, and yet that time now seemed like an eternity. He smoked thoughtfully for a while in silence, watched with great curiosity by the brace of bailiffs, who were undoubtedly much impressed by the fact that the Lady Benedetta Mountmichael, the great heiress and great lady, had deigned to pay a visit to the master of Castle Famine. Then Flynn, because he felt the need of saying something with an audience so blatantly expectant of speech, and, being unwilling to carry on the conversation on the lines that the curiosity of the bailiffs had suggested, began to dilate awhile on the praises of tobacco.

"Was there ever," he mused, "a more blessed, more excellent weed than tobacco? I've never begun a battle yet without smoking a pipe of it, and now that my biggest campaign's ahead of me, I won't break through the habit." As he spoke, he rose again and advanced toward Coin and Gosling with a whimsical smile upon his face. "I suppose neither of you two gentlemen would find it convenient to lend me a hundred pounds to go to Dublin with."

Coin and Gosling shook their heads very emphatically

90

for several seconds in denial of any such preposterous proposition.

O'Flynn's smile widened. "Nor yet fifty?" he questioned further.

Coin grunted.

Gosling answered dryly, "No, nor yet fi'pence."

O'Flynn's face wore the expression of one who, at least, had neglected no available chance of fortune. "No, I thought not," he admitted. "Well, it can't be helped—yet they say Dublin's a fine city."

Gosling nodded approval of the sentiment. He was tired of Castle Famine and its short commons, though he had grown to feel an unbounded admiration for its master, and he sighed not a little for the delights of the capital; delights that must be doubly dear just then with a royal king holding a royal court in the city. "Fine," he echoed, approvingly.

O'Flynn heaved a sigh. "If I had only a horse in my stables, I might be riding there to-morrow," he murmured.

Gosling felt it was his duty, as a representative of the law, to make at least a formal protest against the proposed flitting. "You might if we'd allow you," he said, but he said it half-heartedly, and O'Flynn recognized the half-heartedness with a laugh.

"Is it the likes of you would stop me?" he asked. "Give me some punch." He settled himself again in his chair, thrust his booted legs in front of him, blew several puffs of gray smoke into the air and took a hearty pull at the mug of punch which the obedient Gosling placed in his extended fingers. Then he spoke again.

"Whiles ago I should have thought that there was nothing better in the world than this, to sit with outstretched legs drinking punch and smoking tobacco. But now it's crazy I am to be on the road again." With the words he seemed suddenly to feel a desire to be alone with his thoughts. He turned sharply on the men and commanded them, "Now, clear the table, boys, and be off with you."

With great nimbleness and alacrity the two bailiffs, turned serving-men, did as their temporary lord directed. They removed the remains of the meal that Flynn had shared with Benedetta, that golden meal and worthy of the gods, and withdrawing on tiptoe, left O'Flynn to his meditations and the dusk. For a while O'Flynn sat motionless, the only sign of his animation being the jets of gray clouds that rose slowly from his glowing pipe. He was trying to rhyme a rhyme in honor of the Lady Benedetta and he got the swing of it well enough in the Gaelic, and was now trying to turn it into English for the benefit at some future time of a pretty lady who had no Irish.

"Childeen," it began, for thus the O'Flynn gallantly coined a word to fill a want in the speech of the Sassenach,

> "Childeen, I think the soul of Spring
> Shines in the candor of your eyes."

Beyond that he seemed at the moment to be unable to go on with his task of translation and he abandoned the enterprise and set himself somnolently to the contemplation of the smoke wreaths that swirled about him.

"Pictures in the smoke," he meditated, "wonderful pictures. As those gray clouds spiral in the air they take a woman's shape—they frame a woman's face, they wreathe a woman's hair. God save the king that has her

for his loyal subject. Glory, laurels, honor, success—
Benedetta—" The words he had been forming had come
slower and slower from his lips. His head had dropped
lower and lower as he spoke and now immediately upon
the utterance of the beloved name his chin sank upon his
breast and O'Flynn very actually and positively fell
asleep.

How long Flynn sat there, first smoking consciously,
then, when his pipe had gone out, dozing unconsciously,
and so drifting into the kingdom of dreams, Flynn never
knew. In those dreams he met with Benedetta; she
whom even the magic of dreams could not make more
lovely than she showed to him in life. In those dreams
he walked with her, talked with her, found her more kind
than smiling, believed himself elected her friend, her defender, esteemed himself a god among mortals — for he
was not allowed to kiss her hand without challenge or
question.

He was roused from these raptures, which found, alas,
a physical interpretation in rather vehement snorings, by
a noisy imperative knocking at his front door. At first
these knockings merely translated themselves to his slumbering senses as portion of the pageant of his dreams, but
presently as they persisted and increased in vehemence,
he became gradually and reluctantly aware that he was
not walking in a rose garden with Benedetta who had
just promised to marry him, but that he was huddled in a
hard chair in the bleak hall of Castle Famine and that his
chin was resting heavily upon his breast.

Still the rapping continued, alternating between a series
of taps that seemed almost apologetic and positively
plaintive, and a rattling tattoo that well-nigh threatened

93

invasion. Flynn tugged at the strings of his somnolent senses and tightened them to aptness for use. He lifted himself from the chair in which he had allowed himself to lie embedded, glanced ruefully at the ruins of his pipe upon the floor, and then directed his still uncertain steps toward the door upon whose panels the thumping still persisted. As Flynn reached the portal there came a moment's pause in the summons, a pause in all probability due to the temporary fatigue of the summoner, for when Flynn drew open the door he caught that same summoner, with uplifted hand that clenched a stone in its fingers in the very intent to renew his appeal. On Flynn's appearance the stone was allowed to fall to earth and the hand that had used it to hammer on O'Flynn's timber was extended in salutation and solicitation.

The man who stood before Flynn on the threshold of his ragged castle was such an one as arrested, and indeed appeared desirous to arrest, the attention of the immediate spectator. He was of sufficient height to deny detraction the pleasure of calling him short, and yet at the same time it would take more than flattery to assert him tall. He was plump, he was rotund, he had a full, smooth, colorless face, whose fleshy lips suggested sensuality, whose beady eyes seemed in their mingled hints of insolence and cunning to challenge and to supplicate. The new-comer was clad, after a fashion that was patently intended to suggest a sombre and noble richness, in a body-suit of black velvet, something worn at the seams, indeed the elbows and the knees, but still showy enough for the purpose. This habit was enriched by a considerable display of imitation lace worn in a fashion that was at the least a generation old, and would have recalled the happy days of the great and glorious Restoration to a keener student of the mode than O'Flynn. The not unpleasing apparel was finished as far as the feet were concerned by sable stockings and buckled shoes, and, as to the head, by a massive black hat with its plumage of raven-hued feathers. The whole bulky presence was partially enveloped in a vast black mantle that insinuated the Spanish grandee of a second-rate tragedy.

The O'Flynn stared in astonishment at the fantastic apparition. The fumes of punch, the fumes of tobacco, the fumes of love still clouded his mind, and tags of rhyme about a childeen with fair hair who served King James were buzzing in his ears. He could not feel sure if the thing before him was a reality or a phantasm begotten of nightmare.

"What do you want?" he gasped.

The sable stranger answered him in a voice of muffled thunder that rang through the ancient hall, seeming to echo in the cobwebbed rafters, and fluttered with its vehemence the tattered banners of the past. "Hospitality," he cried, "most noble seneschal of this stately castle —hospitality."

O'Flynn gaped at him. "Hospitality," he repeated, dimly conscious that he was mounting through the waves of sleep to sensibility and so dimly aware of the irony of such a request in such a place at such a time.

The flamboyant man in black explained himself. "Even so, my lord—let me present myself—let me explain my presence, my very necessary trespass."

As the stranger paused at the end of every sentence to observe the effect of his sonorous utterances upon the hearer, O'Flynn felt bound in courtesy to say something, therefore, he said, "Proceed."

The tall man in black wagged his great face from side to side till the curls of his wig shook again. "My name is Burden," he thundered, "Matthew Burden. Perhaps you may have heard of me."

Flynn slowly but steadily collecting his scattered senses made an apologetic gesture of denial.

"Burden," he said, "Burden, well just for the moment I can't for the life of me quite—" he paused, hesitated, stammered, but the stranger took him up with a brisk tonitrous volubility.

"I am," he declaimed, "in all humility, the head of those his Majesty's Servants, the late Riverside Fellowship of Stage Players. Has our modest fame never reached your lordship's ears?"

The full, fat volume of the voice beat against O'Flynn's ears like the volleying of distant guns, or the beating of eager waves against a breakwater. It had, at least, the effect of banging his consciousness awake.

"I have been abroad for twenty years," he said, in explanation of his ignorance. "I know nothing of London." Then feeling that he had said enough on this matter and anxious to set his interlocutor right as to his pompous manner of address, he went on. "And please don't call me lordship, call me O'Flynn. I am the O'Flynn at your service."

There was no sign of embarrassment on the great white face of the stranger. "Well, then, Mr. O'Flynn—" he began, but here O'Flynn, who could endure much, but not everything, interrupted him again impatiently. To be called your lordship was bad, but to be called Mr.

THE COMING OF THE PLAYERS

O'Flynn when he was the O'Flynn, and as such to be addressed as O'Flynn by every man, woman or child that wished to address him, was something more than exasperating.

"Damn it man, no!" he protested, "O'Flynn if you please. That's the way to address me in these parts."

The big black man laid a paw on O'Flynn's shoulder caressingly. "It sounds so familiar," he protested, stroking O'Flynn's sleeve.

O'Flynn shook him off. "You may take it from me that it's not," he said, "and now, sir, what can I do for you?"

The stranger thrust the rejected hand into a fold of his mantle, struck a dramatic attitude and began. "O'Flynn, we are cast naked upon your coast."

Seeing that O'Flynn was somewhat astonished at such a statement coming from a man so thickly garmented, he condescended by the use of a single word, "Hamlet," to explain that he was making a citation from the national poet of England. While Flynn, whose familiarity with the great Master of Stratford-on-Avon was scanty, accepted the explanation with a good-humored grin, the stranger continued, "Less poetically our coach has come to grief, and I and my fellow-players entreat your hospitality till our wheel be mended."

Flynn heard the repetition of the word "hospitality" with a gloomy heart, and he smiled ruefully as he explained: "You are heartily welcome to such shelter as my poor roof can afford. But as to other hospitality, you arrive in an ill-hour. Had you come yesterday, there would have been a haunch of venison, a game pasty, a baron of beef—and—yes, a whole sheep to regale you, but these have gone the way of all roast flesh—"

97

Master Burden uplifted a massive hand in protest. "Say no more, I entreat. We travel well plenished, and if you will permit us to spread our store on yonder table, and will honor us by joining our repast—"

He paused with an air of regal condescension and Flynn, his stomach tickled by this hint of provisions, caught eagerly at his suggestion, though he tried to carry off his eagerness with an airy indifference. "Upon my honor," he protested, "I have been eating so much lately that I don't think I could swallow another morsel." Then with a sudden change of key to sharp interrogation, he asked, "What have you got?"

Master Burden, proud of his pomp, began, "Why, we travel a boar's head—"

Flynn rubbed his hands. "It'll pass—delicious."

Burden went on, "And a string of sausages."

"Admirable," Flynn applauded.

Burden continued, "With a demi-dozen of cold fowls and a ham—"

Flynn continued his applause. "Fowl and ham," he murmured, "magnificent—they're welcome."

Pleased by the O'Flynn's reception of his catalogue of viands Burden shifted his ground. "And as for liquor," he went on, "we have some flasks of prime Burgundy, and a keg of as pleasant a brandy as ever your honor tasted."

He spoke glowingly as if the Burgundy he spoke of were warming his vitals, as if the golden brandy were rolling on his tongue. His enthusiasm stirred the O'Flynn as if it had been the utterance of the sibyl.

"Master Burden," he cried, "you have such a dramatic way with you that you positively make me that am overfed feel hungry. For God's sake, bring in your victuals—"

THE COMING OF THE PLAYERS

He hurriedly checked himself, and continued, "I mean, of course, bring in your companions, at once."

Master Burden made him a stately obeisance and gave a great sweep of his sable-plumaged hat. "I am vastly obliged to you," he said, and then turning on his heel with all the dignity familiar to stage monarchs, he passed solemnly—even portentously—from the hall.

The moment he was gone O'Flynn bounded to the door that led to the domestic offices of the castle and called wildly, "Conachor, man, Conachor—where the devil are you?"

After a few seconds, O'Rourke came in rubbing his sleepy eyes with Coin and Gosling at his heels.

"Where have you been all this while?" O'Flynn questioned.

O'Rourke explained. "Sure, we've been having a bit of sleep in the stable in the warmth of the straw."

Flynn cut him short. "Listen to me," he said. "I've got some visitors, and they have got some provisions, Heaven bless them."

Coin and Gosling caught at the important word and echoed it wolfishly as if they were gnawing bones.

"Provisions!" O'Rourke blinked up incredulously at his master. "Is it food you mean?" he asked.

"No less," Flynn asserted.

He turned to the bailiffs and harangued them vehemently: "Now, I'm not going to pass you off for gentlefolk this time. These people are play-actors, and they'd see through you. You've got to be my servants and wait at table, and if you snatch any of the vivers you'll be sorry."

The little man in the brown coat shook his clenched

99

fists in a kind of impotent rage at O'Flynn. "Curse it!" he screamed, "you won't ask us to stand empty while others fill."

O'Flynn gave him a pat on the shoulder that nearly flattened him into his boots. "Be easy," he said, "I'll pass you bits on the sly. Here they come. Now, then, stand against the wall—as stiff as you can—and keep your hands by your sides, so."

He ranged the three fellows in front of the fireplace according to their sizes, the big man in the blue coat close to the door, the little man in the brown coat next to him, and the diminutive King of Munster, that could scarcely be said to carry a coat at all, ending off a tapering rank of attendants. These matters had scarcely been arranged satisfactorily when the noise was heard of the tread of many feet approaching the doorway, and in another moment Master Burden entered the room with a number of men and women behind him.

XI

THE RHYME OF THE PLAYERS

THE company that entered the room at the heels of Burden represented for the most part types suggesting rather the well-to-do citizen engaged in some reputable commercial business than vagabond and adventurous ministers of delight. Burden himself was bulky of build, solemn of presence, and dignified, even pompous in carriage. Among the foremost of the others was the fat, bald man that might have passed very well for an alderman of experience with his eye upon the chair. He had for a neighbor a fellow that suggested nothing more romantic than a thriving ship's chandler. The third of the males was a stooped, bird-like man with a large nose, who with his small pinched figure tightly habited in rusty umber coat and gray small-clothes, his wrinkled face and little peering eyes, and his thin, lank strips of dusty hair, conveyed to Flynn the impression of a confidential clerk in some not too successful business, who had learned from adversity to look sourly upon the world. Even the earlier of the two women who followed Master Burden was no marked exception to the general atmosphere of the commonplace. Though she possessed some remains of beauty and was dressed with a kind of faded splendor in amber silks and purple velvets, she suggested rather the mayoress of a small provincial town, than an artist who could thrill admiring multitudes with the flowing lines of poets.

The two real exceptions to the general air of respectability were a young man and a young girl who entered the hall together arm in arm, bringing up the rear of the regiment of players. The youth was dressed and over-dressed in what he believed to be the latest mode. Everything about him suggested a character fascinating by pitiful exaggerations. His heels, his buckles, his ruffles, his rings, his chains, his buttons and linen, his lavender coat, golden waistcoat and dove-colored breeches, all asserted themselves aggressively, and, as it were, challenged the spectator to admire the darling of the mode. He had a face that was not ill-looking in a somewhat loutish way; in his gaudy waistcoat and gallant coat he looked for all the world like a footman that was masquerading in the habits of a well-dressed master. Partly cunning, partly impudent, wholly vain and self-complacent, he was such a youth as shopkeepers' daughters might take for the very pattern and example of a fine gentleman.

But the last of the company of players, the girl, the girl that hung upon the arm of this pinchbeck fop, was curiously different from all of them. She was perhaps as obviously the actress as the youth, her companion, was obviously the actor. The stage declared itself in her carriage, in her manners, and in her attitudes, in the overaudacity of her bright eyes, in the insolent assertion of paint upon her lips and cheeks, in the exuberance of her well-displayed bosom. Yet it was plain to see that she was a very pretty woman, and might well prove a very charming woman, and if she had but paid a visit to Castle Famine under other conditions, Flynn might very well have been prepared to welcome her as at least a Thespian deity. Even with the thought of the Lady Benedetta dominant in his brain, and reigning in his heart, he was compelled to recognize that he had seldom or never in all his wanderings seen a more comely or more desirable lass than this. She was dressed with something of the same exaggeration that characterized the attire of her would-be exquisite, but with the skill of her sex she carried her affectations and exaggerations more daintily, and glittered and shone in the dusk of the gaunt hall like some silver bird in a gray forest, like some silver fish in a gray sea. It was evident that the girl from the first was pleased with the appearance of her host, and with the cheerful effrontery of her nature not only made no effort to conceal her approval but was at pains to make it patent, to the obvious indignation of her swain, who seemed to consider that he had certain rights over the lady which he resented seeing infringed.

Flynn, who was only amused at the simmering indignation of the lad, was half unconsciously pleased and flattered by the admiration of the lass. He knew how poor a figure he cut as far as his clothes were concerned, and he was glad to think that this pretty piece of impertinence could forget or ignore the shabby uniform and accept the man that carried it.

Master Burden, however, allowed little time for his host to reflect upon the nature of his guests. With a dexterity and swiftness of an experienced stage-manager, he took command of the situation and proceeded to present his companions to his new host in the grandest manner.

"Allow me," he said, "to present my dear comrades."

He pointed to the opulent lady in amber and purple. "This is our heavy lady—Mrs. Deborah Oldmixon. Her Cleopatra, sir, in *All for Love*—well, there's nothing in the world like it."

The little bird-like man in the snuff-colored coat was heard by O'Flynn to ejaculate, "No, thank Heaven!"

He smiled at the hearing, but his smile faded as the stately lady advancing steadily upon him proceeded to address him in a manner suggestive of much internal anguish:

"The gods have seen my joys with envious eyes;
I have no friends in heaven—and all the world—
As 'twere the business of mankind to part us—
Is armed against my love."

O'Flynn strove to carry an air of the most profound concern. "I am most distressed to hear it, madam," he declared.

But the gorgeous lady, swiftly changing her manner to one of a stately amiability, continued, "Ah, sir, I did but cite our divine Dryden. Whenever I hear his Cleopatra named, I must needs give tongue."

O'Flynn made her his best bow. "Monstrous obliging of you, madam, in my honor," he said.

Hereupon Cleopatra tapped his arm with her fan and whispered, "Flatterer!" She seemed inclined to linger and prolong the conversation, but she was compelled to stand aside by Burden, who now brought forward the pretty girl that had entered the room in the company of the foppish youth.

"This," he said, "this is our comic muse, Mistress **Free**, pretty, witty Fancy, the toast of the wits, the despair of the gallants, gay on the stage, sir, but a saint in the day-time."

Again the bird-like man uttered an exclamation. "Lord, have mercy!" he said, loudly enough, but no one seemed to heed him or indeed to hear him, except O'Flynn.

The pretty girl came close to O'Flynn with a provocative smile on her face. "Have you got any salt on the table?" she asked. "You'll be needing a pinch to season my praises."

O'Flynn looked at her admiringly. "Faith, pretty lady," he protested, "if I were a town gallant, I should lay siege to that same saintliness."

The girl's eyes wooed him invitingly. "Would you so? Will you so?" she asked.

O'Flynn made a gesture of deprecation. "I am but a down-at-heel soldier," he asserted, "an out-at-elbows squire—you'd have no use for my homage."

The girl laughed roguishly. "I think we may be friends, tall gentleman," she said, and would have said more but Master Burden again brought up a member of his company, and Mistress Free had to go her way and rejoin Mistress Oldmixon in the background.

The new-comer that Master Burden presented was a dandified youth that had entered the hall with Mistress Free.

"Here," said Master Burden, "is Master Conamur, prince of juveniles, lord of lovers, the idol of the fair."

The little fop gave an airy wave of his arm. "La, sir, fie!" he protested, in an affected voice, "you abash me." He turned to O'Flynn with a supercilious smile. "It is true, sir, that I am something esteemed in town. I help to set the mode. I will teach you to knot a cravat if you please, after supper."

THE O'FLYNN

The snuff-coated cynic commented, "Lout!" unnoticed.

Flynn looked down good-humoredly at the complacent little dandy. "And I," he said, "can teach you how to twist a halter. I learned it when I was quartermaster of Pandours. Many a pretty fellow like you, have I had the honor to—" He made a gesture with finger and thumb at the side of his neck that suggested the idea of hanging plainly enough, to the most sluggish intelligence.

Master Conamur shuddered, grew pale, and fluttered away to seek solace in the company of the ladies.

Master Burden then brought forward the fellow that had suggested a ship's chandler to O'Flynn. "This," he said, "is Master Winshaw, our noble parent. A fine player, sir, a ripe player, a mellow player."

Master Winshaw looked at O'Flynn with a forbidding frown. "I do my best, sir," he growled. "No artist can do more—or less." With a curt inclination of the head he joined his companions, leaving O'Flynn to murmur, "Very true."

Master Burden now presented the fat, bald man who had lagged behind his comrades with a gloomy expression on his plump cheeks. "Here," he said, "is Master Tulpin, our brisk comedian—'the merriest man within the limits of becoming mirth,' as Will says."

Master Tulpin looked at O'Flynn with an expression of profound despair. "Fate, sir," he said, in a heavy voice, "has chosen that I shall be funny, that I shall make multitudes rock with laughter, but I have that within which knows not mirth."

Flynn's sympathies were instantly aroused by the poor fellow's evident distress. "Indigestion, begad," he suggested; "try a little brandy."

THE RHYME OF THE PLAYERS

The fat man glared at him. "No, sir," he fumed, "it is not indigestion, it is ambition."

"Try a little brandy all the same," O'Flynn suggested, in a consolatory tone of voice.

The fat man nodded. "I will," he said, and going apart to where the players' stores were now displayed upon O'Flynn's table he followed the advice just given him.

Master Burden now pointed a large, white hand dramatically in the direction of the bird-like man in snuff color, to whom he called attention in a commanding voice, "And last but not least, Master Beggles, our man of business."

The little man moved, indeed he seemed to hop, a few paces forward. "I thought you had forgotten me," he said, sourly.

Master Burden protested, pompously, "Faith, I don't think you would let yourself be forgotten."

By this time O'Flynn's hurriedly constituted staff of servants had moved a large table that stood against the wall into the centre of the room to be at the disposal of the new-comers.

O'Flynn addressed his assembled guests: "I am your servant. Welcome to all. Master Burden is aware of the strange chance which finds me somewhat ill-victualled, but you bear your own provender, so spread with my benison."

While he was speaking, Master Burden arranged the table in the best position for an imaginary audience, placed the chairs, still with the imaginary audience in his eye, so that any one of that phantasmal company could be able to see each of his players conveniently, and set down the very substantial viands he carried with him upon the table with as great an air of dignity and magnificence as he was wont to use with the pasteboard mummies which serve to represent the feasts of Alexander and the tragic banquets of Macbeth.

The O'Flynn took his place at the head of the table with Fancy Free on one side of him and Mistress Oldmixon on the other, the two ladies vying with each other in the exuberance of their attentions to their host. Opposite to O'Flynn sat Burden flanked by Winshaw and Tulpin. Master Beggles blinked birdlike by the side of Mistress Oldmixon, and Master Conamur, with a sour smile on his pretty face, strove, with no great success, to distract Mistress Free from her patent interest in the O'Flynn. Coin, Gosling, and O'Rourke busied themselves in the service of the guests, with expressions of countenance that showed how great and how painful were their efforts at restraint in the presence of so ample a display of provender. O'Flynn, himself, for all his sense of dignity, could scarcely prevent an expression of admiration from disturbing the calm demeanor he endeavored to retain at the sight of the magnificent ham which Master Burden was now boldly attacking with dexterous knife and fork.

"What a beautiful ham," he murmured, and Burden, attracted by the gloating rapture in his voice, poised a pink fragment on the fork.

"Pray, take a slice," he said.

O'Flynn waved the proffered gift away. "I really don't think I could," he protested, but then observing, to his horror, that Burden was taking his protestation in good part and removing the coveted slice he made a wild gesture to stay Burden's action, which resulted in the desired morsel finding its way in one moment to O'Flynn's plate, in the next to O'Flynn's mouth, and the third to O'Flynn's stomach. "Well, since you are so pressing. I seem to be always eating," he murmured, as the delectable flesh disappeared from view.

The ice, thus broken, and O'Flynn's effort at stoical resolve melted, the feast progressed gaily. The actors, always good trencher-fellows, ate and drank merrily. Flynn, for his part, fed with an appetite that nothing but a long course of semi-starvation could justify or excuse. At the same time, however, it must be recorded to his credit that he kept his word to his retainers and surreptitiously supplied those hungry vassals with fragments of chicken, slices of ham, and portions of boar's head which he pretended to acquire for himself, and distributed skilfully as opportunity offered. When serious inroads had been made into the players' victuals, and when several flagons of Burgundy had been emptied in the drinking of many healths, the silence that had properly enough brooded over the business of satisfying hunger was allowed to dissipate.

Fancy Free, laying a fairly white hand affectionately upon O'Flynn's dingy sleeve, questioned him. "Do you never feel lonely in this queer old place?"

O'Flynn gave a great sigh of satisfaction. He had eaten, as he calculated, enough to keep him alive for at least a week if no other provisions came his way, and he drained a mug of Burgundy now before answering the player-girl's question, eying her over the dwindling crimson flood with the admiration born of unexpected good cheer. "Devil a bit," he protested, as he set down the vessel with a jolly laugh. "Sure, I've got the ghosts of my ancestors to keep me company."

Mistress Oldmixon, who affected extreme sensibility to an almost old-maidenish degree, though there was nothing old-maidenish either in her opulent appearance or her opulent nature, affected to shiver. "Lud, sir," she protested, "never talk of such things. You give me the shudders."

While O'Flynn was endeavoring to soothe the good lady's ruffled emotions, Master Winshaw, that had caught a word of the conversation and was inspired by it to autobiography, leaned forward and addressed O'Flynn gravely. "I have played the ghost in *Hamlet* with much success."

O'Flynn stared at him, failing to see the relevancy of the remark to which no one else paid any heed.

Mistress Free continued to ply her companion with questions. "Were your ancestors such pleasant fellows as you?"

Flynn laughed louder than before. The repeated bowls of Burgundy, following upon the previous potations of punch, though they could have but little serious effect upon his seasoned head, were producing the result of making him amazingly merry, confidential, and inclined to good-fellowship. "I'm afraid," he said, "some of them were a bit wild, young lady. I could tell you such stories, but I won't—" he paused with a jolly laugh that suggested such possibilities of good narrative that Fancy immediately clasped her hands and entreated him to continue, while Mistress Oldmixon, that was beginning to resent Fancy's undue share of the attentions of their host, protested against the suggestion. "Fie, Fancy, bold girl, for shame!"

The slight altercation that ensued between the two ladies was interrupted by Tulpin, who, with a manner of a man habitually gloomy, levelled a question across the table at O'Flynn. "How do you employ your time?" he asked, in such a voice of melancholy as might have been used by the man that plucked back Priam's curtain and told him tall Troy was burning.

O'Flynn was too merry to be depressed by the quality of Tulpin's question and he answered its purport gaily. "Fine days I tramp the country-side. Wet days, and we have them occasionally—" he admitted, apologetically.

Burden raised his hands in a theatrical manner. "Oh, my dear sir," he said, with mock despair.

Tulpin persisted alike in his gloom and his curiosity. "Well, then, on wet days?"

"Why, I sit by the fire and string rhymes," Flynn confessed.

The confession stirred Fancy to a fresh interest in her companion. "Lord, now, are you a poet?" she cried. "How lively."

Burden instantly rose from his seat and addressed O'Flynn in his most pompous manner. "Indeed, sir, is this so? Have you a tragedy or a comedy in your pocket?"

O'Flynn modestly deprecated the suggestion. "Nothing of the kind," he declared. "I'm not a serious poet. But I got the way when I followed the wars of making verses about this and that to while away the dull hours."

Master Conamur, having failed through all this time to attract the attention of Mistress Free, now made a bold bid for the attention of the company. "Very commendable, too," he said, in a loud voice, "and genteel. Many of my noble friends in town condescend to woo the muse at their leisure."

Nobody paid him any heed. Fancy snuggled closer to O'Flynn. "Dear soldierman," she pleaded, "ring us some rhymes now."

O'Flynn would fain deny her. "Madam," he said, "I

have not Mr. Dryden's mind, to do justice to tragedy and comedy in a breath."

But Fancy was not to be baffled so lightly. "Nay," she insisted, "now something to please me. I never met a poet before that I liked."

By this time Conamur's exasperation at Fancy's admiration for Flynn had reached its height, and he was determined to air his satire. "Nay, nay," he cried, shrilly, "never vex the gentleman. These private poets always need a week or so to prepare their impromptus and extempores."

The rest of the players, and especially the two ladies, looked reprovingly upon the juvenile and his ill-mannered impertinence, but O'Flynn took the insolence in good part. He was so blithe with food and wine that he could have afforded to ignore grosser offences than that of the little fellow in the lavender habit, who looked so like a girl in boy's clothes.

"Come now," he said, jollily, "that rings like a challenge—a thing I never pass. So with your permission, ladies, I will rhyme you some rhymes now on yourselves and your trade after a fashion that I learned from a French musketeer in Flanders."

As he spoke he rose to his feet, his busy imagination already tossing rhymes about and his gaze fixed steadily upon the company.

"Bravo, bravo," Fancy screamed in an ecstasy of delight, while the rest of the players, welcoming the promised entertainment, rattled their knives approvingly upon their plates, with the exception of Master Conamur, who thrusting back his chair a little, sat with his hands in his breeches pockets, the incarnation of sullen discontent.

THE RHYME OF THE PLAYERS

To the O'Flynn, trained as he had been in his youth in the art of improvisation, by the peasants who had been his friends, there was nothing so surprising in the feat he now proposed, as it appeared to his audience. Resting one hand lightly upon the table and glancing alternately at Mistress Free and Mistress Oldmixon, he was already planning the lines upon which his as yet unborn poem was to run.

"And look you," he said, as the storm of applause aroused by his announcement died away, "if I halt or boggle or fail to make good, I will pay what penalty your prettinesses may please to pronounce. So here goes for the ballad of the strolling player." With that the O'Flynn, who had found a scheme for his song, began to recite in a loud and sufficiently musical voice:

> "A stick of paint, a twist of hair,
>   A scarlet mouth—a scarlet nose—
> A velvet coat the worse for wear,
>   A pair of parti-colored hose—
> A gilded crown with glass arrayed;
>   A wooden sword, a buckram shield—
> These are the actors' stock-in-trade,
>   Since Thespis drove his cart afield."

While he had been improvising these lines with a rapidity which astonished a company unused to practice of the art, the players had glanced at one another with smiles of appreciative amusement, and as O'Flynn flung the last line of his verse, which indeed had been the first line that had come into his head, across the table, they renewed their plaudits lustily.

THE O'FLYNN

"A pleasant humor," Tulpin commented, mournfully.
The O'Flynn gave no time for further comment. He
was well in the saddle of his Pegasus now and spurred his
steed gallantly. Rhymes seemed to be tumbling in upon
him from all directions and words shaping themselves
obligingly to his desire. He started again:

> "A merry man, a minion fair;
> A brace of friends, a brace of foes,
> And lovers twain, a troublous pair,
> Full of their wooing and their woes;
> A salary that's seldom paid,
> A hunger gallantly concealed—
> These are the actors' stock-in-trade,
> Since Thespis drove his cart afield."

As he paused he received renewed applause.
Fancy screamed with delight, "What a satirical wit!"
And Burden thundered, "Continue, sir—pray continue."
Flynn, who had taken advantage of the pause to review
his rhythmical forces, was ready to renew the enterprise.
He began again:

> "A-journeying ever here and there,
> Thro' sun and rain, thro' dusts and snows,
> With shoes that sadly need repair,
> The merry-hearted mummer goes.
> And often, when the play is played,
> The audience naught but once will yield.
> These are the actors' stock-in-trade,
> Since Thespis drove his cart afield."

Again the plates rattled on the table, again the roar of
laughter rang from man to man, though Mistress Old-

mixon's sensitiveness was so affected by the picture presented in the later lines that she was obliged to produce a lace-edged handkerchief and to sit for a moment or so like Niobe, all tears.

Master Winshaw leaned forward and addressed the improvisatore with a grim smile. "I vow, sir," he said, "you see us with a roguish eye."

O'Flynn had already perceived that he had allowed his humorous muse perhaps to dwell a little too long upon the tragic-comedy of the players' life and that it was time now to redress the balance. "Nay, nay," he said, "there's a fine moral in my tag," and without a pause he flung himself into his envoy:

"Singer, for shame—a magic blade,
    A magic wand the players wield,
These are the actors' stock-in-trade,
    Since Thespis drove his cart afield."

XII

THE HIDDEN TREASURE

THE players applauded lustily at this honorable conclusion, gratifying alike to their vanity and to the
incantations of their art. Even over Tulpin's solemn
countenance a ray of satisfaction stole and the sneer on
Conamur's face degenerated into a simper. As for the
women, their enthusiasm for their hero flamed into
exultation.

Fancy flung her white arms about O'Flynn's neck,
crying, "I swear you shall have a kiss for your wit." And
Mistress Oldmixon—not to be outdone—did him the same
kind office with her plumper limbs, swearing, "Indeed he
deserves it."

One after another the women gave Flynn kisses, which
he returned cheerfully enough, while Burden rose from
his place at the foot of the table with lifted glass and voice
of solemn enthusiasm:

"Sir, your good health," he said, richly. "I can take a
joke, I thank Heaven, and you have a merry disposition."

The simper on Conamur's face wrinkled back into the
former sneer. "Your muse," he said, sourly, "has a sharp
eye for the players' patches and tatters . . . .yet she is
none too well housed herself, I take it. Your castle seems
to be sadly out of repair." He glanced about him as he

spoke with a malignant irony of observation that missed nothing of the penury and wretchedness of his surroundings.

But O'Flynn's good - humor was not to be troubled. "Ah, you have noticed that," he said, pleasantly. "Clever lad, keen lad. Yes, yes, it is perhaps a thought ramshackle. But indeed I like it thus. It is so pleasantly cool in summer."

Most of the players laughed at their host's pleasant acceptation of his situation, but Conamur was not to be so placated. "And what about the winter?" he snarled.

Burden was annoyed at the ungracious attitude taken up by his leading juvenile, and he showed his annoyance now and plainly speaking with a frowning face, "Keep your questions to yourself, my boy," he commanded.

Conamur surrendered into sulky silence and Fancy Free hugged O'Flynn's arm.

"Never mind him," she said. "He's mad jealous because I show a liking for you."

O'Flynn nodded affably in the direction of the fop. "Nay, nay," he said, "let the young gentleman speak. He shows an inquiring mind, a thing to be admired." He glanced round at the assembled faces with the manner of one who magnanimously made a great admission.

"The fact is, friends, my ancestral mansion is a little shabby. It has been neglected in my absence, but now that I am home again all shall soon be mended."

Burden wagged his great head in approval of the needed restoration. "It will cost a pretty penny, I'm thinking," he mused.

O'Flynn took him up lightly. "What if it does?" he laughed, "money is nothing to me."

Conamur could and would keep silent no longer. He

saw his chance of saying an unpleasant word and said it. "Is it because you haven't got any?" he sneered.

There was a general chorus of reprobation of the young gentleman's effrontery, but O'Flynn only showed amusement. When the hum of disapproval had died away he looked at Conamur with a smile.

"The young gentleman is a wit," he said, "and he hits in the inner ring. But my empty pockets—my empty coffers will be full again—full to overflowing, soon enough."

Conamur grinned a grin of incredulity. "Indeed—when?" he questioned with insinuating disbelief.

Now this was indeed the very question which the O'Flynn found it hard to answer. Flushed with food and wine and applause, with unfamiliar fellowship, and unfamiliar mirth, he had allowed himself to be carried away by the geniality of the situation and he believed himself for the moment to be what each of his ancestors had been one after another, the wealthy and hospitable host of a well-plenished dwelling. Thus he had allowed himself to say what came into his mind without troubling himself very particularly as to its exact meaning or its exact accuracy, and the sudden challenge of Conamur brought him up sharply. He had had some hazy idea when he spoke of his empty pockets and their probable speedy filling, that the proverbial luck of the O'Flynns would perform the necessary miracle, but when that miracle had to be expressed in terms intelligible to ordinary mortals the O'Flynn was for a moment gravelled. Only for a moment, however, then he thought of the legendary wealth which he had wasted some precious hours in pursuing, and he determined to turn the fancy to advantage. He laid a finger to his lips and glanced around at the company mysteriously.

Then he removed the lifted finger and whispered, "When the time comes to make use of the hidden treasure."

The players glanced at each other in surprise.

Burden concentrated the general curiosity into a definite question. "What hidden treasure?" he asked.

O'Flynn was now fairly embarked on the fairy argosy of romance and was not inclined to allow trifles to interrupt his voyage. His nimble fancy rapidly supplied him with what for the moment seemed to him to be facts. He answered Burden's question with a glibness which delighted while it surprised him.

"My grandfather's buried treasure. It's a strange story, but it's worth your attention. Not far from where we sit is a treasure whose possession will make me rich among the rich. My grandfather was a miser—a vile fault. He hoarded and hid, and hoarded again, and hid again, till the walls of this old castle are like so many gold mines." He gave a sigh of satisfaction as he spun this amazing yarn, and felt in the best of tempers with himself because he found that for the moment he was seriously believing in the story he had told so gayly.

But even as he basked in the admiration and the interest which showed themselves on the faces of the players, and even as he tried to close his ears to the ill-suppressed chuckles of O'Rourke behind his chair, Master Conamur nipped in to trouble his allusions with a sneaping wind of cynicism. "But if this be so," he asked, with a snarling drawl, "why do you cut such a poor figure?"

Once again O'Flynn found his invention at first stayed and then spurred by the pertinacity of the sham exquisite. He tossed the problem about in his brain for a second or so and then found a prompt and plausible explanation.

"By the terms of his will," he declared, "I am bound under pain of disinheritance not to touch one penny of the treasure until the midnight of Midsummer Day next. Then I shall be indeed rich. But, as in the mean time I have nothing to live upon, I propose to tramp to Dublin and get a lawyer to raise me a trifle upon my prospects."

The smooth, solemn countenance of Master Burden suddenly rippled with good-natured benevolence, and he raised a full, white hand in friendly protest. "Nay, good sir," he cried, "wherefore should you tramp? Enliven us with your fellowship. We will carry you to Dublin gladly for the sake of your company."

O'Flynn smiled cheerfully at the master player's proposal. It seemed like a good omen which suggested that Fate was giving him a friendly jog. "Faith, it's a kind offer," he declared, "and I've a mind to shake hands on it."

"Do so, do so," Burden urged, warmly. "Our ladies claim the coach, but you are welcome to a place in our wain."

The pretty, impish face of Fancy Free was flushed with delight at the thought of the proposed companionship. She hung on O'Flynn's arms and looked up into his eyes engagingly. "Be persuaded, merry soldierman," she pleaded. "You shall make songs for us through every stage of the journey."

Master Conamur, that was now provoked beyond all patience by the prospect of the further companionship of the mad Irishman, for so to himself he styled his host, made his little effort to prevent the proposed plan. "You will find it mighty rough travelling in the wain, I promise you," he said to the O'Flynn in the tone of one that delivers in time a friendly warning.

THE HIDDEN TREASURE

But O'Flynn was not to be dissuaded by any vague hints of discomfort. "Sir," he answered, cheerfully, "I have travelled on a cannon-carriage and slept like a baby."

What Master Conamur would fain have said to dissaude O'Flynn from his journey was stayed by Master Burden, who laid his large hand affectionately upon O'Flynn's shoulder. "There is but this to it," he said, "that you make up your mind quickly, for I take it our wheel is mended by now and we must be jogging."

By this time all the company were on their feet and full of the bustle of imminent departure. O'Flynn nodded acquiescence. "An old soldier needs little preparation for a march," and, as he spoke, he took up the old valise that lay in a corner of the hall and clapped a pair of pistols into it.

While he was thus engaged, and while the other members of Master Burden's Riverside Fellowship of Players were packing together the remains of their provisions and their cups and other table utensils, the bird-like individual in the snuff-colored garments that had been designated by Burden as Master Beggles, after a cautious glance around him to see that the others were not taking note of his action, drew near to Flynn and plucked him by the skirt of his soiled white coat and addressed him in a low voice. "Sir," he murmured, "I crave your attention."

O'Flynn shut the valise to with a snap and turned to his interlocutor. "At your service," he said, simply.

Master Beggles fixed him with an inquiring eye and pointed a lean forefinger in sign of interrogation. "This treasure you talk of," he said, and there was a kind of anxiety in his voice which for the moment puzzled O'Flynn, "is it very vast?"

THE O'FLYNN

O'Flynn was now so deeply committed to his imaginary treasure that he had come to have a kind of credence in its existence himself, and he was not disposed to let his imaginary wealth suffer any depreciation from his mouth. So, with a jaunty air of carelessness, he answered Master Beggles. "That is as you may reckon it." He paused for a second or so as if to make some swift calculations and then added, "About a million of pounds to an odd penny or so."

Master Beggles held up both his hands with a rapture of admiration. "A million of pounds," he murmured, "magnificent."

By this time Flynn was convinced that his estimate of his mysterious fortune was no more than just, and the joviality of his manner seemed to irradiate warmth and thaw the harshness upon the face of Master Beggles. "I have never had so much to spend in my life," he protested. "I shall enjoy myself, I promise you."

In his fancy he saw himself in Dublin pitching his guineas recklessly, but at the same time, something shrewd in his character urged him to study curiously the appealing countenance of Master Beggles.

Master Beggles, now with hands clasped as if in prayer, began with a stammering eagerness that puzzled and amused his hearer. "If you will pardon my presumption," he said, "in meddling with your affairs I should advise you to go to no Dublin lawyer."

O'Flynn stared at him. "Indeed, and why not?" he asked.

Master Beggles was quick to explain. "Lawyers are queer cattle; best keep clear of them. What you want is some sober reputable citizen who has got a little money put by and is ready to lend it on reasonable interest, reasonable interest, I say, not such as those Dublin sharks expect."

Some vague idea of what the business man of the Riverside Fellowship of Players was driving at began to enter the O'Flynn's head, an idea that seemed preposterous and yet after all was not impossible. But he took good care to show no sign of his suspicions and asked with a great air of innocence, "But where am I to find such an one?"

Master Beggles turned the tips of his fingers against his chest and tapped it significantly. "Just here," he answered, "under your nose. I have put by a considerable sum, but acting is an uncertain trade in these days, and I should like my store to increase and multiply. I shall be pleased to advance you such sums as you may require until you can touch your treasure."

O'Flynn regarded his unexpected friend with gratified amazement. The man was obviously in earnest. The man actually proposed to put money into Flynn's pocket on the strength of a chimerical treasure. To do the O'Flynn justice, that treasure was no longer chimerical in his mind. He believed in its existence firmly and regarded Master Beggles's proposition as a very sensible business offer.

"The devil you will," he said, and tried not to seem too delighted as he said it.

Master Beggles coughed discreetly. "On reasonable interest, of course," he added.

The O'Flynn pretended to be wary, pretended to be prudent, pretended to be business-like. "What do you call reasonable interest?" he questioned with a well-assumed air of cunning.

Master Beggles coughed again. "Shall we say ten per cent?" he suggested, doubtfully.

The O'Flynn pushed the proposal away with a great sweep of the arm. "I wouldn't rob you," he declared, with a ring of indignation in his voice. "It must be twenty or nothing." And then as he saw the gleam of gratified cupidity in the eyes of the bird-like man of business, "Oh, Master Beggles," he cried, "it is the glad man you will be, come midsummer, when we dip our hands into the treasure together."

Master Beggles beamed upon him. "Till then, sir," he entreated, "pray consider me your banker."

In such a matter the O'Flynn required no lengthy process of persuasion. "I will," he answered, instantly, and extended a ready palm. "To begin with, lend me twenty guineas."

Not a little to his surprise, for the whole episode was so like a fairy-tale that he could scarcely credit its reality, Master Beggles dipped his hand into a capacious side-pocket, produced a well-filled purse, and without hesitation counted into O'Flynn's palm the twenty golden coins demanded. O'Flynn eyed them lovingly. It was many a long day since he had even seen so much money, not to speak of possessing it, but he controlled his emotion with spartan fortitude.

"Make a note of it," he commanded his newly acquired banker, with the manner of a man to whom such a transaction is a matter of every-day occurrence. Then while Master Beggles produced from another pocket a note-book and proceeded formally to enter the amount loaned, O'Flynn whispered in his ear, "And now, if you'll excuse me, I've a trifle of private business to settle before we

THE HIDDEN TREASURE

start." He left Master Beggles entering in his note-book the first item of his account with the O'Flynn, and beckoned to O'Rourke, who came shuffling toward him.

"Conachor, old friend," he said, in a low voice, " 'tis to Dublin I'm going this blessed minute to make my fortune."

The little man that ought to be King of Munster cried out upon his master in a wailing voice, "Wirra, wirra, what ails you to go flustering about the world again when you've got a snug place like this to be aisy in ?"

The O'Flynn laid a friendly hand upon the little man's shoulder as he answered, "There's a bugle blowing, whose call I can't deny—there's a flag flying I've got to follow." He took some pieces from his newly acquired store and thrust them into the grimy hand of his retainer. "Here's five guineas for you to keep you cosey till I return."

O'Rourke stared in stupefaction at the unfamiliar coins. "Oh, the beautiful gold pieces," he cried; "the noble effigies."

Leaving his majesty to his ravings over the guineas, the O'Flynn beckoned to Coin and Gosling, who were standing by the fireplace digesting their welcome and unwonted meal, and when they had joined him, he placed eleven of his guineas in Gosling's hand and a single guinea in the hand of Coin. "Here," he said, "is the quittance of your writ, with a guinea apiece to sweeten it."

He paused for a moment, and then an idea occurred to him. A gentleman of his position travelling to Dublin, ought to carry some levy of servants in his train. "What do you say, friends," he asked the two men; "have you a mind to enter my service ? You shall wear fine clothes and pocket fair wages."

The faces of the bailiffs glowed with satisfaction. If they had liked Flynn when he was penniless, they were prepared to idolize him now when he seemed to be the possessor of boundless wealth.

Coin caught at the suggestion with a delighted smile that lent a quaint expression to his little whimsical, wrinkled, twisted face. "I am with you, sir," he said.

Gosling, habitually a man of more restraint than his companion, on this occasion allowed himself to be betrayed into as great a display of emotion. "And so say I," he positively shouted.

O'Flynn gave each a hand on the shoulder. "That's well," he said. "I'll make all our fortunes."

The little king in the corner now shuffled forward. He had pocketed his coins and there was a wistful expression on his pinched physiognomy. "May I go with you?" he said, and there was a pathetically affectionate note in his voice that played on O'Flynn's heartstrings.

The O'Flynn shook his head. "No, no, O'Rourke," he protested, "you must stay here—" He paused and then laughed heartily. "You must stay here to look after the treasure." Fantastic as it was, he believed in the treasure and he did not believe in it, at one and the same time, and his henchman and fellow-countryman was something of his temper, for he, too, was impressed, or pretended to be impressed by the gravity of the charge intrusted to him, and nodded with all the dignity of one that holds high office.

At this moment Master Burden, having ascertained that his coach was in travelling condition again and that the members of his Fellowship had duly packed their belongings and were ready for the road, came into the room with a whirlwind manner that suggested Tamerlane driving his pampered jades of Asia. "Come, friends," he shouted. "Bustle. To Dublin."

Mistress Oldmixon swam across the room and thrust a plump arm into the crook of O'Flynn's elbow. "Your arm, pray," she simpered, "to the coach."

In an instant, Fancy Free, not to be outdone, swooped upon the other arm of O'Flynn as swiftly as ever a kingfisher descends upon its prey. "Nay, then," she insisted, "I must claim the other arm." She looked up with something of surprise and something, it may be, of satisfaction at the smiling face of the O'Flynn. "Why, how radiant you seem. Are you so pleased to be going to Dublin?"

O'Flynn looked at her in a rapture and his heart was in his eyes, but there was no thought of Mistress Free in his mind.

"To Dublin, is it?" he asked, radiantly. "I feel as if I were going to heaven." And with tragedy on one arm and comedy on the other, the O'Flynn of O'Flynn capered out of the ruined hall of his ancestors toward the place where Master Burden's coach and wain were waiting.

XIII

KNOCKMORE

IF the historians of the Jacobean war in Ireland at the close of the seventeenth century appear to be leagued, as it were, in a kind of conspiracy to ignore the famous and marvellous siege of Knockmore, the reason is not far to seek. The historic muse is obsessed—or perhaps it were truer to assert that the servants of the historic muse are obsessed—with a painful sense of the gravity of history, its dignity, its austerity. Now it cannot be denied that there was nothing grave, dignified, or austere about the whole business of the siege of Knockmore Castle from its Hudibrastic beginning to its Gargantuan conclusion. It was a grotesque episode from beginning to end, over which, of the few that concerned themselves with its doings, the most part rocked with Homeric laughter. It was a very burlesque upon all sieges, from Belgrade yesterday to Troy the day before yesterday, and the risibility of its case was, it may be, deemed reason enough for giving it the go-by when the time came for solemn gentlemen in pompous periwigs to play their part as military and political historians. Such as they could not stomach, with any hope of happy digestion, an episode whose stages should have been chronicled by Rabelais, or Lucian, or Butler, or some merry fellow of their kind.

KNOCKMORE

The circumstances of the siege were whimsical from the first. The cardinal humor of the thing was that Knockmore Castle was not, from any point of view, of the slightest use to either of the two powers that were contending, under conditions of so much difficulty, for supremacy in Ireland. Knockmore, in its lonely grandeur in the heart of the Wicklow hills, carried on into an age, indifferent to their glory, the fame of the Norman adventurers that had sought to make Ireland their own by means of havoc and rapine. Hated as they deserved to be, hated by the people they plundered, they had to make good their hold on the soil they polluted by girdling themselves about with girths of Titanic masonry. Behind the grim thickness of their fortifications they housed themselves in safety against the anger of their victims, issuing from their strongholds at the call of lust or hunger, like the robber-barons of the Rhine, to impress the blessings of English civilization upon a thankless multitude.

Of all the strong places that Norman skill, greed, and cunning had called into being in Ireland, no one was more boldly conceived or more nobly executed than Knockmore. The site alone which had been chosen for the building suggested a strategist of genius. Knockmore, the Great Hill, was an elevation so raised by the hand of Nature as to invite any intelligent artificer to crown its summit with some kind of fortification. The curious will find the history of Knockmore, from its foundation-stone to its fall, in the obvious sources of Irish history. They can, if they choose, survey its ruins and meditate on the glories of the past. For all that concerns the chronicle of Flynn O'Flynn, Captain of Austrian dragoons, Chevalier of the Order of the Rose of Lithuania, Knight Commander of

Poland, and Ambassador Extraordinary from His Majesty Conachor LII., King of Munster, to His Majesty James II., King of England, Scotland, France, and Ireland, Defender of the Faith, a few lines will serve the turn.

When the said King James made his raid upon Ireland, Knockmore Castle was in the hands of a more or less honest English gentleman who had inherited it from a less honorable parent that had made a fortune as a swindling army commissioner in the troublous times of the Commonwealth, and had bought the great and famous place for rather less than it was worth, as so much stone and mortar. The Lord of Knockmore was in the latter days of the seventeenth century troubled by a whimsical mental affliction which would never allow him clearly to make up his mind whether his heart was devoted to the cause of the House of Stuart, or the cause of the House of Orange. The right ventricle of that organ, considering it politically rather than physically, was true-blue Tory and was all for oak-apples and hurrah for the twenty-ninth of May; while the right ventricle—to keep up the analogy—palpitated with a fervor of constitutional loyalty to the schism of the great Whig nobles and the lofty virtues of William of Orange.

The worthy gentleman was in this vacillating condition when the regal appearance of James in Ireland seemed to set the seal of certainty upon his legitimistic leanings. He hastened to make public his allegiance to the son of the martyr and to cover with all convenient speed the brief distance between Knockmore and Dublin to lay, as it were, the keys of that vast, ancient, but in a military sense, wholly unimportant stronghold at his blessed Majesty's feet. At the same time he endeavored by a hazardous embarkation on the sea of secret political correspondence to secure the favor of the pliant Whig lords at Whitehall and the confidence of the Dutch notables who plumed themselves upon their ability to govern England as England should be governed. Never was a man wholly unsifted in public affairs and wholly unskilled in the arts of intelligent treachery put to such pains to preserve his estates at the cost of his honor. He lied as vigorously as foolishly, sought to deceive everybody, succeeded in deceiving nobody, and fondly believed that he had accomplished his purpose, made himself *persona grata* with both factions, and secured the integrity of his castle. In all which convictions he counted entirely without the existence of Luitprand van Dronk, of whom indeed he had never heard.

Luitprand van Dronk was an eccentric Dutch general who believed himself to be endowed with the military genius of a Hannibal, an Alexander, or a Cæsar, but who was chiefly remarkable for a strong head against liquor, a bull-like courage, and a kind of savage good-humor that was scarcely less alarming than the ferocity of less genial ruffians. He was dear to William of Orange because of the devotion which he had shown to the prince in the days of his early isolation, a devotion which he had maintained with unchanging fidelity through all the prince's changes of fortune. He was dear to William because of his amazing courage in action, a courage amazing in an age of courage, a recklessness as uncalculated as William's recklessness, which had earned him the magnificent reproof of the great Condé, was calculated. He was dear to William because of his delight in the chase, a delight as keen as his princely master's. But William's affection for the old swashbuckler was not so great as to persuade him that Van Dronk had in him the makings of a military strategist. This difference of opinion between master and man did nothing to lessen the devotion of Van Dronk for William. The old soldier merely held that in this instance, and in this instance alone, his illustrious master had made a mistake, of which he would some day be aware. It is probable that Van Dronk believed that day to be near at hand when he conceived the idea of affecting the capture of Knockmore.

Luitprand van Dronk heard of Knockmore Castle, of the vacillations of its owner, of that owner's presence in Dublin at the Court of James Stuart; he heard also, which interested him even more keenly, that Knockmore was blessed with the most extensive and splendidly stocked cellars of wine in all Ireland. Van Dronk loved fine wine as passionately as Anacreon, and the thought of securing an unlimited supply, and at the same time inflicting a blow upon a probable traitor, and proving his powers of military genius to his august master, combined to turn Luitprand's head.

Discipline was never a matter that gravely concerned the good Van Dronk. He belonged to the dashing, smashing school of soldiery of which Prince Rupert had been so illustrious an example, and if he saw a thing that he wanted to do he did it with little regard for conventionalities and less heed of consequences. In this instance there was Knockmore Castle waiting to be taken by any one who wanted to take it. No ordinary soldier would have wanted to take it, for it could not possibly be of the slightest strategical service in the struggle between James and William. But Van Dronk was not an ordinary soldier and Van Dronk did want to take Knockmore for the reasons already set forth. Therefore, naturally enough, and from his own point of view, logically enough, Van Dronk took Knockmore. Instead of marching to join Schomberg he diverted his course—and himself—and made for Knockmore. He took the castle of course, without the slightest difficulty. It was as easy as picking an apple from a tree. No attack was dreamed of, there were no preparations for defence; there was but a small number of able-bodied fighting-men in the place and they realized instantly the impossibility of resisting this turbulent Dutch general who came upon them from the clouds, as it were, with a well-drilled, well-equipped regiment at his back, and summoned them to surrender in the name of King William. They followed the only sane course open to them: they surrendered. General Van Dronk marched in, flew the Williamite flag from the highest battlements, put the place into fitting condition to sustain a siege, and then proceeded to investigate the wine-cellars.

He found that the reports as to the excellence of the liquors that were stored away in Knockmore cellarage were thoroughly well founded. No better judge of good vintages existed in all the Low Countries than Luitprand van Dronk, and he was quick to perceive that he had secured a treasure in his eyes far above rubies. For many hours, certain of Van Dronk's men, selected for the steadiness and surefootedness, were employed in transferring well-chosen selections of fine French wines from the shady spaces in which they lay below to the quarters the General had chosen in the castle. Then the General began to drink, leisurely, cheerfully, and gloriously.

But the military escapade which seemed so amusing to

THE O'FLYNN

Luitprand van Dronk afforded very little entertainment to King William's advisers in London, and a great deal of annoyance to King James in Dublin. King William's advisers considered, and rightly considered, Van Dronk's exploit to be a waste of time; but, as King William liked Van Dronk and seemed inclined to humor his vagaries, they set the taking of Knockmore down as a victory and made the most of it in despatches and the public prints. Whereby honest citizens in London taverns gaped at the news and talked big of the progress of the war in Ireland and the blow that had been dealt to the pride of King James by the capture of Knockmore Castle. In which talk, as it happened, they were wiser than they knew.

King James's pride had been seriously hurt by Van Dronk's Hudibrastic adventure. Among the weaknesses that marred a great character was a disposition to make too much of insignificant trifles. The taking of Knockmore was just such an insignificant trifle, but it exasperated James beyond all proportion to its importance. He conceived himself dared in his own immediate dominion by this whimsical invasion of the Wicklow hills; he found himself flouted beyond endurance by the flying of the Williamite flag on a stronghold that lay but a few leagues from the walls of Dublin Castle. Naturally enough in all this he was encouraged by the owner of Knockmore, that was furious at finding his hand forced, and was loud in urging King James to avenge the wrong that had been done to the subject and the insult that had been offered to the monarch.

King James, that was too often willing to listen to the counsels of men that in their hearts were traitors to him, listened to the counsels of the owner of Knockmore, and insisted, in the teeth of wiser advice, on sending a small force to redeem Knockmore and send the Dutch general to the right-about. This, however, proved easier to propose than execute. It was true that Luitprand van Dronk had found it easy enough to make himself master of Knockmore Castle, but at that time Knockmore Castle was held by no more than a handful of men. Now it was excellently well garrisoned by a mixed force of Dutch and English, under the command of a seasoned soldier, who, whatever his eccentricities, knew how to make the best of a good situation. When the Jacobean force made its appearance before Knockmore and summoned Van Dronk to surrender, Van Dronk laughed in the faces of the enemy. If they wanted Knockmore, he said, they must do as he did, they must come and take it. And that was exactly what the Jacobean force could not accomplish. Prudence advised its recall, but King James proved obstinate. He set unexpected store upon the reduction of Knockmore, so the Jacobean force proceeded to invest and lay siege to the castle as well as it could.

It well proved ill enough. Only a small number of men could be spared for what was known in Dublin as the folly of Knockmore; such guns as they carried with them were antiquated and worn, and their powder was of a very poor quality like most of the powder supplied to King James's armies. So, though they formally constructed trenches, and carried out all the duties of a solemn and honorable siege, they were able to make no more impression upon the massive walls that frowned above them than if they had attempted to bring about their destruction by pelting them with peas. Van Dronk, on his part, lying snug and comfortable behind his stout walls on his great rock, abstained from doing any particular damage to the besiegers for the very good reason that Knockmore, for all that it was nobly victualled, and liberally provisioned with wine, numbered among its defences but few engines of artillery, and Van Dronk's store of powder was too scanty for him to waste in needless volleys at an enemy that could not possibly, as it seemed, do him any harm.

Soon the siege of Knockmore, if still considered seriously in London news-sheets, became a standing joke in Dublin, a joke at which every one laughed except the various officers and gentlemen that were from time to time despatched into the Wicklow hills to command the besieging operation, and to fail lamentably to make any impression on the defiant fortress and its bacchanalian commander. The royal desire to regain the place grew daily, and daily the royal impatience at repeated failure. It soon began to be bruited abroad that there was no favor which it lay in the king's hands to confer that would not be cheerfully accorded to the captain that was clever enough to retake Knockmore. The knowledge of this failed to attract capable candidates, for it was plain to any soldier that under the conditions existing Knockmore was impregnable. But it impelled my Lord Sedgemouth to conceive the ingenious scheme which he had laid before my lords of Shrewsbury and which had met with the approval of the great man. My Lord Sedgemouth had for some time solicited the post that lay vacant of First Lord of the Bedchamber to His Majesty. The post lay vacant because the nobleman that held it in France was old and infirm, and would not cross the water, and was certain soon to claim to be invalided. James had a liking for Lord

KNOCKMORE

Sedgemouth, who was gay and fair to behold, but for some reason or other he denied his solicitations. Now it came into my lord's head that if he could so contrive it that Knockmore should surrender to him he would have such a claim on James's favor as would entitle him to the post it was so important for him to obtain. There was no difficulty in getting command of the besieging forces. That post was gladly yielded by its leader to any one willing to relieve him of a thankless task. Thus it came about that my Lord Sedgemouth communicated with my Lord Shrewsbury, that my Lord Sedgemouth pledged his knightly word to King James that he would take Knockmore for him on a certain day, and that Roger Hendrigg travelled to Dublin with a paper of importance.

XIV

"THE ISLE OF CYPRUS"

THE Isle of Cyprus inn was, by a curious chance, one of the handsomest buildings in all Dublin. This was because in the beginning, when its beams were set and its timbers trimmed, there was never thought that the great house would one day swing a tapster's sign from its walls and make boon companions welcome within its wainscoted apartments. It was built for a noble that was great and wealthy. He ceased to be wealthy, though he remained great, thanks to the troubles and tumults of the Civil War. Ireland was no longer a place for his safe abiding; Dublin knew him no more, and the great house changed owners time and again. It was a costly house to keep up; times were bad; money scarce; the great house was less and less cared for as time went on. When it last came into the market it looked as if no one cared to buy. But Master Bandy, a London publican on a business visit to Dublin, saw possibilities in the great house, bought it for a song, as the saying is, put it reasonably to rights, named it "The Isle of Cyprus" inn, and soon earned for it a reputation of a most excellent hostelry. He gave good beds, well aired; good food, well cooked; good wine, well kept. He soon grew popular and began to make a fortune. He bought and stocked so much wine—picking up many a cellarful of fine vintages by private treaty from impoverished gentry folk—that at last he lost count of his stock, and had to send to London to a kinsman of his to send him an experienced assistant. The assistant arrived in due time and master Bandy found him invaluable.

The glory of the Isle of Cyprus inn was its spacious hall which the visitor entered directly from the street. It was all panelled in oak; it had a gallery that gave on to many rooms which the quality were fond of hiring for private entertainments; and this gallery was reached by a magnificent staircase that curved nobly away from the hall, that had beautifully carved pedestals and railings, and was probably what Master Bandy always asserted it to be, the handsomest stairway in all Dublin. Master Bandy took care that all the appurtenances of his hall should be worthy of its splendid shell. The dressers were loaded with shining pewter; the cupboards were stocked with costly silver and scarcely less costly glass; the chests were crammed with the finest, whitest linen and napery. It was small wonder that so many noblemen and gentlemen came to make merry at the Isle of Cyprus, when they found that they could count on such regal entertainment. It was small wonder that Master Bandy was making his fortune.

Perhaps the most conspicuous object in the great hall of the Isle of Cyprus inn was a large and exceedingly well executed portrait in oils of His sacred Majesty King James II., which occupied a commanding position above the great hearth. The king was represented in his familiar habit of black with much show of soft white linen, with the blue ribbon of the Garter across his breast and the Star on his coat. The painter had caught fairly skil-fully the air of dignified melancholy which had of late be-come characteristic of the harassed monarch.

In front of this picture, a man was standing on a certain evening some few days after the departure of the players from Castle Famine with their host as travelling com-panion. The man was habited in the humble costume of an inn drawer and he carried a basket of wine in his hand which he had just brought up from the cellar and was about to range upon the adjacent sideboard when his attention had been attracted, not indeed for the first time, by the picture, and he stood for a while observing it, a singular smile upon his face. Any spectator of the scene would have been excused for believing that the humble individual who stood there staring up at the picture of the man who had been a great king and might be a great king yet again, for all he seemed so lowly and obscure, regarded himself as the peer of the paint monarch. What-ever the man's thoughts might have been they were sud-denly diverted by the appearance, on the gallery at the back of the hall, of a little fussy smug-faced man that was squat and stout and self-important with all the self-im-portance that he assumed to be appropriate to the de-meanor of the master of the Isle of Cyprus inn. He had come out of one of the rooms giving on to the gallery and he stood now, holding the door a little open, apparently listening to orders from inside. Through the partly open door came a pleasant gush of talk and laughter and the clink of glasses.

"Yes, your Grace," Master Bandy observed respect-fully, and then drew the door to behind him and the talk and the laughter and the clink of glasses were swallowed up in silence. Master Bandy peered over the balustrade at his dependent who was now ostentatiously removing the bottles from their basket. "His Grace of Tyrconnel calls for more wine," he shouted out, and then he waddled as rapidly as he could down the great staircase to where his servant awaited him.

The servant held up a bottle of wine with an approving look. "There," he said, "here is what should tickle his gills. Master Bandy, 'twas your wise thought to send for me from London to range your cellar. It can't have been overhauled for a generation. Here is some fine old Burgundy that is worth a guinea a bottle."

Master Bandy eyed his lieutenant with something of suspicion in his glance. "How do you know it is fine old Burgundy, Peter Morford?" he asked.

The man whom he addressed as Peter Morford answered him with a knowing chuckle. "By my sixth sense, sir, the art of knowing old wine. Why else did you send for your humble servant?"

Master Bandy nodded agreement with the words of his assistant. "Yes, yes," he said, "with king and court here, there is more calling for wine, and a man had better know what lies in his cellars. Why, his Grace of Tyrconnel likes my vintages so well that he sups here with his friends whenever he has a night's freedom from his duties to King James, God save him." As the landlord spoke he glanced with an expression of extravagant loyalty at the picture of King James which the drawer had been contemplating so steadfastly a little while before.

The drawer nodded his head approvingly, "You are a loyal man." His glance travelled from his pompous little master to the melancholy face above the hearth.

"That's a fine portrait of King James you have there," he said appreciatively.

Master Bandy beamed enthusiasm. "A fine portrait of a fine king, Heaven bless him," he cried.

"Heaven bless him by all means," the man he called Morford echoed with a certain irony in his voice, "but how if Heaven be not so condescending? How if Dutch William win the trick after all?"

Master Bandy started as sharply as if his quiet, well-mannered, deferential servant had suddenly struck him a blow, and he glanced anxiously up the stairs before he found breath to say in little better than a whisper, "Hush, hush, don't talk like that, with his Grace of Tyrconnel up-stairs with the company." He paused for a moment and then gave a little cackling laugh as he grinned cunningly at his companion: "But it behooves a poor inn-keeper to weigh the future. If Dutch William wins as you say he may, 'tis but a turn of the wrist and God save King William."

He advanced slowly toward the fireplace and put his hand behind the lower portion of the mantelpiece, and manipulated a concealed handle. Straightway, to the amusement as well as the surprise of the observing drawer, the picture of King James slowly revolved in its frame till it turned its back upon the spectators and that back represented a life-size portrait of William of Orange habited for battle with a steel breast-plate upon his attenuated person. Master Bandy surveyed his drawer with an air of great self-satisfaction.

And the drawer in response burst into hearty, if suppressed, laughter. "I see," he said, grimly, "you don't turn your coat, you turn your canvas."

Master Bandy nodded, then rapidly handling the secret machinery again, he swung William of Orange out of sight and his Majesty James Stuart once more reigned a melancholy master of the scene.

"Exactly," he said, going away from the fireplace and rubbing his hands, "now give me the wine. I'm glad this is good stuff, for there's a better judge of wine up there than the viceroy, Lord Sedgemouth, no less."

The man that Master Bandy called Peter Morford turned toward the landlord with no great show of curiosity on his expressionless face as he questioned, "And who is Lord Sedgemouth?" he asked indifferently.

Master Bandy stared at him in astonishment. "Man," he said, "'tis plain that you're very new to the Isle of Cyprus to ask such a question. Why, Lord Sedgemouth has been here every evening for the last week and always about this time. Here he will sit and drink with his friends till the world goes round."

Master Morford nodded a certain approval of a gentleman that promised to make so good a patron by his master's tavern. "Then, my Lord Sedgemouth is a pretty drinker," he observed.

"Pretty and neat," Master Bandy cried. "He can carry more wine without taking color than any nobleman of my acquaintance. He will drink and drink and keep pale, and wear a grave bearing, while he is crazy drunk behind his white face. Hush! Talk of the devil, here comes the pleasant gentleman."

Even as he spoke the door on the gallery out of which Master Bandy had issued a few minutes earlier now opened again letting through the same little gush of pleasant sounds, and letting through also a very tall and distinguished-looking gentleman, who closed the door behind him and, walking with a certain unsteadiness along the gallery, began to descend the steps. The new-comer was dressed in a rich wine-colored coat—and his flowered waistcoat, his silk breeches and stockings, his red-heeled shoes, his rich laces and jewels asserted his right to be regarded as a master of the mode. Indeed there was no one in Dublin, in London, or in Paris likely to question the right of my Lord Sedgemouth so to be regarded.

All those writers of memoirs in the seventeenth century, who treat at all of Philip Defford, Earl of Sedgemouth— and it would have been hard for any contemporary chronicler wholly to overlook him—are agreed in one thing, the praise of his person. It seems clear that to him, as to few men in any given generation, the epithet beautiful might pertinently be applied. He resembled, he recalled, as he had rivalled, my lord of Monmouth in a comeliness of carriage and countenance that most men found excessive, and that few women refrained from adoring. For all his comeliness and pride of port my lord had, or considered himself and was so considered by many, to have a deplorable ancestry. The first Earl of Sedgemouth, crested by James I. for services rendered, married toward the close of his clouded life a market-wench whose beauty, which was great, happened to be no greater than her virtue, her chastity, or her prudence. The old earl saw her, took fire like dry heather and was prepared to go to any lengths in guineas. The market-maid was politic, intractable; all the gold she wanted was a hoop of the fine metal upon the fitting finger. This she asked and was laughed at for asking; this she stood out for stoutly; this she obtained at last because the old lord's desires were hotter than his prejudices, because also, it may be, he realized that the gulf between an Inns of Court rogue and a Covent Garden apple-woman was none so unbridgeable. The certain result is that the third Earl of Sedgemouth had a marked dislike for apples and never permitted them to grace his table.

My Lord Sedgemouth descended the stairs leisurely, and even gracefully for a man that carried so much wine. He paused for a moment to glance at his pale comely face in a mirror that hung against the wall, tapped his forehead with the kerchief he carried in his hand and called to the obsequious landlord, "Now, Bandy, the wine, man—the wine. Tyrconnel is swearing like the fiend!"

"Coming, my lord, coming," Bandy answered, respectfully. As he took up a couple of bottles from the sideboard he whispered to his drawer, "You would not think it to look at him, but he is half drunk already."

Master Morford said nothing. His expressionless face revealed no hint of interest in the splendid gentleman who had now descended the stairs and advancing toward the fireplace stood there warming his slim fingers daintily.

"I'll bide here awhile," my lord said with a yawn. "It's hot in the room there, and the ladies are a check on drinking. Leave me a bottle to keep me company."

"Yes, my lord," Bandy answered. He handed a bottle to the man he called Morford, filled the drawer's basket with wine and hooking it on his arm ascended the stairs, opened the door of the room where the viceroy's party were amusing themselves, and let out again a little ripple of mirth which was silenced as he closed the door behind him.

Master Morford meanwhile was busying himself with the

drawing of the bottle, which Master Bandy had intrusted to him for the delectation of my Lord Sedgemouth. It proved to be an elaborate process needing much examination, first of the corkscrew, then of the bottle, then of the cork before inserting the twisted steel into its substance. Very slowly Master Morford drove the instrument home, standing the while with his back to my lord there at the fireplace.

My lord seemed to watch his proceedings at first with some amusement, then with impatience. He glanced at the clock and noted the time it told with a frown; he drew out his watch and compared its statement, apparently to his dissatisfaction, with that of the clock, then he advanced to the table and drummed on it sharply with the tips of his fine, delicate fingers. "Brisk, man, brisk," he cried, "am I to die of thirst?"

The drawer still kept his back turned to his magnificent client, but he answered with a voice that was more mocking than deferential, "I thought your lordship was growing impatient."

Sedgemouth stared at the fellow. He had thought his form strange to the inn and now the voice sounded strange, too. "You have an unfamiliar back," he said, "who are you?"

Master Morford drew the cork and turned on his heel in one and the same instant, facing my Lord Sedgemouth and holding the bottle in his extended left hand. He tapped himself on the breast with the cork on the end of the corkscrew as he introduced himself, "Mat Bandy's new drawer from London, Peter Morford, at your service." He came close to the table where my lord had now seated himself and poured out a glass of the precious liquor. "This is a rare wine. Will your lordship drink the first glass to the king?"

My lord looked at him with a smile. "You are an original," he protested. "By all means!—the king!"

As he spoke he was for lifting the filled goblet to his lips, but the drawer laid a finger on his sleeve and stayed him. "But which king?" he asked, ironically. "King Lemon here in Dublin, or King Orange yonder in London?"

My lord let the goblet descend to the level of the table again and he frowned a little at what he conceived to be the impertinent presumption of the man. "Fellow—" he began.

But the drawer with perfect composure interrupted his lordship's show of anger: "Your lordship," he said calmly, "is impatient because you haunt this tavern nightly for a message and the message does not come. I do not marvel that your lordship is fretful."

There followed a pause of several seconds during which the man that was called Morford stared steadfastly at my Lord Sedgemouth, and my Lord Sedgemouth stared no less steadfastly at the man that was called Morford.

Then my lord said with something of anxiety in his voice, "Have you something to say to me?"

The man that was a servant came close to the man that was a great nobleman and addressed him emphatically, "I have but one word for you," he said, "and that word is 'Whitehall.'"

My Lord Sedgemouth's anxiety now grew keener and he questioned his companion eagerly, "Are you the man?"

The man that was called Morford suddenly and easily abandoned his humble manner and spoke to Lord Sedge-

147

mouth with ease and authority: "I am the man," he said. "I am Roger Hendrigg, one of King William's humblest, but also one of his most useful servants."

My Lord Sedgemouth's habitually pale face seemed to grow paler as Hendrigg spoke to him. "You must make me sure," he said, and there was fear and suspicion in his voice as he spoke.

Hendrigg nodded his head coolly: "Of course," he said. "You were to have three tokens. One was my Lord Shrewsbury's signet-ring; one was a guinea of James Stuart with a hole in the middle of it; one was a piece of paper with some words and a signature."

My Lord Sedgemouth tried to preserve his familiar carriage of nonchalance in the presence of this strange messenger of Fate. He took out his snuff-box and helped himself to a pinch with fingers that he tried to keep steady but which betrayed, in spite of his effort at mastery, the agitation of the man. "Where are these tokens?" he asked, and his voice shook a little as he questioned.

Hendrigg slipped his hand into a side pocket and produced a gold ring. "Here," he said, "is my Lord of Shrewsbury's signet-ring. A pretty motto 'Prest d'accomplir.' His lordship is always ready to accomplish his own advancement." He laid down the ring as he spoke.

And Lord Sedgemouth took it up and examined it and knew it to be the expected signet. "Lord Shrewsbury is my friend," he said with a show of anger which Hendrigg wholly disregarded.

From another pocket he drew a gold coin which he laid upon the table before Lord Sedgemouth. "Here is the guinea of James with the hole through it, which shows that we have nailed that false coin to the counter."

"THE ISLE OF CYPRUS"

My Lord Sedgemouth took up the coin and scrutinized it. It was, as Hendrigg said, a James guinea and it had a hole in it, punched right through the effigy of the king. He looked up at Hendrigg thoughtfully, "And the third token ?" he asked.

From an inner pocket Hendrigg instantly produced a paper. "Here it is," he said. "It is an order to the Dutch Governor of Knockmore, commanding him to surrender the castle to the bearer if allowed to march out with the honors of war. It is dated from Whitehall, and it is signed, William. Is not that the paper you expected ?"

My Lord Sedgemouth brought his finger-tips together and spoke through compressed lips, "Perhaps," he said, softly.

Hendrigg looked approval of his caution. "You are politic," he commented. "You are thinking that I might have killed the true carrier, and stolen his tokens—for all you know to the contrary, as I killed the fellow that was coming here to be drawer to the landlord yonder."

My Lord Sedgemouth lifted his fine eyebrows a little. "Why ?" he questioned.

Hendrigg replied: "To take his place. What better office for a William spy with a message to deliver than drawer in a tavern hard by Dublin Castle ?"

My Lord Sedgemouth smiled faintly. "You stick at little," he said.

"I stick at nothing," Hendrigg asserted, emphatically. "He that plays at politics with a half heart had better keep out of the game. Chew that wisdom, my dear lord."

Sedgemouth looked at the quiet man, at the quiet figure,

at the quiet, expressionless face and felt assured. "I think you are the man," he said.

Hendrigg came closer to him, resolved to silence all doubts. "Let me convince you," he said, slowly. "Let me whisper in your ear a piece of secret history. Though you, my lord, profess allegiance to King James in Dublin, you are really a secret agent of King William, and here on a special mission."

My Lord Sedgemouth gave a little laugh. "Am I so?" he said.

Hendrigg went on without heeding. "That mission is in the first place to obtain the post of First Lord of the Bedchamber to James Stuart."

By this time my Lord Sedgemouth had regained full control over himself. His airy manner had returned, and he played with his snuff-box in security, letting no grain of the precious powder fall upon the splendor of his brocaded waistcoat. "I have," he drawled deliberately, "asked King James to give me that place of honor."

Hendrigg grinned. "But James Stuart has not made you his First Lord of the Bedchamber."

Lord Sedgemouth shrugged his shoulders: "I have rivals," he said. "The king has whims. There are times when he is as hard to manage—I was going to say as a woman, but I have never found women hard to manage—" Here he paused and laughed again, a laugh of infinite self-satisfaction, for my lord was very famous for his successes in love.

"Let us say as a mule," Hendrigg commented, gruffly. He cared nothing for my lord's love-affairs.

My lord went on with his story. "Service for service, says his Majesty to me, tells me I have done nothing for him yet, that I shall be rewarded when I deserve it. Well, one of King James's armies has been besieging Knockmore for the last month without success. The place seems impregnable, but James has set his heart on taking it. I see my chance, I promise to take Knockmore as a present for his Majesty, and if I do the king promises me the post I covet. I let my Lord Shrewsbury know of this, and he, as you see, sends me the paper which is to insure the surrender of the town."

"Yes," said Hendrigg, "and when the town is taken you know what you have to do?"

My Lord Sedgemouth answered him in a low voice. "I am to bring about the abdication of James Stuart. Holding the post of First Lord of the Bedchamber, I should have daily, nightly, hourly access to the royal apartments."

Hendrigg spoke in the same low tone as my lord had used. "As such you could be the means of introducing at the right time a certain number of persons to the presence of James Stuart, men of strong will, men of strong hands, men of stern purpose."

My lord took another pinch of snuff. "And that purpose?" he asked, with a faint air of gay indifference.

Hendrigg spoke gravely, spoke sternly. "To get rid of James Stuart—to force him to sign an Act of Abdication —to kidnap him back to France—to kill him if necessary."

My Lord Sedgemouth yawned a little, checked the yawn with a gracefully lifted hand and then said, languidly, "That need not be necessary."

Hendrigg grunted again: "Maybe not. All we want is that on a certain morning Dublin shall wake up to find

11   151

that there is no Stuart king in Dublin Castle, and that every wall in the city is labelled with a copy of his Act of Abdication, the original of which myself will carry to Whitehall. You understand?"

My Lord Sedgemouth nodded, "I understand."

"When you are master of Knockmore," Hendrigg went on, "when you have your post of attendance of James Stuart's person, look to see me again. I shall find the man we shall need to lay our little game of abdication."

My Lord Sedgemouth stretched himself and spoke a little fretfully, "I wish it were done," he said.

Hendrigg looked at him reprovingly: "I am never impatient. If a thing cannot be done quickly, then it must be done slowly, that is all. The great thing is that it be done."

"Philosopher," my Lord Sedgemouth commented, and laughed.

Hendrigg leaned forward toward the objects he had laid upon the table. "As for these tokens," he said, "the ring goes back to my Lord Shrewsbury as soon as may be. The James guinea I shall hold for myself as a pocketpiece. This paper is your part of the plunder. Keep it carefully. If it were found with you I think you would hang."

My lord smiled a little sourly at Hendrigg's humor. "It shall not be found," he promised.

Hendrigg had moved a little apart from my lord as he pocketed the ring and the coin, but now he drew near to him again. "And now, my lord," he said, "before we part, tell me, for my private satisfaction, why you follow James Stuart?"

My lord looked at him with something of amusement

152

on his fine face. "Whatever happens to James, I want to marry Lord Mountmichael's daughter."

Hendrigg seemed to approve. "Lord Mountmichael is very rich," he said, "and Lady Benedetta is his only child."

My lord went on merrily: "And Lady Benedetta loves me with all her silly heart and soul. But Lord Mountmichael is hot for King James, and will have none but a James man for his daughter's suitor. Happily, Lord Mountmichael's estates and fortunes are, for the most part, in France. My Lord Shrewsbury knows that I must be outwardly a James man till I marry the pretty ninny."

Even as my lord finished speaking, Hendrigg's demeanor changed in a flash. He was no longer Roger Hendrigg conveying orders from Whitehall to my Lord Sedgemouth, treating my Lord Sedgemouth with equality. He assumed in an instant the humble and deferential bearing of a tavern drawer and it was with a humble and deferential voice that he said, aloud, "I am proud to learn that your lordship esteems our Burgundy."

My lord was taken by surprise by this shift of demeanor. "What the devil"— he began, and then lifted his eyes to the gallery and understood.

XV

THE Lady Benedetta had come out of the room where
the viceroy and his friends were revelling, and stood
for a moment in the gallery, her hands resting lightly on
the balustrade, as she looked down into the room below.
My Lord Sedgemouth looked up at her and found her very
fair to behold. He could never remember the time when
he had not been in love with some woman or with several
women, and he was not very deeply in love with Lady
Benedetta. But he found her eminently desirable now
as he saw her with his wine-stained eyes, standing there in
her youth and her beauty, and knew that she loved him
and knew that she was rich. My Lord Sedgemouth had
no passionate wish to marry; his knowledge of other men's
wives inspired him with no great enthusiasm for the possession of a wife of his own, but my Lord Sedgemouth's coffers
were empty; my Lord Sedgemouth's lands were mortgaged;
my Lord Sedgemouth's luck at cards had been, of late, unfortunate. Scandal had always represented my lord as a
gentleman that was willing to be kind to ladies that sought
his kindness for a substantial monetary consideration, but
even this means of filling his pocket had not, of late, presented itself with sufficient frequency to be regarded as a
substantial item in my lord's uncomfortable budget.

MY LORD SEES FANCY FREE

Therefore, my lord was willing to make the best of a bad business and to marry a fortune; and under these circumstances, had gratitude been part of his composition, he should have been grateful to the chance that flung fortune in his way with so lovely a lady seated on the top of it. As it was, he professed to be content with his condition and he accepted Lady Benedetta's very simple, childish, and open admiration with a condescending tolerance which he regarded as a conclusive proof of his own extreme good-nature. He pushed the drawer aside with a careless left hand.

"Yes, yes, my good fellow—I never tasted better—" he said, and made the Lady Benedetta a stately bow.

Benedetta leaned a little farther over the gallery and called down to her lover, "My dear lord, why do you abandon us?"

Hendrigg, with no sign of intelligence on his expressionless countenance, made a profound salutation to Benedetta and another to Lord Sedgemouth and quitted the room.

Lady Benedetta came running down the steps toward my lord, who moved with leisurely grace to greet her.

He lifted her hand to his lips very courtierly and kissed it. "Most dear lady," he said, tenderly, "dare I believe that you noted my absence?"

Benedetta gave a little sigh and smiled faintly into the handsome face before her. "Indeed," she protested, "it has all grown dull for me without you."

My lord made an apologetic gesture toward the table with its freight of wine and glasses. "I did but taste a vintage on which our landlord asked my judgment," he explained. "Forgive me, sweet lady." He held both her hands in his as he spoke and looked into her eyes with

155

that keen regard wherein fierceness and homage were ingeniously blended—a regard that had made many a woman, before Benedetta's day, believe that Lord Sedgemouth loved her.

Benedetta gave a little cry of pleasure. "I think I could forgive you anything when you plead so prettily." She looked joyously into her lover's face as if to challenge him to the utterance of further pretty speeches.

But my lord was in no humor for such romantic traffic. Although he carried himself so airily, he had been drinking deep for some hours and his interview with Hendrigg had stirred him beyond his wont, and he needed more wine and more excitement, and not aimless dallyings with a foolish girl. It was, therefore, with a scarcely veiled weariness that he answered Benedetta's pleading glances with a question. "Shall we return?" he asked, and glanced up toward the gallery and the room which Benedetta had left so lately.

But Benedetta was not to be denied. She had stolen away from her company in the hope of finding her lover, and she had found him and did not want to lose him immediately. "Nay," she protested, "let us linger here a little. Why, I have not seen you—to have any speech alone with you—for a day! Do you not find it a long time?"

My lord swallowed a yawn. "It is a very desert of time, an age of ages," he declared, as fervently as he could. His glance still travelled in the direction of the gallery. "What are they doing within?" he asked.

Lady Benedetta began to explain. "Why, Her Grace of Tyrconnel is all of a sudden for playing games, and 'tis 'Hunt the slipper' and 'Forfeits' and 'Puss in the Corner,' and such romps, till I wearied and slipped away to seek you, my truant knight."

My lord clearly perceived that it was expected of him to play the gallant and he forced himself to the task with a fair show of enthusiasm. "I have no other picture of happiness than to be ever by your side," he said, passionately. "When will that picture prove a living fact with my sweet love for my sweet wife?"

Benedetta sighed again. "You know my father will not have me wed any man that has not done some great service for the king."

My lord flourished his kerchief with a great air of heroism. "I shall be that man," he asserted. "I shall do that great service. I have promised the king to give him Knockmore Castle as a midsummer present. To-morrow I set off to take command of the besieging force."

Benedetta looked at him in admiration; fond confidence in all his heroic qualities shining in her eyes. "I think you are sure to succeed," she said, and pressed the hand that still held one of hers.

Lord Sedgemouth returned the pressure and answered with a significance that was greater than Benedetta knew, "I know I shall succeed." He thought of Hendrigg as he spoke and of the paper Hendrigg had given him which now lay comfortably bestowed in an inner pocket close against the organ which he was pleased to call his heart. Cheered by his sense of security he continued, caressing the girl with his glances. "Fired by the hope of winning you, I feel that nothing can stand in the way of my purpose."

Benedetta looked up at him as some devout votary

might regard a sacred image. "My hero!" she cried, "My St. George, my Paladin!"

She looked so pleasing in her pretty vehemence that my lord felt some stirring of the spirit and clasped the child in his arms. "Beloved," he said, and kissed her passionately and felt for the moment quite a thrill of pleasure in the embrace. A thrill of pleasure that allowed him to feel a thrill of annoyance when there came a great noise and clatter outside the inn door and the ringing of the inn bell.

Benedetta, startled by the interruption, broke away from his encircling arms. "What is that?" she cried.

Sedgemouth shrugged his shoulders. "Some late arrivals, probably," he said.

Then, as the inn door opened, my lord gave Lady Benedetta his hand, and the pair moved slowly up the staircase to the gallery as the new-comers entered the hall. The new-comers were the members of the late Riverside Fellowship of Stage Players—Master Winshaw, Master Tulpin, Master Conamur, Mistress Oldmixon, and Mistress Free with Master Burden at their head. They swarmed into the hall making a great noise. They all looked travelstained; they all looked tired; they all looked hungry. Over the din the voice of Master Burden volleyed like muffled thunder: "Holloa, landlord! Come forth, thou fearful man!"

My lord and Benedetta had paused at the top of the stairs to observe the intruders. My lord's appreciative eye discerned the attractiveness of Fancy Free standing out from her associates and, with his characteristic carelessness of the feelings of women, he pointed her out to Lady Benedetta. "Is not she a pretty piece in the flowered silk?" he asked.

MY LORD SEES FANCY FREE

Lady Benedetta was frankly vexed and did not try to dissemble her vexation. She found it aggravating to have the comeliness of other women pointed out to her by her own lover, and being a very jealous maid betrayed her jealousy in her speech. "My dear lord, I protest, there is nothing in the wench."

My lord saw his mistake instantly and, because he did not wish to vex Benedetta unreasonably before she was married to him, he strove hastily to make amends. "You are right," he declared, in a loud voice that carried farther than he knew or heeded, "now I see clearer, she is very ill-favored."

He was so occupied with the endeavor to placate Benedetta, who, indeed, was easily placated by her lover, that he did not note a mocking smile on Fancy Free's face, or the disdainful toss of Fancy Free's head. In the meantime the players were bustling about below relieving themselves of their baggage and explaining to each other their immediate needs of refreshment. Mistress Oldmixon confided to Fancy in a stage whisper, "I could fancy pig's feet for my supper, couldn't you, dear?"

Burden, beating the table with his fist, thundered vociferously, "What ho! Within there."

Summoned by the unexpected clamor Master Bandy made his appearance from the recesses of his hostelry. "Coming, coming," he shouted, as he made his way into the hall, and then gazing at the newly assembled throng he questioned, "What can I do for your honors?"

Master Burden advanced upon him majestically portentous and addressed him in his richest voice. "You can do much, master landlord. Here are we, the Riverside Fellowship of Stage Players, come to Dublin to en-

tertain his Majesty." As he spoke he paid a florid salutation to the picture of King James above the fireplace.
"Here we will feast, here we will sleep, here will we warm
our bloods that are chilled to jelly with our travels in this
savage island."

Master Bandy might not, under ordinary conditions,
have been overpleased to welcome the coming of a cry of
players to the Isle of Cyprus inn, but he was shrewd
enough to perceive at a glance that Master Burden and
his comrades were far from common strolling players, and
to infer from their seeming and carriage that they would
be able to pay for what they desired. So he rubbed his
hands and nodded his head friendly enough and grinned
approvingly at Master Burden's comment upon the country. "Well may you so name it!" he declared.

Master Burden beamed upon him. "Are you an Englishman?" he asked, and when Bandy nodded agreement
the master player thrust out his hand. "Give me your
hand," he cried. "My name is Matthew Burden, and
this is my company." With a spacious sweep of his arm
he indicated his companions and those same companions
instantly closed around the landlord, each voicing his immediate wants, noisily.

Conamur cried, "Landlord, have you got any orange-
flower water?"

As he spoke he plucked at Bandy's right arm and Mistress Oldmixon seized Bandy's left arm and questioned,
"Landlord, are you sure the linen is well aired?"

Winshaw shrieked into one ear, "Landlord, do you
know how to mull ale?" And Tulpin groaned into the
other, "Landlord, I need a pipe and tobacco."

Master Bandy extricated himself with some difficulty

from the attentions of the players and strove to lessen the
hubbub by waving his hands deprecatingly at them.
"Gently, sirs, gently," he pleaded, and in response
to his gestures the players expressed their wishes more
quietly.

Now, while Master Bandy was dealing with these new
customers my lord turned to Benedetta where they stood
on the gallery and said to her, "Were it not sport to get
these mummers to clown for us?"

Benedetta clapped her hands joyously. "A good thought,
dear one. Her Grace of Tyrconnel loves stage plays —
and so do I."

My lord leaned over the balcony and called to Burden, "Master player, master player, a word with you."

Master Burden heard the voice, swung round and struck
an imposing attitude. "Who calls from the gods?" he
cried.

Bandy came close to him and whispered behind his
hand, "'Tis my Lord Sedgemouth, a great noble."

My lord asked Burden: "Are you and your fellows too
weary with travel to play something shortly for our entertainment?"

Master Burden rebuffed the suggestion of fatigue cheerily. "Never say it, never think it," he protested. Then
he turned to the others, who were now grouped together
and staring up at the fine lady and the fine gentleman
on the gallery. "How say ye, my hearts, shall we give
his lordship a taste of our quality?"

Mistress Oldmixon swam a little forward and dipped a
profound courtesy for my lord's benefit. "I ask nothing
better than to please his lordship," she declared.

Conamur following her lead made Benedetta a profound

salutation. "Nor I," he declared, "that to please her ladyship."

Mistress Free said nothing; she only laughed quietly to herself.

As for Winshaw, his inclination was to grumble and he grumbled. "I need some immediate refreshment," he said, surlily.

"So do I," declared Tulpin, backing him.

Perhaps my lord heard them, at least he continued his conversation with Master Burden as if he had done so. "You shall sup at my cost and a guinea apiece for your pains over your lawful charges," he promised.

Master Burden was delighted. "Say no more, my lord," he cried. "We are yours to command."

It was now Benedetta's turn to speak, and she addressed Master Burden very graciously. "What can you play, sir?" she asked.

Master Burden spread out his arms as if with the intention of suggesting universal ability. "Our heads are stocked with comedies, *D'Urfey, Killigrew, Glorious John* —what you will. But taken as we are, I should say that *The Emperor of the Moon* would be as apt as any."

Benedetta turned with a delighted smile to Lord Sedgemouth. "Yes, let it be *The Emperor of the Moon*, my dear lord."

Sedgemouth made her a bow. "As you please, sweeting. Will you tell Her Grace of Tyrconnel of the pleasure we prepare for her?"

Benedetta smiled upon him and moved quickly toward the door that masked the viceroy's party. She opened it, letting out a little breeze of laughter, then she passed through and shut it behind her.

MY LORD SEES FANCY FREE

My Lord Sedgemouth slowly descended the stairs, while the players waited upon his pleasure until he had reached their level. Then he spoke to them again. "As for you, friends, when you have had bite and sup, Master Bandy will show you the way to our presence."

Burden bowed deeply. "We humbly thank your lordship."

By this time Master Bandy had been reinforced by the appearance of his drawer, to whose care he committed the players while he himself retired into the background and busied himself with his bottles.

Hendrigg bade the players follow him and he led them out of the hall through a door at the foot of the stairs. All had passed through save Fancy Free and she was about to follow when my Lord Sedgemouth tapped her lightly on the arm. She turned and faced him, and there was a mocking smile on her mischievous face.

"You are a pretty girl," Lord Sedgemouth said, coolly.

Fancy looked at him pertly. "Do you think so?" she questioned.

My lord looked surprised. "Do not you think so?" he asked.

Fancy smiled demurely. "I know it," she said, decisively. "But I heard what you said to your great lady just now, and I think your mind is not fixed as to my good looks."

My lord laughed heartily. "Bah! she was jealous," he declared, "as well she might be, for I'll swear you are radiantly fair! Here is a kiss for forgiveness." As he spoke he caught her in his arms and made to kiss her on the lips, but the girl, being by no means taken unawares, was too dextrous for his purpose and evaded him.

163

"I do not kiss for nothing," she declared, as she slipped away from his arms.

My lord laughed again and lifted her hand to his lips. "Then I hope we may come to terms," he said, quietly.

Fancy looked steadily at him; then she smiled enigmatically and went after her companions.

My lord took snuff, slowly mounted the stairs again and disappeared in his turn into the room on the gallery.

Master Bandy, that had been a witness of the by-play between my lord and the player, lifted up his hands with an air of mock horror. "Oh, my lord, my lord," he murmured. He then went to the table where Lord Sedgemouth had been sitting at the time of his interview with Hendrigg. He examined the bottle and finding it unfinished, poured out a glass for himself and drank it off with evident satisfaction. As he set down the glass his attention was caught by the sound of a lusty voice in the street singing a lively snatch of a lively song. "There goes a merry fellow," he said; then he corrected himself, "No—he doesn't go, he stops."

XVI

NEW PLUMAGE

THE door of the inn was thrown noisily open and Flynn O'Flynn entered the hall with a swaggering manner that seemed ill-assorted with the dingy garments which he still wore. He was followed at a respectful distance by Master Beggles, who appeared to regard his new leader with a curious mixture of admiration and awe. The reason why the O'Flynn did not put in an appearance at the Isle of Cyprus inn at the same time as the rest of the players was a simple matter enough. Though the coach travelled a little swifter than the wain, the two vehicles had both made their appearance in Dublin at the same time and the players at once made their way to the hostelry of their choice. Their one wish was for rest and refreshment, but O'Flynn, whose war-hardened carcass the discomforts of the wain had failed to trouble, had other thoughts than food and drink and repose.

Promising the Fellowship to join them speedily, his first course was to ascertain the whereabouts of a barber's shop. This found, he directed Coin and Gosling to seek out the best tailor in the neighborhood and bring him with a choice assortment of his wares to the Isle of Cyprus inn. Then the O'Flynn, with Beggles in tow, entered the barber's shop, and was duly shaved and trimmed and essenced till his head, thus suddenly made modish, formed a whimsical contrast to the ragged apparel of the body. Now, fresh from the barber's and at the top of high spirits the O'Flynn strode across the floor of the hall. Master Beggles, whose frame was less calculated to resist the hardships of travel in a country wagon over a country road, dropped wearily into a chair. The O'Flynn addressed him, cheeringly:

"Courage, comrade," he cried, "the devil is dead." Then he turned to Master Bandy. "Is this the Isle of Cyprus inn?" he asked.

Master Bandy, who had been surveying his new visitor with a great air of disfavor, nodded his head. "It is," he said curtly.

O'Flynn, not noticing or not heeding the surliness of the man's manner, continued his questioning. "Are you the landlord of that same?"

Again Master Bandy answered with the same uncivil brusqueness. "I am."

Flynn now assumed his grandest manner. "Then I'm heartily glad to see you. My friend and I have been travelling in a country cart—a vile method; the others fared better in the coach, but here we are at last! for which give praise. Oh, by-the-way, I have sent a couple of friends of mine to find a tailor to fit me some clothes. Let them be sent to me the moment they arrive."

As he gave his orders in this magniloquent manner the surliness of the landlord's demeanor increased. "And who, pray, may you be?" he asked, offensively. "Are you one of the players?"

The O'Flynn slapped his chest sonorously. "Am I one of the players?" he asked. "Do I look like one of the

166

players? I am the O'Flynn, of Castle Famine—of Castle O'Flynn, I should say—Chevalier of the Order of the Rose of Lithuania, Knight Commander of Poland, and Ambassador Extraordinary from his Majesty King Conachor LII., whom Heaven preserve!"

Master Bandy looked at him suspiciously and began to believe that he had now to deal with a madman. "King who?" he asked.

The O'Flynn condescended to repeat, "Conachor LII., King of Munster."

"King of what?" Master Bandy asked, scratching his head.

The O'Flynn eyed him scornfully. "The ignorance of these English," he said to himself. "They think their own little whipper-snapper kinglets are the only tenpins in the world." He turned to the landlord again and addressed him peremptorily. "Now, fellow, which is the best room in the house?"

"Mine," Bandy answered, gruffly.

"Then I take it," Flynn declared, promptly.

Bandy shook his head. "You do nothing of the kind. You can shake down with the playermen, if they be willing, and you can pay your share."

The suggestion was not to the O'Flynn's taste and he made speed to decline it. "Sure, I like the playermen well enough, but I've a mind to have a room to myself this night."

Master Bandy laughed rudely. "I should have thought," he said, "that the middle of a field was the most likely place of your honor's lodging."

O'Flynn seemed to take no offence at the insolence of the landlord's speech. On the contrary, he laughed loudly.

"I take your meaning, you rascal," he said. "You think that these rags and tatters are more suited to a scarecrow than a gentleman." Then, suddenly changing to a ruder manner, he caught Master Bandy by the ear before the alarmed publican could escape and addressed him sternly. "But I'd have you know, my fine fellow, that this coat, for all its troubles, is the uniform of a captain of Austrian Dragoons, and that in the countries I come from we'd think mighty little of slitting the ears of any blackguardly publican that lacked respect."

As he spoke he released Bandy's tingling ear and gave him a push which sent him staggering across the floor, till he brought up against the staircase, on which he fell in a sitting posture, which he retained ruefully, evidently fearing a further attack from his dangerous visitor. That visitor meanwhile had turned to his companion and commanded him with a lordly air, "And now, Beggles, give this fellow a fistful of guineas on account, and see that he does my bidding."

The words roused Master Beggles from his fatigue and his chair. "Dear sir," he protested, advancing toward the O'Flynn, "consider—a fistful of guineas!"

The O'Flynn frowned disapproval of his paltry spirit. "Man, man, we are playing for great stakes, and must not haggle over trifles. Give him five guineas as I tell you."

With an air of sour disapproval Master Beggles crossed the floor to the place where Bandy was sitting and, producing a well-filled purse, arranged five guineas in a row on the table hard by. The sight of the coins had a remarkable effect upon Master Bandy. He rose to his feet with alacrity, forgetting his physical injuries, and swiftly pocketing the gold pieces he saluted the O'Flynn as respectfully as if he had been the viceroy himself. As for Master Beggles, he ostentatiously produced a note-book and entered to O'Flynn's account the amount expended.

"Your lordship has but to command," Bandy said.

And Flynn nodded approval. "Come, that's better. Guineas buy manners. Now, in the first place, I want your room."

Master Bandy abased himself. "Yes, my lord."

Flynn went on: "And in the second place as good a supper as you can muster, with the best wine in your cellar. Send it soon, and send it good, and set it here." As he spoke he pointed to the table near the fireplace, the table at which my Lord Sedgemouth and Hendrigg had held their conference earlier in the evening.

Master Bandy bowed again. "Yes, my lord!" he repeated.

At this moment Hendrigg entered the room through the street door and advanced to his master. "There are a couple of fellows without," he said, "and a tailor asking to see a nobleman that bade them come here."

The sound of Hendrigg's voice conveyed the sense of his words very clearly to the O'Flynn's ears, but it conveyed something else besides; a memory, a suspicion, a wonder. He answered first the sense of the words. "I am that nobleman," he said.

Hendrigg turned and looked at Flynn. Perhaps any one who knew Hendrigg well might have detected a slight glance of recognition in his seeming indifferent eyes. Those who did not know Hendrigg well would not have seen so much. He made as if to move away, but Flynn, answering now to the second interest that the sound of Hendrigg's voice had aroused in him, signed to him to stop, and Hendrigg came to a halt, standing respectfully before him.

"Wait a bit, my fine fellow," O'Flynn said. "Where have I heard your voice before?"

Hendrigg shook his head. "I cannot tell, your honor," he answered, quietly. "In London, belike. I am a London man. But I cannot recall ever seeing your honor before."

O'Flynn tapped his forehead meditatively. "Where was it?" he asked, "where was it?" Then with a sudden inspiration he cried, "By glory, you remind me of my highwayman on the Cork road."

Hendrigg eyed him with a look of offended virtue. "Your honor is uncomplimentary," he protested. "Your honor is mistaken. I am an honest publican's drawer of London, come over here to aid Mr. Bandy." He turned to Bandy as he spoke and the honest publican backed his words:

"That is so, sir. He came to me with the best of characters."

O'Flynn accepted the statement. "Then it's mistaken I am," he said, "and I ask your pardon."

Hendrigg was for making off when with a gesture O'Flynn detained him while he added, "But if you are an honest man, it's a pity you have the face of a rogue. Be off with you."

Hendrigg, impassive and expressionless, quitted the room.

Flynn turned to Master Bandy, "Now tell me, honest landlord, where are my friends the players?"

"Why, your honor," the landlord answered, "as soon

as they arrived they were commanded by my Lord Sedgemouth to do some of their tricks for the entertainment of
Her Grace of Tyrconnel's company up yonder."

The O'Flynn seemed annoyed. "And who the devil
is your Lord Sedgemouth that he deprives me of my
friends ?"

Master Bandy explained volubly. "My Lord Sedgemouth is a great noble that honors me much with his
patronage. To-night he is one of a fine company—the
viceroy and Her Grace of Tyrconnel, and my Lord
Fawley, and Sir George Mayhew, and the three B's."

O'Flynn stared at him. "What are the three B's ?" he
asked.

"Your honor must be strange to Dublin," Master Bandy
went on deferentially, "not to have heard of the three B's.
The three B's are the three greatest beauties in all Dublin, or in all the world, it may be for that matter, and
they are called the three B's because the Christian name
of each of them begins with that letter. They are the
Lady Belinda Fanshaw, the Lady Barbara Jarmyn, and
the Lady Benedetta Mountmichael."

As the words came from Bandy's lips Flynn gave a cry
of joy so loud in its exultation that the astonished landlord
fell back in alarm and eyed his eccentric guest warily as
if fearful for his reason. Flynn advanced upon Bandy
with gleaming eyes, and Bandy retreated before him with
a great air of apprehension. "Stop, man, stop," Flynn
cried. "Do you mean to say that the Lady Benedetta
Mountmichael is under your roof at this blessed and holy
minute ?"

Bandy was something reassured as to his guest's sanity
by this question, though it puzzled him not a little to im-

agine any degree of acquaintanceship existing between the Lady Benedetta Mountmichael, the beauty, the toast, the adored of the gallants, and this astonishing ragamuffin that was so shabbily clad and yet made so free with golden guineas. "Yes, indeed," he asserted.

The O'Flynn lifted up his hands in an ecstasy. "Then this is not a tavern, this is paradise. I shall see her at once! But I can't see her like this. Where is that damned tailor?"

Even as he spoke the door opened and Hendrigg entered the room followed by Coin and Gosling, who were carrying a box between them. Coin and Gosling were gorgeously and grotesquely arrayed in showy liveries of gold and crimson that fitted them very ill, but with which they appeared to be vastly pleased. They were followed by a little man in a dark suit who bowed very respectfully. Coin tapped himself on the chest to call attention to his change of raiment.

"We took this occasion to make ourselves spruce for his honor."

Gosling grinned with delight. "We'll do you credit now, I'm thinking," he said.

Flynn was almost as pleased with the appearance of his followers as they were. "Splendid, splendid," he declared. He turned to Beggles, whose face was wrinkled with indignation. "Don't look sour, man; I suppose we must have clothes."

Beggles pawed the air protestingly. "Usage, warmth, and decorum suggest as much, but fashion is folly, fashion is costly."

The tailor hastened to interfere in the argument. "Good-evening to your honor," he said. "Sure, you've hit upon

the right man in all Dublin to give you a new outside."

Flynn surveyed him steadily. "Now, you'll please to
understand that it's mighty well dressed I mean to be.
Sure, I know that fine feathers don't make fine birds, but
all the same your fine bird has fine feathers."

The tailor knuckled his forehead. "Yes, your honor,"
he said. Then, with the aid of Coin and Gosling, he produced from the depth of the chest various suits of clothes,
the most of which were handsome and in good condition.

As Flynn eyed them he continued his harangue. "Also,
I am going into the presence of a king—but that's nothing.
Sure, I'm used to kings. But I hope soon to be in the
presence of the sweetest lady now alive, and that means a
great deal, my friend."

The tailor nodded. "Yes, your honor," he said.

The O'Flynn smiled benignly. "I'm glad you agree
with me," he observed.

At this moment the tailor produced a very gorgeous coat
of blue and silver brocade which caught and captivated
the O'Flynn's fancy.

"That seems to be a handsome thing, that blue and
silver; I like that. finely! With a flowered waistcoat now
and some gallooned small-clothes I ought to cut a pretty
figure."

"It's the very thing for your worship," Coin agreed, enthusiastically.

"I'll be trying that same on this minute," Flynn declared.

The landlord pointed out that the public hall of an inn
was no place wherein to effect a change of wardrobe. But
Flynn was too impatient to bring about his metamorphosis
to consent to ascend to his room. So he agreed to the

landlord's suggestion to avail himself of a kind of bar-parlor in which Master Bandy took his ease. Here, with the aid of his faithful varlets, he shifted from his shabby clothes into his fine new suit and came forth into the hall of the Isle of Cyprus with great majesty. He admired himself in a small mirror Master Bandy offered him from the dresser and protested cheerfully:

"It's a dream of delight I'd call myself if I met myself on the street."

Gosling sunned himself in the splendor of his master. "Faith, you're finer than the lord mayor," he declared.

Flynn laughed, but he was flattered none the less at the intended compliment. "You're very polite," he said. Then he bade Coin and Gosling convey his discarded garments to his bedroom and ordered Beggles to pay the tailor, a task which that worthy man fulfilled very reluctantly.

When Coin and Gosling and the tailor had departed, O'Flynn turned eagerly to Bandy. "And now, landlord, for the love of Heaven find me pen, ink, and paper."

"They are here, your honor," the landlord answered, producing the desired articles from a drawer in the dresser.

Flynn seated himself at the table and began to write, murmuring as he did so, "Well, if this isn't too wonderful!" When he had written he read the letter over to himself in a low voice: "To the Lady Benedetta Mountmichael, these. The ambassador from the King of Munster presents his humblest respects and begs to be allowed to wait upon her ladyship's pleasure."

He closed the letter, sealed it and handed it to Bandy. "Honest man, will you take instant occasion to convey this to the Lady Benedetta Mountmichael? Then, but not till then, you can set about supper."

Bandy took the letter, staring in surprise at Flynn as he did so. Then he went slowly up the stairs and entered the room occupied by the viceroy's party.

When he was out of sight, Flynn hurried to Beggles triumphantly. "Man, man," he cried, "isn't it glorious to think she is here—under the happy roof of this sacrosanct tavern? Why don't you dance man, why don't you sing?"

"You will pardon me," Beggles protested, "but I do not understand your raptures."

Flynn raged at him. "Oh, sluggish churl! I am speaking of the loveliest lady in the world."

"For Heaven's sake, sir," Beggles pleaded, "have a care of lovely ladies. They are mostly a sad bar to fortune."

"I tell you, you reptile," Flynn said scornfully, "it is the fairest fortune in the world to be permitted to serve such a lady."

Beggles pricked up his ears. "Is there money in it; is there advancement?" he questioned.

Flynn took him by the shoulders and shook him. "If you talk like that any more I shall do you a mischief. Oh, by the Lord, there she is." His quick ear had heard the door above open and a light footfall on the gallery. He seized Beggles' hand and laid it against his breast. "Put your hand on my heart, man, and feel how it beats the reveille. And now, begone! Join the landlord, watch the supper, do what you please but begone!"

XVII

BENEDETTA DESCENDS THE STAIRS

FLYNN pushed Beggles away from him, and the poor man, with a gesture of despair, quitted the hall.

The Lady Benedetta was standing on the gallery looking down and smiling.

Flynn advanced and saluted her.

Benedetta leaned over. "It is you then, O'Flynn. I guessed it must be when I got your mad message."

"Never call it mad," Flynn protested, "when it gave me the sweet sight of you like this."

The girl laughed at his rhapsodies. "What are you doing here?" she asked.

He made her a bow. "Doing your pleasure, lady," he answered.

"Have you come to serve the king?" she questioned eagerly.

And he answered her instantly, "I have come to serve the queen."

Benedetta shook her head. "The queen is in France."

"The queen I mean is in Ireland," Flynn asserted. "The queen I mean is the girl for whose sake I have come to Dublin—the queen I mean is at the top of those stairs, and I wish she would come down them."

"Oh, I cannot come down," Benedetta declared, "I

must not stop away a minute — the company will miss me."

"If you are the girl I take you for," Flynn said persuasively, "it's mighty little you care for the company. Come down, angel, while I tell you what brings me to Dublin."

Benedetta seemed firm. "You are an imperious pleader, but I must deny you."

The O'Flynn was never a man to take "no" for an answer in the Courts of Love. "Don't do that same," he entreated, "don't do it! Sure, you were never made to refuse a kindness to a very deserving soldier of fortune. Now, listen to me. If you will come down here to me for a minute, I will rhyme you a rhyme for each step of the stair that brings you nearer to me."

Benedetta looked at him with an amused smile that was not without a certain malicious perverseness. "Will you so?" she asked, teasingly.

And the O'Flynn answered her with a cheerful alacrity. "I will so. I am a bit of a poet as I told you the other day, though I am brisker at the Gaelic than the English. Come now—is it a bargain?"

He gave his great plumed hat a jaunty cock to one side and looked up at his lady with a smile in which roguish impudence and passionate adoration were so whimsically blended that Benedetta did not know whether to laugh at his insolence or to weep over his inevitable woe. She decided to laugh, tempted not a little in her decision by curiosity to see if this astounding gentleman of fortune could keep his fantastical promise. She moved to the head of the stately stairway and stood there, light and fair, her delicate coloring a little deepened, maybe, by the strangeness of the situation and the oddness of her wooer —the wooer for whom, as she assured herself, she cared nothing, but who certainly diverted her, and who certainly had contrived to safeguard his gentility through the stress of adventurous years.

"Well, essay," she said, "but I warn you that if you fail at a single stair I fall back instantly and vanish."

Flynn looked at her longingly with the desire to draw her nearer to him burning hotly in his heart. "You shall come down, you shall come down," he whispered to himself, and his fanciful, passionate thoughts began shaping themselves into rhythms and rhymes. He made a splendid gesture as of appeal to the unseen powers. "Here goes then—" he cried to his angel, and followed his cry with a fervent appeal to the goddess of song, "Oh, my vagabond Muse, befriend me."

Then, with his eyes fixed on the enchanting creature above him, he began to improvise, words coming trip-toe to his call as was their wont when he needed them:

"Most dainty, most gracious, most radiant, most fair,
I will rhyme you a rhyme for each step of the stair."

As he paused to take breath after this auspicious beginning, Benedetta advanced a small high-heeled shoe from where she stood to the stair immediately below her, and stood poised there with a tantalizing smile upon her face as if she were defying her mad Irishman to keep to the terms of his fantastic contract. But the O'Flynn was not to be daunted. He felt the spirit of song swelling within his breast, and he rattled out another brace of rhymes with a rapidity which surprised Benedetta and himself:

BENEDETTA DESCENDS THE STAIRS

"For each fall of your foot that draws nearer the place
  Where I wait and I worship the light of your face."

Benedetta came down a pair of steps this time. She
was tickled by his whimsical proposition and was ready
to give him good measure of encouragement.

Flynn, with his eyes fixed eagerly on his nearing divinity,
essayed a third couplet:

"Are you woman or angel? Whichever you be,
  Entertain the kind thought and draw nearer to me."

The appeal was promptly answered by a further ap-
proach of the fair lady, but for a moment Flynn's inspiration seemed to halt and Benedetta made a feint to retire.

Thus spurred, Flynn found new words for his purpose:

"Sure the king has his ribbons, the king has his stars,
  To give to the faithful that serve in his wars."

Benedetta came graciously down some three steps in
response to this strophe, and Flynn pursued the thought
in a further verse:

"But I'd change all the gifts that the king can command,
  For one smile of your eyes, for one touch of your hand."

Lured by Flynn's fluent muse, Benedetta continued to
descend the stairway. She was more than half-way down
now and Flynn's fancy was still fertile.

He drew breath and spoke again:

"And there's never a deed that a hero would do,
  But myself would achieve it in honor of you."

Benedetta seemed to think that her poet's powers were flagging, for she only accorded him the favor of a single stair's descent in return for this verse.

Flynn noted the change and his voice grew stronger, his manner more animated as he rolled out two new lines which he strove to charge with all the vehemence of his passion:

> "I swear me your soldier, your servant, your slave,
> To the height of my hope, to the depth of my grave."

Benedetta was taken by the fervor of his words, of his speech, and she glided down several of the steps as a proof of her approval. There were now only three steps between her and the floor of the hall.

Flynn's face glowed and he went to it again rapturously:

> "So long as the blackbirds that dwell in my breast
> Can sing of the wonderful world you have blest."

Benedetta came down two more steps, leaving but one to be overtrodden, but now Flynn paused, seemed to hesitate, to have lost command of words and ideas. Instantly Benedetta, roguish and tricksy, gave a little turn and made as if to scamper up the stairs again at full speed.

Now, whether Flynn's hesitation had been natural or no more than the plausible artifice of the artist, he certainly recovered his wits quickly before this menace of Benedetta's. With renewed vigor he shouted aloud the continuation of the thought of the just finished verse:

> "My song shall be yours, like my life and my prayers"—

BENEDETTA DESCENDS THE STAIRS

He waited for an instant playfully, pretending to be troubled, though he knew very well what was coming; then he delivered his line in a rush:

"And behold you have come to the foot of the stairs."

Even as he said the last word Benedetta, smiling very sweetly at the winner of the wager, stepped daintily on the floor of the hall.

Flynn sprang forward to greet her, and, dropping on his knee, took her hand tenderly in his and kissed it reverently. "Lady," he said jubilantly, as he rose to his feet, "the last time we met I promised that Dublin should know me soon. You did not believe me then, yet here I am in Dublin, kissing your dear hand. You have given King James another soldier, for behold me eager to serve him." He paused for an instant, and then concluded emphatically, "Ah, I will please you against your will."

Benedetta looked at him with very kindly eyes. "Indeed, O'Flynn," she declared, "you have pleased me, and greatly."

O'Flynn gave a little gasp of delight. He twirled a pirouette, fluttering his sky-blue skirts as he swung on his heels, then he faced the girl again, and pranced, as it were, before her in the pride of his brand-new apparel. "What do you think of these clothes?" he asked with a kind of boyish simplicity of pleasure in the sporting of unfamiliar finery that diverted Benedetta, but that also touched her.

She was used to splendid gentlemen splendidly garmented, but she seemed to understand the delight of this rough-and-ready soldier of fortune in his bright habiliments. "They are beautiful," she averred, sincerely enough, for if the coat that O'Flynn had chosen was a trifle gaudier than the precision of the mode would wholly justify, his stalwart person and manly carriage carried it off properly enough and minimized its brilliancy.

"Lady," he declared, "I lay them at your feet—" He checked himself abruptly as if recognizing the incongruity of the remark, and added hurriedly, "metaphorically, of course." He was silent for a whole second that seemed to him an eternity; then he cried out in an ecstasy of delight, "Ah, Benedetta, I could fly out of my skin for joy of seeing you again. I love you so that nothing can withstand my love. I have had a revelation from Heaven which tells me that the earth itself was created that I might meet you. I am the most important man upon the earth because I love you." He was prepared to go on this strain so long as his breath lasted, but Benedetta lifted a finger and checked him.

"You are very gallant, Flynn," she said, gayly, "but I like your way of talk. It makes me think of the fountains of Versailles on a fine day, all the little drops of water dancing in the sunlight. I suppose you could go on like that forever?"

The O'Flynn laughed. "What good for a man to be a bit of a poet if he couldn't find words for his heart if his heart is happy?"

Benedetta smoothed out the dimples of her smiling face to an expression of great gravity. "Well, Chevalier," she said, with an air of mock earnestness that became her vastly, "it's well I don't take you too seriously, or your heart wouldn't be so happy as you say. I told you I was ear-deep in love with a man, and now the man is ear-deep in love with me, happy wretch that I am: and we are to be married whenever I can get my father's consent."

"And mine," O'Flynn commented dryly.

Benedetta went on unheeding him, thrilled by her theme. "He is the handsomest creature in the world, and the gallantest; the face of an angel, the figure of a god, the carriage of a hero, perfect courtier, perfect soldier, perfect lover! Nay, I must tell you no more."

If Flynn were at all dashed by the girl's praises of her to him unknown lover, he showed no sign of his discomfiture in face or bearing. "What is the name of this nonpareil?" he asked jauntily.

Benedetta denied him a straight answer. "That I must not tell you," she said, "for we have not yet got my father's consent. But you shall know in good time."

Flynn shrugged his shoulders. "Oh, there's no hurry," he declared, truthfully enough. He felt there was more he wanted to say, but while he was seeking how to say it the quiet of the place was disturbed by a distant sound of applause that came to them by way of the gallery and the stairs, through the closed doors of the viceroy's room.

Benedetta started at the sound. "Hark!" she cried, "I hear them clapping their hands. I must go. Likely the play is beginning. Farewell!"

She made to go, but Flynn clawed at the air and delayed her. "Wait a bit, lady," he said, "don't think I'm dashed by this news of yours. I don't care a damn for your Apollo. I'm your wooer still and mean to be your winner sooner or later."

Benedetta looked at him with a little quizzical grin. "Ah, you fantastical madman," she cried, and then swing-

13   183

ing round on her high heels, she ran swiftly up the stairs, paused for a moment on the gallery to wave him a salute that was half derisive and half kindly, and so disappeared behind the panels that masked the viceroy's pleasures.

O'Flynn bore himself defiantly enough till the last whisk of the girl's skirts had vanished, but then his devil-may-care carriage abandoned him and he dropped very despondently into a chair by the table near the fire.

XVIII

FANCY FREE PROPOSES

"DAMN your Apollo," he murmured, and buried his head in his hands. "Oh, the devil, the devil, the devil," he said to himself, raging and despairingly.

A door into the hall opened, the door hard by the foot of the stairs through which Master Bandy's drawer had conducted the players to their quarters. Through the open door a head was popped, a head of a girl, pretty, impudent, appealing—the head of Mistress Fancy Free. Fancy saw that the O'Flynn was alone and she slipped into the room, crossed the floor cat-foot on tiptoe and made to put her arms about the Irishman's neck. At the soft pressure of the plump flesh O'Flynn turned with a wild unreasonable cry of joy. He thought for a moment, being a hot-headed madman, that somehow or other Benedetta had changed her mind and returned to him, and that he was free to clasp her in his arms. When he looked into the impudent mutinous face of Fancy Free he drew back with a little start and some stammering apologies of which the girl took no notice. It was plain that she had something to say and was eager to say it.

"I have just learned of your arrival," she said in a low voice, "and as I'm not to play for a while I choose to chat with you. Why, what have you been doing to yourself?"

Flynn, who had risen to his feet, made her a bow. "Making a fine gentleman of myself, little lady," he answered.

Fancy dipped him a courtesy. "I think the angels had a hand at that before you," she said. She said it as if she meant it, but Flynn answered her as if she jested:

"It's making game of me you are, Mischief," he said.

Fancy shook her head. "No, my faith," she protested, "do you know there's another fine gentleman up yonder been making wide eyes at me. I believe he'd like me well enough for his lady-love."

Flynn looked with a kindly interest at the audacious creature whose looks wooed him so boldly. "Do you mean honorable?" he asked.

Fancy laughed loudly. "Lord, no, man. Great lords don't think honorably of the likes of me."

"Then give him the go-by," Flynn suggested. He was exalted by his own romantic passion into a mood for philosophic advice; yet, even as he gave it, his sense of humor suggested that it must sound incongruous from the lips of such a free-companion as himself.

Fancy's laughter continued full and frank and childlike. "Why, you dear droll man," she cried, "he wouldn't be the first and he won't be the last—if I go on as I am going."

He looked at her musing. "It's a pity, I'm thinking," he said, slowly.

Fancy hunched her pretty shoulders and made a mocking face at him. "Is it?" she asked. "I don't know." She sidled a little nearer to Flynn and nudged him caressingly with her elbow. "Tall soldierman, I have a tale to tell you."

Flynn surveyed her with good-humored curiosity. "I

hope it's prettier than your last," he said, "for such pretty lips to tell."

Fancy suddenly reached out her hands and caught at the lappets of Flynn's gorgeous new coat as if she had a mind to draw his face nearer to hers, while she spoke after a fashion that was part bravado and part earnestness, "I have taken a great fancy to you, soldierman," she said.

O'Flynn made a wry face. He was not taking the girl seriously, but he was thinking serious thoughts. "I wish others shared your taste," he murmured, ruefully.

Fancy persisted. "I'm as earnest as a hungry owl. Shall I tell you I like you—love you ?"

O'Flynn began to realize that he was in the whimsical position of being wooed by this delicious creature and that by the irony of Fate he must be wooed in vain. He strove to put her off. "Be easy, minx! Is it me with this face on me ?"

Fancy derided his humility. "Do you think I'm a fine lady," she asked, "to be snared by a pretty face ? I'm a play-actress to whom looks are no more than make-up. But you are a bit of a true man, tall soldier."

Flynn looked at her between laughing and crying. The situation was not of his choosing, was not to his taste. He wished himself well out of it. "Thank you kindly for thinking that same," he said, soberly.

The girl nestled temptingly against his side. "Couldn't we make a match of it?" she whispered. "Wait now, don't speak for a minute. You needn't marry unless you like, but I love you and I'd be true to you. We've both been in the wars and been wounded. You are no more of a perfect man than I am a perfect woman, but we might be happy together."

THE O'FLYNN

There was no mistaking the sincerity of Fancy's words, there was no mistaking the look in Fancy's eyes, there was no mistaking the tender pressure of Fancy's fingers. Flynn took the girl's hands gently and put them away from him. "Mistress Fancy," he said, gravely and simply, meaning all he said, "you do me a great honor, and so long as I live I shall think better of the world and of myself because of your favor. And you mustn't think that anything that's happened in your life would go against you with me. It's the love that's everything—the love of a man for a woman, the love of a woman for a man. If this had happened a little while ago I should have been blithe to take you in my arms. But now I can't."

Fancy looked up at him tearfully blinking away tears. "Do you love some one else?" she asked.

Flynn drew himself up. "Yes," he answered, "through God's anger and God's mercy I love some one else, and I mean to make her love me before I've done with her. But it will take a bit of doing, I'm thinking."

Fancy looked steadily at him. "You are in earnest?" she questioned, and then reading the answer on his set face, she sighed: "yes, you are in earnest. Then I think I will go back to my fine gentleman."

"Don't do that, child," Flynn entreated.

Fancy tossed her head. "Nay," she protested, "I must feather my own nest since you will not make one for me."

As she turned to leave him the door on the gallery above opened, the door that helped to sequestrate the viceroy from the rest of the world, the familiar ripple of mirth flowed forth for a moment as a small party of gentlemen issued from the apartment, and, closing the door behind them, began to descend the stairs with different degrees

FANCY FREE PROPOSES

of unsteadiness. The gentlemen were my Lord Sedgemouth, my Lord Fawley, Sir George Mayhew, and Captain Scully—the three last-named being bloods and wits in the Dublin society of the day. They were talking together as they descended.

"I am weary of the players," Sedgemouth protested with a yawn.

My Lord Fawley tittered foolishly to mask a hiccough. "Yet they divert the ladies," he said, "and the viceroy, vastly."

Scully, who seemed less deep in wine than either Sedgemouth or Fawley, observed, "Her grace must needs have them to it again."

By this time the party was more than half-way down the stairs, and Sir George Mayhew caught sight of Fancy where she lingered in the hall, lingering purposely, indeed, because of the coming of the gentry. "Why, there's one of the players," he called out.

Sedgemouth, following the direction of his extended finger, recognized Fancy. "And the best of the bunch," he cried, hilariously.

He descended the rest of the stairs at a run that came near to a disastrous conclusion, but rallied himself against the pedestal. He lurched forward amorously toward Fancy, who waited for his advances simpering and mincing. "Shall I see you to-morrow, sweet?" he asked, thickly.

Fancy dipped him a courtesy, tipped him a mischievous wink. "Very likely, your lordship," she answered, demurely, and then as he made to lay hands on her she slipped away and disappeared through the door by which she had entered, leaving him like a new Ixion to close his fingers on empty air.

XIX

HOT PUNCH AND COLD STEEL

SEDGEMOUTH and his companions had seated themselves about the table that stood at the foot of the stairs and prepared to enjoy themselves. So far they took no notice of Flynn where he stood apart by the hearth staring moodily into the fire. Sir George Mayhew produced a pack of cards from his pocket and proposed cutting for ten guineas a cut.

My Lord Sedgemouth slapped the table noisily with his open palm. "Landlord, landlord, I say, landlord," he shouted.

From the distant regions of the kitchen Bandy's voice was heard in answer, crying, "Coming, my lord, coming."

A moment later Master Bandy entered the room bearing the O'Flynn's supper on a tray, and followed by Beggles. Bandy placed his tray on the table near the hearth, left its contents for Beggles to set out, and hastened to give his attention to the gentlemen at the foot of the stairs, who by this time were deep in their cutting of the pack and changing piles of guineas briskly.

Sedgemouth greeted Bandy impatiently. "Punch, man," he shouted, "punch."

Bandy bowed. "Yes, my lord," he said.

Flynn, seated at the table and already busy sharing his

supper and his Burgundy with Beggles, turned to Bandy and commanded him with his mouth full, "You may brew me a bowl of the same elixir, landlord."

Bandy bowed again. "Yes, your honor," he answered, and sped toward the kitchen to compound the punch.

Flynn's order for drink had drawn the attention of the gamblers to him, and the rich coloring of his new clothes seemed to attract the fancy of Lord Sedgemouth. He rose to his feet with some uncertainty and advanced a little way across the hall toward Flynn's table. "Is the sun in my eyes that I see strange sights?" he asked, affecting to shade his eyes with lifted hand from the brilliancy of O'Flynn's attire. "Is it real? What is it?"

Scully still seated at that table but joining in the jest, questioned, "Is it a popinjay?" and my Lord Fawley, carrying on the game, suggested, "Or a peacock?"

Sedgemouth, standing in the middle of the hall, waved them down with an extended left hand. "I take it," he said, with tipsy solemnity, "for a scarecrow stained by a rainbow."

By this time Flynn, who had his back to the group, and was sturdily engrossed in his supper, became aware that he was the subject of the gentlemen's comments. Muttering to himself, "the rascals," he made to rise from his chair, but Beggles, leaning across the table, restrained him with pleading words and gestures. "For Heaven's sake, sir, let them be," he entreated, "they are drunk beyond understanding of speech, unworthy your honor's notice."

"If I pull their noses," Flynn answered, furiously, "it will sober them." He glared round as he spoke, but by this time my Lord Sedgemouth had lost all interest in the parti-colored stranger, and returning to his companions was hard at it again, cutting the cards and losing his guineas.

Master Beggles took advantage of the changed situation to homilise. "Consider, dear sir, the consequences of a quarrel now. Risking your new clothes, risking your life, your precious life."

Flynn sighed and swallowed a glass of Burgundy at a draught without seeming solaced. "There are moments," he said, "when I wish you were not my banker, Master Beggles." He turned to the consideration of his supper gloomily as he spoke, and he and his companion proceeded with their meal untroubled for some minutes.

Then the quiet of the room was disturbed by my Lord Sedgemouth, who banged his handful of cards on the table in a rage. "Curse the cards," he screamed in a rage, "was there ever such infernal luck?"

Mayhew, pocketing my lord's guineas cheerfully, protested. "Damn it, man, you can't have everything. You are lucky enough in love."

Sedgemouth stretched out his legs and thrust his hands into his breeches pockets. "Luck in love won't fill my pockets," he grumbled.

My Lord Fawley leaned over and said in an audible whisper, "A little bird sang that you sometimes take toll for your favors."

Sedgemouth greeted the innuendo with a grunt, and Scully continued, "Well, your exchequer will be replenished when you win Lady Benedetta."

O'Flynn, that had been wholly inattentive to the doings of his neighbors, caught the name that fell from Scully's lips, and instantly alert, "Lady Benedetta," he echoed angrily and turned his head toward the others.

HOT PUNCH AND COLD STEEL

Those others were paying him no manner of attention. They had forgotten his existence; they were occupied solely with their own immediate concerns, with their own idle, loose talk, with their own idle, loose thoughts. My Lord Sedgemouth chuckled with an air of vinous sagacity. "Why, I have won her already," he said. "The child would die for a smile."

Flynn struck the table a furious blow with his clenched fist that set all the glasses reeling and the ware rattling. He swung himself round in his seat and glared balefully at the gentlemen. "Silence!" he bawled, and the sound of his voice thundered through the room and rolled among the rafters with all the fulness and fury of a storm.

The attention of the gamblers was naturally attracted by this astonishing diversion and the eyes of the four gentlemen were fixed with varying steadiness upon the infuriated O'Flynn, whose efforts to rise from his table were impeded by Master Beggles, who had flung himself upon him at the first symptom of indignation and who now clung to him with all the passionate energy of a limpet.

My Lord Sedgemouth rose to his feet and advanced somewhat totteringly toward the O'Flynn, eying him with derisive insolence.

My Lord Fawley propped against his table hiccoughed out, "What is the matter with Harlequin?"

The O'Flynn took Master Beggles by the collar between his fingers and thumb, plucked him from his person, placed him in his chair, and advanced to meet Lord Sedgemouth. Addressing him and his grinning companions that were about the table, he called out savagely, "You silly committee of jackanapes, you must not toss a lady's name abroad in a tavern."

My Lord Sedgemouth chuckled drunkenly. He had taken more wine than was good even for his hardened head, and was inclined to be jocose. "Are you Gog, Magog, or Punchinello?" he asked, leering at the O'Flynn. Then he plucked off his feathered hat and made a swish with it in the air before O'Flynn's face as if he were brushing away some objectionable insect. "Go away," he shrilled, "I do not want you."

He pivoted on his red heels as he spoke and made unsteadily for his companions.

Flynn followed him up, raging. "Air a civil tongue when you speak of women," he commanded, but my lord paid him no more heed than if he had not spoken. Sinking into his seat with a languishing air he took up a glass and held it toward Fawley.

"Give me some wine?" he asked, with drunken malice. "I want to drink to the kisses of Benedetta."

The O'Flynn's action was instant and swift. He snatched up the full glass that stood before Captain Scully and dashed its red contents straight into the white face of my Lord Sedgemouth. The Burgundy ran over his pale cheeks and dribbled hideously on to the lace about his neck and his embroidered waistcoat. The unexpected insult quickened Lord Sedgemouth's wits to a sudden explosion of rage. He scrambled to his feet, clawing at the hilt of his sword, but Mayhew and Scully caught him by the arms and controlled him. Beggles by this time had flung himself forward, and hung about Flynn's body hampering him sadly. At this moment Bandy entered the hall followed by Hendrigg. Each was carrying a large china bowl full of punch in his hands. Seeing that a brawl was toward, the two men set their burdens down upon the table near the fire which Flynn had been occupying and stared in amazement at the unexpected scene.

My Lord Sedgemouth, whiter than his drinking, wont with passion, strove to liberate himself from the claspings of his friends. "Blast you," he screamed at O'Flynn, "I will slice you into tripe," and, as he spoke, he shook off Scully and Mayhew and plucked his sword forth of its scabbard. In the same instant O'Flynn's blade saw the light.

Master Bandy in an anguish flung himself between the antagonists. "Be easy, sir," he entreated the O'Flynn. "Sure, my lord is mad drunk, and you are sane sober. What kind of a match would it be ?"

The O'Flynn pushed the beseeching landlord away from him with scarcely an effort. He looked sternly on Lord Sedgemouth who stood before him, vacillating a little in carriage, but resolute for combat, holding his sword with the manner of a master of the weapon, as indeed my lord was.

A wild thought danced in O'Flynn's head and sent him nigh crazy with delight. "We can set that right easy enough," he said, exultantly: "I can fight drunk as well as sober. Give me the punch." As he spoke he lifted from the table the great china punch-bowl that Master Bandy had but just set down, and raised it to his lips, "Your health!" he said, with a comprehensive smile at the astonished company. Then he slowly tilted the bowl and sucked steadily at the subtle and aromatic compound, drinking and tilting, tilting and drinking, till the inverted vessel almost hid his head from the amazed spectators. He put the bowl down on the table again with a jolly laugh. "Now I think we ought to be pretty equal," he cried, triumphantly.

195

Master Bandy flung up his hands. "Glory! At a draught!" he ejaculated.

Beggles, fidgetting with uneasiness, vainly tried to attract Flynn's attention. "Sir, sir, consider your health!" he entreated, but Flynn in a voice perhaps a trifle thicker, and his gait maybe a shade less steady, pushed Master Beggles aside and addressed himself to the gentlemen who were by main force restraining my Lord Sedgemouth: "Let your friend go!" he commanded, and as he spoke he drew his sword. "Now, sir, let's see the color of your cutlery." He turned aside for a moment to address Bandy, "Faith, landlord, that was a noble brew; give me the other bowl!"

Sedgemouth, being now released by his friends, reeled across the floor and faced the O'Flynn. "Damn you!" he growled; "you are drunk!"

"And damn you, you are drunk," Flynn retorted, "so there's a pair of us. Perhaps two pairs. I think I like your twin brother that's standing there by your side better than yourself. Now, sir, will you fight or shall I help you to some more Burgundy?"

"I shall kill you?" my Lord Sedgemouth said, savagely.

Flynn wagged his head wisely. "I doubt it. The drink makes you too confident: you don't take it the right way. Now, is there any part of your person which you may wish to have pinked? I promise you, for all I have drunk, I will skewer you where you please."

Captain Scully now pushed between the two antagonists, protesting loudly: "No more of this, Sedgemouth," he said; "you are both too drunk."

Sedgemouth looked at his friend steadily; his anger had

sobered him a little. "I never pass an affront," he said; "I am going to kill this yokel."

O'Flynn leaned against the table and mocked my Lord Sedgemouth, fleeringly. "Come on, pretty gentleman, come on!" he chanted. He turned to Bandy: "Is that punch ready? Look here, landlord, you have a goblet ready on that table, and as fast as I empty it, fill it up again. I can drink and fight at the same time."

By this time Hendrigg began to lose patience: he had watched the squabble so far with something like indifference, believing that the tipsy altercation would have no serious conclusion and that O'Flynn's feat with the punch-bowl would render him powerless to do harm. He now realized that Flynn, in spite of his draught, was able to hold a sword and also able to use it. He began to fear for the success of the scheme on which he was employed. Injury to my Lord Sedgemouth at this juncture meant injury to the cause that Hendrigg was content to serve, so forgetting for a moment the important point he played in the eyes of all present save only my Lord Sedgemouth, he raised his voice in angry protestations: "Sirs, sirs," he cried, "this must not be."

Mayhew turned on him angrily. "What the devil have you to say to a brawl between gentlemen?"

Hendrigg continued to speak hotly: "I protest for the credit of the house," he said, and made as if to ascend the stairs and alarm the house, but my Lord Fawley gripped him by the collar and held him fast. "Hold your tongue, you fool!" he cried, and apparently because my Lord Fawley was very strong, and apparently because Hendrigg realized the danger of any action that might reveal his identity, he kept still while the two antagonists faced each other with lifted weapons.

"Are you ready, gentlemen?" Mayhew asked.

"Ready," Sedgemouth answered.

"And willing!" Flynn responded, cheerily.

In the fight that followed Sir George Mayhew and Captain Scully played the parts of temporary seconds; Sir George acting for the Irishman and Captain Scully for Lord Sedgemouth. The moment that the swords met it was plain to both the seconds that O'Flynn in spite of the liquor he had taken was more than a match for my Lord Sedgemouth in his then condition, and would prove more than a match for my Lord Sedgemouth if my Lord Sedgemouth were stark sober.

Duels had been fought before in that wonderful inn that had once been so wonderful a mansion, but never a duel so magnificent as that in all the days of its history. For the O'Flynn kept off the angry attack of Lord Sedgemouth with perfect ease, his sword meeting and parrying swift lunges as his enemy played with marvellous rapidity, and while he thus baffled his antagonist he ever and anon reached out his left hand for the glass that Master Bandy filled from the dwindling punch-bowl and drained it derisively to Lord Sedgemouth's health. "The loving-cup!" he had cried out as he emptied the first glass, and now a few minutes later Master Bandy ladled the last drop of punch into the goblet that he handed to the O'Flynn.

"Is the punch all gone?" Flynn asked.

"Every drop!" Master Bandy answered.

"Then," O'Flynn responded, "we'll make an end of the business." He parried a vicious stab from Lord Sedgemouth, feinted, reposted, and ran my Lord Sedgemouth through the body.

Lord Sedgemouth dropped his sword and clapped his hand to his side with a silly laugh. "Blast me! I'm drunk!" he cried, and then plucking his fingers from his side held them to his face and seemed to wonder to find them bloody. Then he gave an ugly groan and fell heavily on his face. Beggles gave a shrill scream as Scully and Mayhew hastened to the side of their fallen friend.

Hendrigg instantly seized the opportunity to tear, at full speed, up the stairs crying out: "Help! Help! My Lord Sedgemouth is slain!"

"You've killed him!" Beggles gasped.

Flynn shook his head. "Be easy! I've only pricked him a little."

"Is he much hurt?" Mayhew asked.

Scully looked up from the wounded man. "Not badly," he answered. "Give me a hand to carry him to a bed."

14

XX

O'FLYNN'S OWN

BY this time the Isle of Cyprus was all in confusion: uproar reigned above, below, everywhere. The door of the room on the gallery where His Grace of Tyrconnel was feasting flung open, and the mingled crowd of ladies and courtiers richly attired, and of players in their hurriedly assumed costumes, came pouring out to learn the meaning of the hubbub.

While Mayhew, Scully, and Fawley carried their wounded friend into an adjoining room to have his hurt attended to, O'Flynn, seizing the great punch-bowl he had emptied, filled it with water from a ewer on the sideboard and thrust his glowing face into the cool liquid, whence he emerged a moment afterward and dried his dripping countenance on a towel hastily provided for him by Master Beggles, ever solicitous for his well-being. Flynn's elevation of spirit was sufficiently tempered to enable him to realize clearly what was going on about him; he saw the thronged galleries and the crowded staircase filled with eager faces; he saw the inn door leading to the street open and passers-by come into the hall attracted by the noises within; he recognized, with a confused sense of merriment, the faces of his friends, composed of the Riverside Fellowship of Players, staring at him; and then he beheld with a sudden rapture the lady for whom he had fought his drunken fight—Benedetta herself pushing her way through the throng on the gallery and stairs in a fierce anxiety to reach the hall. This anxiety O'Flynn was, for a moment, rash enough to believe was worn for his sake, but he was soon undeceived.

Benedetta spoke to Bandy feverishly. "What has come to my lord?" she asked.

Bandy looked grave. "My lord is ill," he replied.

"Ill?" Benedetta cried, and put her hand to her heart. "What has happened?"

At this moment the O'Flynn, casting aside his drenched towel, believed the moment had come for him to clear up the lady's doubts. He advanced and began with a melancholy smile: "Forgive me, gracious lady, if I attempt to explain the unpleasing concatenation of events. My Lord Sedgemouth, having had the misfortune to fall against a sharp point, has been obliged to take to his bed. Nothing to be alarmed about, absolutely nothing. A little letting of blood will do him a world of good—ease his spleen, cool his liver."

Benedetta, who had listened with amazement to Flynn's speech, wrung her hands. "God's love, what has happened?" she moaned.

At that moment Sir George Mayhew returned from the adjoining room and, hearing her question, answered, "In a word, madam, Lord Sedgemouth and this gentleman had a passage of arms, wherein my lord was worsted."

Flynn strove to waive him on one side. "Prithee, peace, meddler," he cried, pompously, "you spoil all with your parleying." He turned to Benedetta again, "It came about thus, exquisite creature—"

THE O'FLYNN

Benedetta looked at him with blazing eyes. "You have fought with Lord Sedgemouth?" she asked, in a voice that trembled with rage, but Flynn did not interpret its tones rightly.

"I have done that same, lady," he returned, cheerily, "fought him with his own weapons—hot punch first and cold steel afterward."

Benedetta flamed at him. "Are you a fool or a devil or what to do this thing?" she screamed, and Flynn staggered as if she had struck him.

"I do not understand," he faltered; "he spoke lightly of you—of the loveliest woman in this world—and I taught him his manners."

Benedetta raved at him with clenched fists. "You beast, you— Oh! I have no word for you! He is my dear lover, he may speak of me as he pleases; it is not for you to school him!"

She turned from the abashed and bewildered Flynn and questioned the landlord: "Where is he?"

"Madam," Bandy answered, deferentially, "his friends are with him. Captain Scully is a surgeon. No one, for his life's sake, may intrude."

"For his life's sake!" Benedetta echoed, in a breaking voice; then she turned again and faced Flynn, furiously: "He is in danger, and you stand grinning there! What shall I do?" She glanced wildly about her and saw that Bandy was holding in his hand a naked sword, the sword that my Lord Sedgemouth had let fall so short awhile before. She sprang at the startled landlord and snatched the weapon from his grasp and confronted Flynn, Amazon-like, with the blade held as if the use of the sword were familiar to her, while she shrieked at him, "I can handle a sword, too—will you fight me, too, you savage, and kill me, and make an end of both of us that were young and comely, and loved each other well?"

There were tears of shame and despair in Flynn's eyes. "Lady, for God's sake—" he pleaded.

But Benedetta cut him short. "God on your mouth, and the devil in your heart," she cried. She would have said more, but her tirade was interrupted by the entrance of Captain Scully, to whom she turned at once. "Your news, sir?" she asked, eagerly.

"Lord Sedgemouth," Scully replied, "is suffering from a fairly deep flesh-wound between the first and second ribs; there is much loss of blood, but no serious danger. He may perhaps need to keep his bed for a week, no more."

Flynn turned to her apologetically: "Didn't I tell you so? Sure, I know how to knock a man out without hurting him, as easy as A, B, C."

Benedetta paid him no heed. "May I go to my lord?" she asked of Captain Scully.

"If you will not excite him," Scully answered.

"I will be very quiet," Benedetta promised. She made to enter the room from which Scully had just come, but Flynn made a quick movement and stood before her. "Now," he pleaded pathetically, "how was I to know that he was your lover?"

Benedetta looked at him with the steady eyes of hate. "Let me pass, please," she said, coldly, and before her withering glance Flynn could do nothing. He fell back and Benedetta passed him and entered the room where her lover lay.

For a moment, silence reigned over the amazed assemblage: then the silence was disturbed by a new interruption. A big, elderly, red-faced man, very gorgeously dressed and seemingly very drunk, broke noisily out of the room in the gallery and pushing his way furiously through the throng of ladies and gentlemen, began to stagger rapidly down the great stairway. Flynn learned from the murmurs about him what he would readily have guessed, that the new-comer was the viceroy himself, the Duke of Tyrconnel.

"Blast me!" Tyrconnel shouted savagely, "what is all this noise about? Sink me! Can't a gentleman drink his wine in peace?" He came to a halt at the foot of the stairs and clung heavily to the pedestal for support, glaring around him with angry eyes like a boar at bay.

Hendrigg, that had followed his drunken progress, stood by his side. "Your Grace! Your Grace!" he declared; "he has killed my Lord Sedgemouth."

Flynn advanced to meet the viceroy with a stately bow: "I assure your Grace," he said, "I have done nothing of the kind. I found an unknown person here, on whom I will not waste the name of gentleman, using lightly the name of a lady I respect and revere beyond all women living—and I wished to teach him a lesson in manners."

"Blast me," the duke roared, mollified by Flynn's gallantry, courage and frank speech, "if I blame you for it!"

"I took him up short on the word," Flynn continued, "just as you would have done, if you had been there and the man I take you for. Then we out with our bilboas, and I gave him a dig in the ribs that will make him keep his bed a sennight—no more harm done."

The Duke of Tyrconnel turned to Captain Scully, who was standing hard by. "Captain Scully," he asked, "was all this business conducted according to honor?"

"Quite, my lord," Scully answered candidly.

The answer seemed to content his grace so far as the conduct of the duel was concerned, and he turned now to the O'Flynn with a fresh note of quarrel in his voice. "Do you know, sir," he shouted, "that you have done a damned awkward thing? My Lord Sedgemouth had promised to give his Majesty Knockmore Castle, now in the hands of the Dutch, as a midsummer present, and your silly meddling will make him break faith."

Flynn laughed cheerily. "Is that all?" he asked. "With his Majesty's gracious permission and the loan of a regiment or so, I will take Knockmore for his Majesty whenever his Majesty pleases."

My lord duke glared at him. "Who the devil are you?" he asked, "that you talk so free?"

Flynn gave him his favorite formula, "I am the O'Flynn of Castle Famine—of Castle O'Flynn, I should say—Chevalier of the Order of the Rose of Lithuania, Knight Commander of Poland, and Ambassador Extraordinary from His Majesty King Conachor LII., whom Heaven preserve!"

My lord duke gasped at this fluent enumeration of strange titles. "I do not think, sir," he answered, "that his Majesty has regiments to spare for unknown adventurers."

Flynn's head and heart were all in a whirl; the increasing excitement of his drink, his duel and his denunciation by Lady Benedetta had whipped his blood to madness, and he was now ready for any and every rashness or insanity. Tyrconnel's refusal of his offer chaffed him with an appealing insanity. "Then if the king won't lend me a regiment," he cried defiantly, "I'll raise one for myself."

THE O'FLYNN

His grace, that was a good judge of a pretty man, eyed him with something like admiration. "Strike me frightful!" he swore, "but you are a bold bully."

"And I'll begin enlisting at once," Flynn declared; "only I'll do better than the king, or the king's shilling, I offer O'Flynn's guinea!" As he spoke he sprang on to a chair and from thence to the table, and looked around him upon his strange audience.

The hall of the inn was now crowded by strangers from without—strangers representing all classes of the social life of Dublin: gentle folk, burgesses, beggars, red-coated soldiers, white-robed, black-robed, and brown-robed priests, honest tradesmen, and nimble thieves. Above the motley assemblage were ranged the crowd on the stairs that included the quaintly garbed players and the fine folk of the gallery, beautiful women and gallant gentlemen.

Flynn surveyed his hearers as Mark Anthony might have surveyed the crowd in the Roman forum, and began his harangue: "Is there a man here that would not wish to be a soldier and serve King James? If such an one there be, to him I address myself, that he may repent of his past, rejoice in his future, and enlist in this present. For I promise you from long knowledge that the finest and the wisest thing in the world is to follow the drum. Look upon me that preach to you! Here am I, a simple soldier of fortune, no better nor no cleverer than my hearers. I have fought under every flag in Europe, and behold me with the silk upon my limbs and laces at my wrists and pockets brimmed with guineas. None of these could I have owned if I had not been a soldier, and all these comforts ye shall know if you will but serve.

Remember the ladies, too, how dearly they love a soldier-man, how their eyes dazzle at the glow of a soldier's coat. Who loves full purses, let him follow me: who loves fair women, let him follow me: who loves fine garments, let him follow me! Come, who will take a guinea from my fingers and fill the lists of O'Flynn's Own ?"

He stooped and snatched a purse from Master Beggles' hand and drew from it a shining guinea piece and held it up for the admiration of the spectators.

My lord duke banged his hand against his thigh. "Blast me flat!" he swore, "but I would if I were a younger man and not already engaged in his Majesty's service."

Coin pushed his way through the crowd to the table. "Tip me the guinea," he cried. "I am with you!"

He was closely followed by Gosling. "And I!" Gosling shouted.

Flynn tossed each of the bailiffs a guinea, and the guineas were skilfully caught. "Come, there's a bold beginning!" he cried. "Two heroes that will be shaking hands with themselves in a fortnight for taking this chance. It's wise men all are that use the wars, for their lives move blithely to a marching measure and last longer than civilians', too, which is a gain worth weighing. Sure no man can live forever, but I have known more old soldiers than old stay-at-homes. A man may fall in battle, very true! But also he may slip in the street on a bit of apple-skin and break his inglorious neck! Look at me that have fought in fifty actions, and am ready for fifty more!"

He addressed himself to Master Burden whose white face he saw on the staircase: "Come, Master Burden, will not some of your fellowship join me ?"

THE O'FLYNN

Master Burden shook his black mane. "Nay," he protested, "we are players—not soldiers."

"A sad answer!" Flynn cried; "a bad answer. Let me tell you, Master Burden, that when King James's father, King Charles of blessed memory, was fighting for his crown, many of your trade made his best soldiers. Hart, that was the handsomest lover on the stage, was Lieutenant of Rupert's Horse; Burt and Shatterley, noted players both, served in the same troop; Mohun, that was famous for stage tyrants, won nobler fame as a captain of dragoons, and Allen of the Cockpit Theatre, as funny a man as ever set an audience rocking, was a major at Oxford. What they did, you can do, with a laced coat on your shoulders, and a feathered hat on your heads. Come and play great parts on the world's stage!"

If Flynn's appeal had no effect upon Master Burden, it touched the hearts of some of his followers. Master Conamur cried from the staircase, "I am tired of play-acting—" He turned to argue with Burden that sought to restrain him; "I don't get good parts enough," he cried. He pushed his manager on one side and stretched out his hand through the balustrade toward Flynn. "I will be with you, sir, if you make me an officer."

"You shall be my lieutenant," Flynn promised, and added with a laugh, "I think we'll all be officers in O'Flynn's Own!"

The example of Master Conamur proved infectious. Tulpin, his habitual gloom dissipated by a sudden wave of martial ardor, came hurrying down the stairs, crying, "I am with you!"

He was followed by Winshaw, calling, "And I!"

By this time the military enthusiasm, warmed by the

sight of Flynn's guineas, was spreading in the crowd and hand after hand was reached out to catch the coins that Flynn was tossing in all directions with generous profusion. Almost delirious with excitement, O'Flynn began to sing the famous Stuart song:

> "Here's a health to his Majesty,
> With a fal, lal, la, la, la, la:
> Confusion to his enemies,
> With a fal, lal, la, la, la, la, la:
> And he who will not drink this health,
> I wish him neither wit nor wealth,
> But just a rope to hang himself,
> With a fal, lal, la, la, la, la, la!"

The exultants caught up and repeated the stirring words and the stirring tune.

"Three cheers for Captain O'Flynn!" Coin shouted, and Gosling led the enthusiastic cheers that followed to the call.

O'Flynn was lifted in triumph on to the shoulders of two of his recruits, and thus, under whimsical conditions, O'Flynn's Own came into being.

XXI

RING A RING OF ROSES

IT was not to be expected that the whimsicality of the siege of Knockmore would be suffered to diminish with the appearance of the O'Flynn and O'Flynn's Own on that scene of serio-comic conflict. Flynn was ever the man for heightening the humor of any humorous situation, and in the position of affairs before Knockmore he found abundant opportunity for amusing himself and others.

His progress in Irish arms had been brilliant and swift. He had raised a regiment of stout rascals, a hundred strong, with his friends of the Fellowship of Players as his subordinate officers. He had clad his gang of rascallions in gaudy uniforms of the royal scarlet plentifully enriched with gold lace—all this to the great agony of paymaster Beggles. He supplied them with the best muskets money could buy —another throe in Beggles' lacerated bosom, and through the interest of Tyrconnel, who had taken a great fancy to him, he was given the king's permission to swell the strength of the force encamped before Knockmore. The O'Flynn was not, however, to his great disappointment, accorded the desired position of commander of that force. That post had already been given to Lord Sedgemouth, and Lord Sedgemouth was not going to relinquish it, in spite of his wound.

RING A RING OF ROSES

As a matter of fact the wound was a very trifling matter, and it was more my lord's intoxication than my lord's injury that brought about his collapse in the Isle of Cyprus. On the very next morning, with a clear head and a body properly plastered and bandaged, my lord insisted upon being conveyed on a litter to the camp before Knockmore, where he took over the command to the infinite relief and gratitude of his predecessor.

Thus when O'Flynn arrived at the seat of war at the head of his redcoats, he found himself condemned to a season of inactivity, which he resented, and which he did his best to enliven. He quartered his men apart, devoted himself heart and soul to their drill, and before forty-eight hours had passed he had knocked them into sufficient shape to present at least the appearance of men at arms. But thereafter he yearned for new interests, and being a creature that liked to gratify his desires, he cast about him for means of entertainment. Most of all things imaginable and unimaginable, he yearned to look again upon the Lady Benedetta Mountmichael, and to effect this purpose he conceived and carried out a plan so daringly impudent that only the O'Flynn would, under the conditions, have dreamed of attempting it.

What that plan was will be seen in due course. It was part and parcel of the plan that the O'Flynn should on a certain afternoon some five days after his arrival at Knockmore, convert his encampment, as far as possible, into a bower of roses. If Luitprand van Dronk, up in his eyrie, could have taken the trouble to eye through his spy-glass that portion of the encampment of the beleaguering force over which a green flag flew, he would have observed, to his surprise, that the garden of Flora seemed suddenly to flourish on the field of Mars. Wreaths of deep-colored roses were wound in festoons around those seeming grim, if real innocent engines of war, the cannons, ranked against the castle: long ropes of roses crept from tent to tent and shed their sweetness upon the friendly summer air. Seldom had any camp of warriors shown so gay and gracious a seeming as the O'Flynn quarters before Knockmore on that blithe and kindly June day.

Festoons of roses floated from a tent that stood hard by on a rising bit of ground, a tent that carried a placard over its opening. This placard bore the words "Master Burden's Riverside Fellowship of Stage Players." As, however, for the moment, the Riverside Fellowship of Stage Players had ceased to exist, thanks to the O'Flynn's sudden enthusiasm for the cause of King James, the tent was only occupied by the two ladies of the company, Mistress Oldmixon and Mistress Fancy Free. The placard and the companionship of Mistress Oldmixon gave Mistress Free a plausible excuse for her presence in the camp, if she had needed one.

In the midst of their elaborate entanglement of roses O'Flynn's heroes took their ease. Some played cards; others dice; all smoked and drank cheerfully, blessing the munificence of the O'Flynn, who, leaning against a rose-garlanded cannon, studied the fortifications of Knockmore through a spy-glass. But there was one of that company that in no wise blessed the munificence of the O'Flynn, and this was Master Beggles, that sat apart from the hilarity of the others upon an unused mortar, and scowled upon a note-book.

Presently Master Beggles put his note-book into his pocket with a wry expression and advancing to where the

RING A RING OF ROSES

O'Flynn stood contemplatively, plucked him gingerly by the sleeve. "Good sir," he said, "a word in your ear."

The O'Flynn took his spy-glass from his eye, placed it under his arm and turned to his dependent with a gesture of acquiescence. "Both organs are at your service," he said, politely.

Master Beggles rapped his breast pocket where the note-book lay. "Touching my accounts," he murmured deferentially.

Flynn made a disapproving gesture. "The devil, the devil," he said. "I trust entirely to you; I never had a head for figures."

Master Beggles' finger jumped to his breast pocket and the note-book came into evidence again. "I find," he said, "that from first to last, since I had the honor to enter your honor's service, which is, as who should say, no less and no better than a week, I have expended—"

The O'Flynn interrupted him with a magnificent gesture. "Pardon me—I have expended."

Master Beggles coughed apologetically and continued, "You have expended no less a sum than five hundred guineas."

Flynn eyed him with an affected sternness. "Well, what of it?" he asked.

"What of it?" Master Beggles repeated in a shocked voice; "what of five hundred guineas?"

"Yes," said Flynn, "what of it? What is five hundred guineas to me with my millions? Gold is dross, Master Beggles. It's what gold can do, that is the true ingot."

Master Beggles did not look convinced. "No doubt, but—" he began.

Flynn would not let him continue. "Haven't I raised

213

a troop for King James, with the finest uniforms in his service? Sure, I've served under kings galore and never known a finer pack of rascals than O'Flynn's Own. They'd be a credit to an emperor."

Master Beggles sighed heavily. "But they're a debit to me," he groaned.

Flynn reproved him. "Hush, usurer, hush! At the rate of interest agreed upon, I owe you six hundred guineas. Put it down, Master Beggles, put it down."

"Of course, of course," Master Beggles concurred, putting away his precious note-book. "But don't you think we might economize a little?"

The O'Flynn reeled as if he had been struck by a bullet. "Economize! There's a dirty verb to use to a gentleman. Will you be telling me why I should economize? Fie the foul word. It was never the way with the O'Flynns."

Beggles gave a cry of despair. "Then whatever possessed you," he cried, "to go giving this grand entertainment for all the world as if you were a Roman emperor?"

Flynn addressed him confidentially. "Let me tell you, my boy, that an O'Flynn of O'Flynn considers himself a cut above any Roman emperor that ever walked in sandals."

Beggles began to enumerate items of extravagance, ticking them off on his fingers. "Fiddlers from Dublin. Fine wines from the Isle of Cyprus. Made dishes and pastry and all such kickshaws, with tents set out for lodgings as if they were apartments in a palace."

The O'Flynn checked him. "My friend," he said, "when the O'Flynn gives a party he knows no half measures."

Beggles groaned again. "Suppose they don't come," he suggested lugubriously.

But Flynn declined to be depressed. "Suppose nothing of the kind," he said. "It's glad enough of a change they'll be from dear old dirty Dublin."

Master Beggles stood still; he seemed to have a point to make. "But, excuse me," he said, "is it necessary or sensible to adorn our artillery with garlands of roses?"

The O'Flynn looked properly indignant. "Necessary?" he cried. "Essential! Do you know whom I serve?"

Master Beggles began faithfully to enumerate, "His Majesty James II., King of England, France and Ireland, Defender of the Faith—"

Flynn interrupted him. "Thank you. Nominally I serve King James. Actually I am the soldier of the loveliest lady God ever made."

Master Beggles lifted up his hands in despair to the skies, a gesture familiar with him whenever his new master spoke of lovely ladies. "Lord, Lord!" he groaned.

But Flynn paid him no heed and continued, "And that it's ten chances to one that the said loveliest lady will grace the camp with her presence this blessed and holy day."

Master Beggles continued his lamentations. "I could have got paper roses from Dublin for a fiftieth of the money," he wailed.

Flynn turned upon him fiercely: "Paper roses, is it, you skinflint? If I could get roses from the Elysian Fields, they wouldn't be good enough for my lady's presence."

Master Beggles endeavored to continue his protest. "Yes, but after all—"

Flynn cut him short peremptorily. "Say no more,

Master Beggles, say no more. If you are tired of being my paymaster, I'll find others more complacent at a lesser rate. Why, tell me now, didn't I force twenty per cent. upon you, just because I took a fancy to the thing you call a face ?"

Master Beggles was apologetic. "No offence, O'Flynn," he declared, "no offence."

O'Flynn looked at him disapprovingly. "It's the ungrateful devil you are, Beggles, and I making your fortune. If I wasn't so fond of you, I'd give you back your dirty money—"

At this suggestion Master Beggles, whose confidence in the future wealth of the O'Flynn was unabated, broke in imploringly. "Don't say that, O'Flynn, for the love of Heaven, don't say that!"

O'Flynn met his request cheerfully. "I won't," he promised. "Now don't be distressing me any more with your finances. I know what's good for you, and I know what's good for me, and I know what's good for everybody without your interfering. Put that in your pipe and smoke it."

As he spoke he moved away from his treasurer, who sat down upon the mortar and joined the little knot of his soldiers who were making merry together and whose merriment attracted him. As their leader approached, they arose and saluted him, but seated themselves again in obedience to a gesture from him while he addressed them.

"Well, boys, it's the fine time you're having here, I'm thinking. Never a siege like this have I seen in all my days. We eating, drinking, and smoking comfortably here; the enemy eating, drinking, and smoking comfortably up yonder. We don't fire at them because we can't do them any damage. They don't fire at us because they know they're quite safe and they don't want to waste their powder. Sure it's the golden age come back again, and it seems a pity to spoil it by taking the old place."

The wearing of a soldier's coat had not materially lifted Master Tulpin's spirits. "The place will never be taken," he said gloomily.

The O'Flynn turned his head sharply. "Who says the place will never be taken?"

Conamur, looking up from his book, explained, "Only Tulpin, always grunting."

Flynn turned his gaze upon his melancholy adherent. "Why do you say that, my merry friend?" he asked.

Tulpin, with a wry face, condescended to explain: "Because the thing is as plain as a pikestaff. Look at the place!"

Flynn nodded. "I have been looking at it."

Master Winshaw put in his oar. "Our comrade is inclined to the lugubrious mood, but in this I am with him. Consider its walls."

"Those walls are a wonder," Coin said wisely. "It would take a century to knock them down. Leastways, with such powder as we have."

Gosling approved of his comrade's remarks. "Walls, is it? They've no need of a wall at all on one side. Sure the smooth of the rock would defy a goat to climb it."

Coin confirmed his judgment. "Aye, or ten goats either," he added sagely.

Conamur pressed the point. "And they are victualled to stand a year's siege moreover, and right well victualled, too, very different from King James's army."

His words reached Master Beggles' ears where he sat apart, and roused his just indignation. He rose in protest. "Come, come," he said, "you've got no call to complain of your rations. O'Flynn's Own is well fed to my knowledge, whatever may be the case with the Frenchies and the rest."

O'Flynn imposed silence upon his treasurer. "O'Flynn's Own," he said, "shall eat well and drink well so long as O'Flynn has a guinea left of his millions. O'Flynn's Own is the finest troop in the king's service, and 'tis sorry I am to hear one of us say that yonder castle cannot be taken."

Tulpin was not to be shaken. "Yet such is my conviction," he persisted.

Winshaw supported him, "And mine."

Flynn began to lose patience. "'Tis talking through a horse-collar, you are, for foolishness," he cried: "My head to a halfpenny that I could have taken it any day myself since we came here."

Coin dug Gosling in the ribs. "Don't you love him when he talks like that?" he asked, in a hoarse whisper.

Tulpin riposted the O'Flynn's assertion. "Then why didn't you?" he asked gloomily.

Flynn explained: "Because when my Lord Sedgemouth was carried here from Dublin—and it's much to his credit that he would be brought here for all he was wounded— he gave orders that nothing was to be done until he was well enough to take command."

Gosling chuckled. "Faith, for a sick man he has been fairly comfortable, with pretty Mistress Free to keep him company."

Conamur looked up from his book again with a gentle

sigh. "I wouldn't complain of a flesh-wound myself," he said; "if I had that sweet minion to nurse me."

The O'Flynn cast a reproving glance about him. "Hold your tongues, boys. No light talk about ladies. If Mistress Free brightens the camp with her presence, 'tis because my lord likes stage plays—"

"With one player," Conamur supposed with a faint hint of malice in his voice.

"Be easy," Flynn nodded. "Sure you know very well that Master Burden, poor man, is busy in Dublin, trying to whip up a new cry of players since I turned his old company into Trojans; besides, Mistress Free is under the care of Mistress Oldmixon, so there's no more to be said, and if any one wants to say it I'm quite ready to forget for five minutes that I'm his captain and to settle the question as gentlemen should."

Conamur hastened to apologize. "Indeed, I intended no innuendo," he protested.

Master Winshaw took advantage of the momentary pause to put a question. "May I ask, Captain, if you would be willing to confide to us your ideas touching the capture of yonder castle?"

Flynn replied: "With all the pleasure in life. Now, I've been studying the position carefully ever since we came here, and I've seen a few sieges in my time, but never a one like this for silliness."

Coin applauded loudly. "Hear him, hear him!"

Flynn continued: "If we had ten times the men we have and they ten times better equipped, that place would still be too strong for us. No, boys, I've come to the conclusion there's only one way to get at that old castle—"

"And that way is—?" Coin questioned.

Flynn answered intersely, "The way up the rock."

Gosling shook his head. "There's no way up the rock."

Conamur again deserted his book for a moment. "You might as well talk of a way up the side of a house," he declared.

"You couldn't do it unless you were a fly," Winshaw said, solemnly.

Tulpin improved upon his comrade's suggestion. "You couldn't do it if you were a fly," he grunted.

Flynn regarded his comrades with a look of philosophic disdain. "Wait a bit, wiseacres. It would be easy enough for fellows like us to climb up that rock if only old General Van Dronk, that sits there so snugly and grins at us, were obliging enough to lower us a rope."

Gosling grinned. "Is that all you want?" he asked.

Conamur smiled satirically. "I doubt General Van Dronk is likely to prove so obliging," he said.

Flynn laughed. "I have my own private doubts on that matter. I fought against Van Dronk in the Low Countries. A wicked old devil he was, too; a hard-hearted—hard-hearted son of a Dutch gun."

Then said Beggles deferentially, "Then he is scarcely likely to lower us a rope."

Flynn motioned to Beggles to be silent and addressed his comrades: "Now listen to me, boys, and don't be talking so much. Did you ever hear of a man named Ulysses?"

Coin scratched his ear thoughtfully. "Was he a judge on the Munster circuit?"

"He was not," Flynn answered. "He was a foxy old fellow that lived in Greece yonder, ages and ages ago, and it was ever the idea to him that you could go farther in this world by cunning than by force."

RING A RING OF ROSES

Gosling slapped his knee. "Then he must have been a lawyer," he asserted.

"Whist!" Flynn ordered. "In the course of his life this Ulysses and a party of friends were besieging a town called Troy, much as we are besieging this old place, and were doing no better than we, seeing it was such an elegant stronghold. So at last, Ulysses stands on the two feet of him and says what I say—where force fails try cunning."

Coin looked at his revered leader with keen interest. "Captain darling, what egg are you hatching?" he asked.

And Flynn answered him, "I'm going to get inside that castle; I'm going to lower you a rope down that rock."

Master Winshaw spoke in his most monumental manner. "I opine, sir, that you are pleased to be facetious," he said, solemnly.

Flynn shook his head. "Devil a bit! Listen to my intentions. First I slip into my shabby clothes again— and that's the part of my scheme I like the least—and round my body inside my waistcoat I wind a coil of silk rope as slender as catgut and as strong as steel. Between twilight and dusk I slip over the trenches and run like a deer toward the castle. You, Coin, and you, Gosling, fire your muskets after me—"

He paused, and Gosling questioned him. "For why should we do that?"

Flynn explained: "To elude the enemy that I am a deserter, flying from our lines. But as I don't want to be hit the best thing you can do is to aim at me as closely as you can."

For the first time for many days something in the nature of a smile was observed to steal over Master Tulpin's mournful countenance. "Ha! that's good," he gasped

221

convulsively; "as he doesn't want to be hit, you must aim at him as closely as you can. Oh! that's monstrous good."

Conamur continued to question his chief, "But if the enemy take you for a deserter, what then?"

"Once they let me inside their walls," Flynn replied, "you may wager a doubloon to a duck's egg that I am master of the castle."

Tulpin, who had now mastered his brief attack of mirth, questioned him with his accustomed gloom. "How, pray?"

O'Flynn was in an explanatory mood. "I know old Van Dronk well enough. I know the way I can take to make friends with him. Can't I talk Dutch to him, and can't I flatter him, and isn't he a man that drinks like a fish?"

Winshaw nodded portentously, "It is so reported."

Flynn went on with his plan. "Just let me get a chance, one chance at him alone and I'll settle his business. Sure I could knock him on the head easy enough, but I'd rather not do that unless I'm driven to it. So I've got a little syrup here"—as he spoke he produced from his pocket a little phial which he held up for a moment before his comrades, and then restored it to its hiding-place—"which I got from an apothecary in Dublin; if I can tilt it into his drink, it will send him to sleep like a child, though I swear he'll awake with a headache. Once Van Dronk is out of the way, the rest is easy."

Winshaw seemed puzzled. "I do not follow your thought," he said, doubtfully.

Flynn continued. "When I'm off, you'll find in my tent, under the truckle, a rope-ladder; with this you'll steal across in the dark to the foot of the crag and wait there till I throw down my hat to you."

"Why your hat?" Tulpin questioned sullenly.

Flynn turned sharply upon him: "Because it's more convenient, not to say decent, than throwing down my breeches, you idiot. 'Tis my signal to you that I have managed Van Dronk somehow or other. I lower my cord; you attach ladder; I haul ladder up and make fast. Up that ladder you climb and join me,—presto! we command the castle."

Coin clapped his hands. "Well said, Captain darling," and the applause was taken up by the rest of the group.

Under cover of the noise, Master Beggles twitched Flynn by the sleeve. "Lord's sake, sir," he pleaded, "refrain from this insane enterprise. Consider, if anything should happen to you, where should I be?"

The O'Flynn laid a heavy hand on Beggles' shoulder. "Master Beggles," he said, "if anything happens to me, I've left Castle Famine to you in my will, treasure and all, so you are all right anyhow."

Master Beggles did not seem satisfied. "But how will you ever persuade the Dutchman—" he began.

But Flynn promptly silenced him. "That's my business. Enough! Some one's coming! Why, 'tis Mistress Free!"

XXII

MY LORD SEDGEMOUTH RECEIVES VISITORS

FANCY FREE came dancing daintily along, treading her way to the tents of the quarters of O'Flynn's Own; she greeted her familiar friends with a cheerful wave of the hand. "Good-afternoon, all," she cried, gaily, and then suddenly observing the floral display about her, she exclaimed in wonder, "Why, what a world of roses!"

Flynn smiled a smile of satisfaction. "'Tis an invention of mine, Mistress Fancy," he said, "for making the war-god foppish."

Conamur came a little forward and looked at Fancy with admiring, reproachful eyes. "We thought you had forgotten us, Fancy," he said plaintively.

"Never in all the world," Fancy shook her head vehemently protesting; then she said, "I have news for you, gallant heroes, but first you shall have each a kiss for the sake of old comradeship." As she spoke she flung her arms round Conamur's neck and kissed him, and then she stepped daintily from him to Beggles and from Beggles to Winshaw, and from Winshaw to Tulpin, kissing each affectionately. "I could scold you," she continued, "for leaving the fellowship, if I did not like men to be men."

Flynn looked at Fancy with a smile that was not all

joyous. He knew very well why she was there in the camp, and all those that were with him knew the truth as well as he, and he wished almost pathetically that he did not know the truth, though after all, as he told himself, if Mistress Free were content with her existence and had a liking for my Lord Sedgemouth, it was no concern on earth to a battered adventurer to vex himself over the matter. "What is your news, Mistress Fancy?" he asked of the girl.

Conamur, who had been watching him, suggested slyly to Fancy before she could answer, "Have you never a kiss for the captain?"

Fancy laughed a laugh that was not quite hearty. "He was not of our brotherhood," she said; "I am not on such kissing terms with him. 'Tis my thought that he would deny me if I aimed at his cheek."

The O'Flynn shook his head. "Little rogue! May I remind your flightiness that you carried news?"

Fancy clapped her hands. "Brave news, rare news! There be visitors coming to the camp."

Flynn stared at her good-humoredly. "Sure it is no news, child," he said.

"No news!" Fancy echoed; "and it only comes to my Lord Sedgemouth this minute. I was reading a comedy to him but now to divert him, when in dashes Captain Scully that Lady Tyrconnel and a bevy of ladies are coming to the camp."

Flynn looked hilarious. "Of course they are, the darlings," he said joyously.

Fancy looked surprised. "Of course they are!" she said. "What do you know about it?"

Flynn struck an imposing attitude. "Sure, and didn't

225

THE O'FLYNN

I invite them? The O'Flynn of O'Flynn's Own has the honor to present his respectful homage to the Lady Tyrconnel and to request her presence with her suite at a ball within the lines on this blessed and holy evening."

Fancy stared at him with uplifted eyebrows. "You never did that!"

"I ever did!" Flynn answered, emphatically. "And all the beautiful ladies are coming like flies after sugar. There's to be an elegant collation when they arrive in the big marquée yonder, and dancing the moment it's dark enough to light the flambeaux. 'Tis the evening of evenings, it's going to be, please the pigs."

Fancy gave a little laugh and a little shiver. "It's a towering rage my lord will be in."

Flynn shrugged his shoulders. "Let him tower," he said, complacently.

Fancy went on without heeding him. "Why, when he heard the news he cursed and swore as famously as a pagan, and bade me go about my business while the visitation endures. I have it in my mind that there was something he wanted to do with this day, for no sooner does he hear of his intended visitors than—though he is whole of his hurt and has left his bed, though not his tent these two days—he calls upon his physician to witness that he is still too sick to play the host, and even now they are carrying him hither in his chair to meet her ladyship, though he can walk as well as I can."

Flynn gaped at her. "What does the good gentleman do that for, in the name of the crows?"

Fancy suddenly looked cunning. "There!" she protested; "I'm talking too loosely. He'd be mad with me if I babbled."

Flynn reassured her. "Sure, I am not heeding you. 'Tis little I care what he does with his time."

Fancy glanced apart and pointed: "Here he comes!" she said, "as if he were in the Mall instead of this wilderness. So good-bye to you, Captain O'Flynn."

She darted away as swiftly as she had come. Flynn, following the direction indicated by her pointed finger, saw, as she had said, a chair was being carried in the direction of the encampment. He turned to his men where they lay scattered upon the ground and gave the word, "Fall in!" The O'Flynn's Own, rising obediently, scrambled and scuffled into some kind of order to receive their commander.

"Present arms!" O'Flynn next directed, and the direction was obeyed with a moderate degree of military precision as my Lord Sedgemouth came upon the scene, carried in his chair and accompanied by a sober-looking man in black, who was his physician. The bearers set down their burden and the physician opened the gilded door, and my Lord Sedgemouth, leaning on the arm of the man in black, got out of the chair with much apparent show of difficulty and advanced toward Flynn, leaning heavily upon his stick. He looked around him angrily as he advanced at the profusion of roses.

"Why, what a devil is all this foolery?" he asked, sourly. "Who gave you permission to stick up these gimcracks?"

Flynn tapped his chest significantly. "I gave myself permission," he replied. "'Tis a way of the O'Flynns. Sure, the vice-reine's coming to see me and I wish to receive her decently."

Sedgemouth swore at him: "Damnation! Do you

mean to say that you have brought these cursed women here?"

Flynn raised a rebuking hand. "Easy, my lord, easy! I have done myself the honor to invite her grace to a small entertainment, and her grace has done me the honor to accept my invitation."

Sedgemouth glared at him furiously. "By God! sir, who are you to dare to—"

But Flynn interrupted him without ceremony: "I am the O'Flynn of O'Flynn, an Irish gentleman of unblemished descent. My grandfather served the first Charles when your grandmother was selling turnips in Covent Garden."

Any allusion to his unfortunate ancestry always irritated my Lord Sedgemouth beyond words, but now he strove to restrain himself, and with livid countenance spoke scornfully to the O'Flynn. "The first time I had the privilege of meeting you, you were drunk. You seem to be drunk still."

The O'Flynn laughed, indifferently. "Let bygones be bygones. I am sober enough this day."

Sedgemouth's anger grew in spite of his efforts to keep calm. "Drunk or sober, let me tell you, sir, that though you are here by the favor of His Grace of Tyrconnel, because you happen to have the money to raise a troop, you are not master of this camp, and if you ignore my authority I will drum-head you and hang you for a mutineer."

O'Flynn drolled him, gleaning at his fellows as he spoke: "I'm thinking O'Flynn's Own might have a word to say to that, seeing they're the best troops in the camp, even if O'Flynn himself didn't raise any objection—and he is inclined to be disputatious."

At these audacious words of O'Flynn's his followers expressed their approval with significant gestures and grunts of approbation, which my Lord Sedgemouth thought it wise under the circumstances to overlook.

"I am a fool," he said, "to bandy words with you. Thanks to you, the camp has visitors of distinction who will arrive in a few minutes. Send your fellows to form a guard of honor for the vice-reine. They have got coats on their backs, which few of ours have."

O'Flynn saluted him. "I'm obliged to your lordship for noticing the fact." He took off his hat with a magnificent gesture. "Sure, if you are civil, I can be civil too. It's wrong I was about your ancestor. 'Twas apples she sold, not turnips."

Sedgemouth glared at him ferociously. "Damn you!" he said, and said no more, as O'Flynn gave the command to his men: "Left wheel. By your left. Quick march!" and, putting himself at their head, marched briskly away in the direction of the spot where the ladies were expected to arrive.

No sooner were O'Flynn's Own out of sight than my Lord Sedgemouth, abandoning his air of illness, turned to the tent which served as a shelter to Mistress Fancy, and called to her: "Fancy! Are you there, Fancy?"

In obedience to his summons Fancy made her appearance. "Here, my lord," she said, and dropped him a courtesy.

Sedgemouth addressed her pettishly: "I am sorry to banish you, child, but these damned women are cursedly interfering."

Fancy looked at him in surprise. "Is it less than high

treason to talk thus of the viceroy's lady? Not to speak
of the lady you want to marry."

Sedgemouth's temper got the better of him. "Keep my
marriage out of your mouth," he cried, "curse you!"

Fancy drew a little way back and looked at him with
cool disdain. "Hark you, my dear lord," she said, "if it
pleases me to be civil to you, it must please you to be civil
to me. You are a pretty man enough while your speech is
sweet, but if you swear at me again, I'll show you my
heels."

Sedgemouth did not wish to quarrel with Fancy, so he
made an effort to appear amiable. "Keep your temper,
child. I ask your pardon if I forget your humor to be
treated like a fine madam."

Fancy made a face at him, but Sedgemouth still sought
to conciliate the girl.

"I want to be treated," she said, "as a decent man
would treat a decent woman, and that's too much to ask
from you or for me."

"Pish! devilkin, don't be a ninny. You should have
none of this sick-a-bed whimsies. Why, I like you as well
as another, and shall like you better if you will do me the
good turn."

"What is it?" Fancy asked.

Sedgemouth explained, "I have urgent reasons for
quitting the camp for an hour or so at sundown; 'tis to
see no woman, I promise, so you need not prick up your
ears."

Fancy shook her head. "My lord, my lord, I am not
jealous. I think you are more anxious to hold me than
I you."

"Prithee," Sedgemouth continued, "when it darkens,

go to my tent, and stretch there at your ease on my sofa covered with a cloak. If thereafter any should come to my quarters, my physician, that knows my wishes, will swear I am sleeping and must not be troubled; will, if need be, point to a seeming sleeper on the couch. Will you do this for me, minx?"

Fancy nodded. " 'Tis no great strain of complaisance to do such."

Sedgemouth smiled approval. "You are no politician, I think. You are not for one party more than another?"

Fancy laughed. "I am but for one party," she protested; "the party that pays."

Sedgemouth patted her hand. "Egad, you are a most sensible woman," he asserted. Then, glancing away from her, he saw to his irritation that the O'Flynn was returning alone to his quarters; he hastened to dismiss Fancy. "Now to earth, vixen, for I see my Rapparee returning."

Fancy vanished into the tent again, and my Lord Sedgemouth carefully reassumed his invalid manner and appeared very feeble, indeed, as Flynn again came into his presence.

Flynn saluted. "The ladies are sighted, my lord; I have placed my men to form a guard of honor, under my lieutenant."

Sedgemouth frowned at him. "Why have you returned, sir?"

"Sure," Flynn answered, breezily, "I want to receive my visitors on my own doorstep, as it were."

Sedgemouth looked steadily at him. "You carry yourself very arrogantly. Who would think to hear you speak that I was in command. But while I can stand on my feet, sir, you must concede me the privilege of receiving the vice-reine. And here, I perceive, come the ladies.

XXIII

"IF EVER YOU CAN DO HIM A SERVICE"

THE Duchess of Tyrconnel was no longer a young woman, but she still retained much of the beauty which, in the days when she was known as Frances Jennings, had won the heart of Richard Talbot, who, in his maturity, had made her his second wife, and a duchess in the fulness of time. She moved now a noble centre of a circle of gracious girls of whom the most beautiful were the three that were called, in Dublin, "the three B's"— Lady Belinda Fanshaw, Lady Barbara Jarmyn, and Lady Benedetta Mountmichael. A number of gallant gentlemen escorted her, Captain Scully and Sir George Mayhew chief among them.

O'Flynn's Own, making up in gorgeousness of uniform for what they had lacked in precision of drill, formed an imposing line through which the procession of fair ladies and gay gentlemen advanced toward Lord Sedgemouth.

The Duchess of Tyrconnel looked frankly surprised to see Lord Sedgemouth. "Why," she cried, "my lord, we did not hope to find you afoot."

My lord paid her his profoundest bow. "Indeed, madam," he said, with an air of melancholy dignity, "by rights I should not be abroad, but when I heard of your coming I would not be constrained from greeting you for all my physician urged to the contrary."

"IF EVER YOU CAN DO HIM A SERVICE"

The duchess shook her fan at him. "I fear you are over-gallant, my lord. Return to your quarters, I entreat. We shall not do as well without you as with you, though I make no doubt as shall do very well."

Sedgemouth bowed again. "Your ladyship is most gracious, and my infirmity accepts your dispensation."

The vice-reine turned and looked at her little court of ladies; she singled out Benedetta with a gesture. "There is a child here," she said, kindly, "who would gladly keep you company for a while. Shall we lend you, Benedetta, to his lordship?"

Benedetta's fair face flushed with pleasure. "I thank your ladyship," she said, gratefully; then, passing with a reverence before her grace, she came to her lover's side. "Let me be with you, my lord," she pleaded.

My Lord Sedgemouth again saluted the duchess. "Your ladyships are too good," he said, gratefully. He turned to Benedetta, and there were tears in his voice if he could not bring any show of tears into his eyes. "Dear Lady Benedetta," he said, "it is a second grief to me to deny myself your company awhile. But my physician will have it that I must needs be alone and I dare not cross him. I trust I shall be better to-morrow, but for the time I entreat your consideration and your permission to retire."

"You have them both, my lord," the duchess declared warmly.

Sedgemouth made as if to depart, and then paused to speak again: "But ere I go, I would ask your grace's permission to present to you the gentleman whose lively Irish wit devised this festivity. This is the O'Flynn, of O'Flynn's Own. Though he has blooded me as weak as

233

a kitten I bear him no other grudge than this, that I am prevented from sharing in your grace's entertainment."

O'Flynn made his best bow to the Duchess, who eyed him approvingly. She knew a pretty man when she saw one and in her gallery of gallant gentlemen she recalled no more soldierly figure than that of the O'Flynn.

"Why, O'Flynn," she cried, "you seem the Anacreon of the battle-field and we are glad to be your guests."

O'Flynn laid his hand to his heart. "Your ladyship does me great honor," he protested.

My Lord Sedgemouth interrupted the duchess and O'Flynn with a malign smile. "It is unfortunate," he observed, "that his duty prevents Captain O'Flynn from playing your host in person to-night."

O'Flynn looked at him coolly; he was surprised and angry, but showed no sign of either emotion. So this, then, was what my lord had meant when he threatened to put him in his place; my lord knew well that O'Flynn could show neither resentment of my lord's conduct nor disobedience to my lord's commands in the presence of the vice-reine and in the presence of Benedetta. After all, however, he reflected, it mattered very little; his purposes might be best served by Lord Sedgemouth's prohibition. But if O'Flynn was silent and resigned, her grace was less complacent.

"Oh, my lord," she said, "can he not be relieved of this duty for the nonce?"

My Lord Sedgemouth smiled a dignified denial. "No soldier, your ladyship, ever wishes to be relieved of a duty, and I know that Captain O'Flynn is no exception to this rule. But I request Captain Scully and Sir George Mayhew to act as his deputies, and to make you forget him and me."

Her grace shook her head. "Not so, we vow, though they make excellent company."

My Lord Sedgemouth allowed himself to slip a little and placed a hand in the neighborhood of his heart. The physician darted forward to support his failing strength. "I am growing faint," said my Lord Sedgemouth, faintly; "may I retire?"

The duchess gave her permission. "Surely, surely. We shall hope to know you stronger to-morrow."

Sedgemouth bowed. "I thank your ladyship." He then turned to Benedetta and spoke with the rare tenderness which he could infuse into the tones of his voice when he wished to charm women. "Farewell, for the present, dear lady, I am almost well, and the sight of you will go far to complete my recovery." Then, moving very feebly and weighing heavily upon the extended arm of his physician, my Lord Sedgemouth crept into his gilded chair that was lined with crimson silk, and was carried away at a brisk pace toward his own quarters.

Her Grace of Tyrconnel addressed the Irishman, whose appearance she admired. "We are sorry to lose your company, O'Flynn," she said.

The O'Flynn bowed again. "I could not have better delegates, your ladyship." He turned to Sir George Mayhew. "Sir George, you will find a trifling entertainment spread in the pavilion yonder, and the violins will tune up whenever you please."

Her grace addressed Captain Scully and Sir George Mayhew. "Well, gentlemen, 'tis your task to divert us in the absence of our host. Take us everywhere, show us everything; but before we part, tell me, O'Flynn, what put it into your head to turn a camp into a nosegay?"

"Faith, your ladyship," O'Flynn answered, "an old soldier is always superstitious, and 'twas ever the thought with me that our good cause might be rewarded by a visitation of angels; and your ladyship sees I was right."

Her grace applauded, "A pleasing conceit and a gallant interpretation."

While the O'Flynn had been speaking he had gathered from the garlands about them a large handful of the brilliant flowers that made his camp appear so fantastically fair. He advanced toward the duchess with his arms full of blossoms. "May I offer your ladyships posies from my roses?" he asked, and as the duchess graciously gave her consent he presented her and each of her accompanying ladies with a bunch of the blooms; to Benedetta as if by accident he came last, and again to her as if by accident he gave but a single flower, the last that was left in his hands.

Her grace beamed upon him. "We thank you," she said; "we shall hope to welcome you shortly at Dublin Castle."

O'Flynn bowed, "I shall do myself the honor to wait on your ladyship."

Her grace smiled her fairest, "Good-day, sir." She turned to the gentleman nearest to her, "Captain Scully, conduct us." And so her grace with her bright and lively company went their way beneath the arches of roses to the distant pavilion where the O'Flynns awaited them.

Lady Benedetta lingered to the last, paused for a second before O'Flynn, and then let fall at his feet the rose he had just given her; O'Flynn swiftly stooping picked up the flower and stood for an instant uncertain whether to restore it to her or to understand that she had purposely rejected it. Benedetta shook her head and laid a finger on her lips as she followed quickly in the direction of the departed duchess.

Flynn stood with the rose in his fingers wonderingly. He had seen no sign of unkindness in his lady's face. He turned to his Lieutenant Conamur: "Faith," he said, "that same peevish gentleman served me better than he knew. I was at a loss for occasion to slip away from my guests and try my luck with the castle yonder, and sure my lord presses opportunity into my fingers."

Conamur looked at him with eager interest. "You'll try it to-night then?" he questioned.

Flynn nodded: "Of course I'll try it to-night. Could I have a finer audience for so bold an adventure and could I give my visitors a pleasanter gift than the keys of the castle? Now to your tents, O Israel. Dismiss! I'll be with you by-and-by."

O'Flynn's Own fell out and departed to their tents in obedience to their captain's orders. O'Flynn stopped Beggles for a moment as he passed: "Beggles, my friend, put out my old clothes. I'll have a use for them again this night, and it ought to please you to see me practising economy," he said. Then he gave Beggles a friendly pat on the back and sent him after the others, remaining alone in contemplation of Benedetta's rose. He walked slowly up and down for some time, shuffling rhymes and phrases in the attempt to make some verses about the flower. After various experiments he got some lines into shape and he repeated them to himself in his solitude:

THE O'FLYNN

"Oh, Rose of the world, if I gave you a rose
  From the heart of the Garden of Love,
The garden so green, where each blossom that blows
  A tear or a smile is of angels above,
Would you wear or disdain it, protect or reject it?
Would you guard or discard it, preserve or neglect it?
  The Rose from the Garden of Love."

He shook his head over them; they were not what he meant; they were not what he wanted and he was for beginning over again when a light step distracted him from idle verses to more serious thoughts. Benedetta had returned and stood before him. She looked at him whimsically, "I have dropped my rose," she said.

O'Flynn sighed, "I picked it up."

"I let it fall of purpose," Benedetta said, rapidly, "for I wanted a word with you and those others not by. O'Flynn, I spoke harshly to you the other night, gave you bad names, upbraided you—as, indeed, you deserved to be upbraided."

Flynn repeated his earlier assurance, "I had sooner be railed at by you than praised by another."

"I thought, then," Benedetta went on, "that you had forced a quarrel upon my Lord Sedgemouth with some fantastic idea of getting rid of a rival."

Flynn protested, "Haven't I told you a thousand times that I don't admit the existence of a rival?"

Benedetta frowned a little frown upon him. "Will you be still, amazing gentleman?" she asked. "I know now that it was your belief that my name was taken lightly, which made you do as you did. I know all that happened, for my Lord Sedgemouth told me all."

"Come, that was mighty honorable of him," Flynn approved.

"He is all honor," Benedetta said, gravely. "His friends were praising this lady and that, and he, because he is pleased to deem me handsome, must needs thrust in my name as the fairest of ladies. This, you overhearing, took for a slight that was but a homage."

Flynn sighed again. "It's the devil I am for jumping to conclusions."

"I was rightly angry with you then," Benedetta went on, "for you made yourself my eneny, though you meant to be my friend. But I am not angry with you, for my lord is well-nigh whole of his hurt. I want you and him to be friends."

Flynn shook his head. "I'm afraid that's impossible."

Benedetta entreated: "Come, come, Chevalier, when can a lady's wish prove impossible? I love him—"

"Are you sure?" Flynn questioned, quietly.

"Surely I am sure," Benedetta affirmed; "I love him, and I like you, and because he is first in my love and because you are high in my liking I cannot abide it that you two should be enemies."

There was a moment's pause and then Flynn spoke again, looking steadily at the girl. "Let us understand each other, pretty lady. You want me that loves you to be friends with him that you think you love."

Benedetta strove to silence him. "You must not speak of loving me, I forbid it. And you must not say that I think I love my lover; I forbid it. If you and I are to be friends, O'Flynn, it must be on my terms, or else goodbye to the friendship. And if we are to be friends, then I command you to be friends with him."

"If I were for being friends with him," Flynn said, dubiously, "I doubt he would be friends with me."

"Indeed, he will be so," Benedetta insisted. "Did you not hear him say but now that he bore you no grudge for your victory?"

Flynn smiled ironically. "I heard him say so."

"If he can be so generous," Benedetta continued, "you must be generous, too. You beat the wind when you woo me, for I am not to be wooed. But, because I believe in you and your true good-will to me, I say this. You would make a great enemy: do better, and prove a great friend. If ever it be in your power to do him a service, do him that service for my sake."

Flynn slowly repeated her words: "Do him that service for your sake. You ask a great deal, lady, but you have the right to ask all, and I will give you all, even my hope."

Now, even as Flynn was making in all earnestness this magnanimous promise, his conference with the lady of his heart was sharply interrupted. As the Lady Belinda Fanshaw came running toward them swift and nimble as a hare, ineffectually followed by Captain Scully, Lady Belinda rushed forward to Lady Benedetta with a little cry of delight just as Captain Scully, panting and flushed, reached her side and endeavored to restrain her.

"Lady Belinda," Scully gasped, "I entreat you—"

Lady Belinda laughed maliciously. "No, no, no," she cried; "I vow I must tell her; she will laugh herself fat."

She addressed Benedetta, "Child, dear, dear child, just a jest for your ear." Then she turned to O'Flynn with a slight inclination of her head, "Pray pardon me, sir," she said, "if I intrude an instant, but my news is peremptory."

Flynn made the mischievous lady a bow and withdrew a little, leaning against a field-piece and surveying the distant castle indifferently.

Captain Scully still vainly protested, "Nay, it is a misunderstanding—a mistake."

Benedetta looked in wonder at the jangling man and woman. "What is all this noise?" she asked.

Lady Belinda explained eagerly. "Why, what do you think, child, that desperate lover of yours, that terrible Lord Sedgemouth, for all he is so death-bed sick, entertains a woman here in the camp."

Lady Benedetta looked at her coldly. "Indeed," she said, and said no more. Captain Scully interrupted the girl. "Indeed, dear ladies, let me explain; Lady Belinda mistakes—"

Lady Belinda would not allow him to continue. "Nonsense," she said, "I do not mistake. You told me, broad and long, that this player-woman was here under Lord Sedgemouth's protection."

Benedetta spoke quite calmly: "But if this is so, what has it to do with us? Surely my Lord Sedgemouth's private pleasures are my Lord Sedgemouth's private property, and no concern of another's."

Lady Belinda looked at her maliciously. "No concern of yours, dear Ben?" she asked.

"Not at all," Lady Benedetta answered positively. "Surely, dear Belinda, a woman of fashion does not expect her lover to be a simpleton, that neither plays, drinks, nor kisses. Shame on you for a Puritan."

Lady Belinda looked and felt disappointed. "Well,"

she said, "If you take it so, I am content. For sure I meant to amuse you, not to distress you."

"You neither amuse nor distress me," Benedetta said calmly; "I am not so easily diverted or disturbed. You must come with more blood-curdling tidings."

"And are you never a tiny bit jealous?" Belinda asked.

Benedetta shook her head. "Nonsense, Belinda, jealousy is not in the mode."

Lady Belinda was disappointed. "Then I have no more to say. Good-bye, pretty philosopher," she said, and turning to Captain Scully, who stood looking a picture of misery by her side, "Come, sir, escort me."

When Lady Belinda and her protesting escort were out of sight, Lady Benedetta suddenly abandoned her show of fortitude; she sank on the carriage of the mortar and hid her face in her hands.

O'Flynn was by her side in an instant. "Don't cry, childeen," he entreated; "it's my heart you'll be breaking if you weep salt water."

Benedetta looked up at him: "I am not weeping, O'Flynn, never fear. But I am so angry that I would I were a man for a minute that I might swear and stamp as men can; for I am jealous, horribly jealous, though I down-faced that mew-cat I was no such thing. Why, I know well enough that our men are seldom single lovers, with their man-gallant's law of life that suits them finely, but I did think that I held the whole of his heart."

Flynn looked wistfully at her. "'Tis the queer fish we are, and we swim in a queer sea."

Benedetta rose to her feet. "I could have sworn I was my lover's only love; I believed him so bound by my bonds that he had no eyes for another face, no ears for another voice, no clasp for another hand, no kiss for another lip. And now he brings this player-jade to camp: I am mad with the rage and shame of it." She was pacing up and down in the fierceness of her rage.

Flynn murmured softly to himself, "If ever it be in your power to do him a service." He turned and said aloud to Benedetta, "Listen, Colleen ma chree, you need never taste the heartache for a spiteful hussy's sting. 'Tis true that Fancy Free is here in the camp, but that fly-by-night Fanshaw Madam is misled when she thinks that the girl is here for the sake of my Lord Sedgemouth."

Benedetta, who had paused in her impatient promenade, looked oddly at him. "For whose sake, then ?" she asked.

"Good faith," Flynn replied, "a man cannot be too chary with a woman's name. But what I say will do the girl no wrong, nor will she wish to deny it."

"What do you mean ?" Benedetta questioned.

Flynn shrugged his shoulders. "Well," he confessed, "the girl is here for no other a man than me."

Benedetta stared at him. "For you ?" she said.

Flynn smiled ruefully. "For me, no less."

Benedetta's mood seemed suddenly to change, though she still showed great anger, but her anger now was not with my Lord Sedgemouth, but with the man to whom she was speaking. She laughed bitterly: "For you, for you—how excellent a jest! You, who talked so tall and rhymed so blithely; Romeo in a soldier's coat, can you, the pattern of Roman ticks, easy emperor of the realm of sentiment, find consolation with any Doll Tearsheet or Moll Cutpurse to hand ?"

Flynn tried to interrupt her. "Lady Benedetta"—he began.

243

But she swept on at him: "Lord, sir, do not apologize. I am very much your debtor for enlightening my simplicity. I suppose you will scarcely credit it that I took your tinkling cymbals for true music, from the very choir of chivalry believed in your passion, was cheated by your phrases. Well, sir, well, have you nothing to say?"

"I have nothing to say," Flynn said, sadly.

Benedetta looked at him scornfully. "Pray, do not think I am angry with you. It was only your lively Irish way that must needs try its wit on any woman that passed." She lowered her angry tone a little as she spoke the last words, for she saw Captain Scully approaching; that worthy gentleman, indeed, was returning to endeavor to repair his recent blunder. Benedetta greeted him with a radiant smile that filled him with delight; she turned and bowed coldly to O'Flynn: "Good-night, Captain O'Flynn. Captain Scully will escort me."

O'Flynn saluted her gravely. "Good-night, Lady Benedetta," he said, and went his way, leaving her alone with the apologetic Scully.

"Your pardon," Scully began, "if I importune in returning thus, but I am so anxious to set matters right—"

Benedetta stopped his explanation. "Matters are set right, I assure you; there is no harm done. Will you bring me to her ladyship?"

"With pleasure, Lady Benedetta," Scully answered. He offered Benedetta his arm and she was about to take it when her attention was attracted by the figure of a girl who came out of the tent on the little inclination that dominated the place where she and Scully were standing; she called her companion's attention to the girl: "Is not that the girl we spoke of? Is not that Fancy Free?"

Scully glanced at the girl and glanced away. "That is she, indeed," he said. "Shall we go on ?" And he made as if he would lead Benedetta from the spot.

Benedetta had now an idea in her head and would not go. "Please do not wait for me, Captain Scully," she said; "I will join her grace presently."

Scully would fain have protested, but the expression of Benedetta's face silenced his protestations: he obeyed and left her alone.

XXIV

FANCY FREE EXPLAINS

FANCY FREE came down the slope humming a tune. The evening was dusking down and she was on her way to Lord Sedgemouth's tent to keep her promise to his lordship. She suddenly became aware of Lady Benedetta standing in her path.

Lady Benedetta spoke to her, "You are Fancy Free?"

Fancy, who knew Benedetta well enough, answered with veiled hostility as she dipped a courtesy, "That is the name I sail under."

Benedetta spoke to her with slightly patronizing disdain, "I saw you act awhile ago; you are a pretty player."

Fancy courtesied again. "Your ladyship is very condescending."

Benedetta scrutinized coolly the pretty, impudent face of the girl. "Now, that I look at you nearer," she said, "I do not wonder that men find you to their liking."

"Neither do I," Fancy answered, impertinently.

Benedetta went on without heeding her impertinence, "Yet I should scarcely have thought you would prove the O'Flynn's choice."

Fancy started at the name and repeated it. "O'Flynn!"

Benedetta laughed scornfully. "You need not pretend to be surprised, though I must say it has surprised me."

FANCY FREE EXPLAINS

"On his account or mine?" Fancy asked, insolently.

Benedetta answered her sharply: "You are pert and foolish to assume that I think about you. But O'Flynn, as a gentleman whose love any woman might be proud of, that he, who professed—oh! it is too grotesque, too monstrous." She moved away, but Fancy followed her up.

"Pray, fine madam, what is O'Flynn to you?" she questioned.

Benedetta answered her still speaking sharply: "To me —nothing, girl. And if you think I am angry about him, you are vastly mistaken. I was vexed, indeed, at a scandal which coupled your name with that of a gentleman whom I know to be the flower of chivalry; it is only amazement I entertain at O'Flynn's taste."

Fancy looked Benedetta full in the face. "You talk very foolish," she said. "The O'Flynn is no lover of mine. I'd just give my ears that he were, but though I wooed him plainly, being a bold piece, he would have none of me."

"He would have none of you!" Benedetta repeated, amazed.

"Even so," Fancy affirmed. "He was all flame for some nameless lady; at least, he left her nameless, and I have never bothered to guess. There was no other woman in the world for him; he would sooner be disdained by her than loved by all others. Oh! he was neck deep in devotion, and I could not entice him. All this I tell you, though O'Flynn is nothing to you, fine madam."

Benedetta gave a little cry and caught Fancy by the wrist. "Ah! then, if this be true, what are you to Lord Sedgemouth?"

Fancy shook off Benedetta's clasp: "I think you

question me too liberally," she said coolly. "If you are curious about Lord Sedgemouth's concerns, can you not ask him yourself? I have the honor to wish your ladyship good-evening." She dipped another courtesy, swung coolly on her heel and went away swiftly, leaving Benedetta alone with her anger, her sorrow, and her surprise.

Benedetta had stood for a few minutes in the deepening dusk, struggling with the tumult in her heart, when she saw in the distance O'Flynn enveloped in a long mantle and followed by two men, going across the opening in the trenches. Instantly and impulsively she ran toward him: at the sound of her voice O'Flynn looked round but did not stay his course.

"O'Flynn! O'Flynn!" she cried, "I want to speak to you." But O'Flynn still continued on his way. She cried again, "Where are you going?"

By this time O'Flynn had reached the gap in the earthworks, and at a signal from him the two soldiers accompanying him, that were Conamur and Gosling, and that carried their muskets, passed through and disappeared into the darkness.

"Where are you going?" Benedetta repeated.

Flynn saluted her with a melancholy smile on his face. "For a walk in the dark," he answered, and leaped down after his companions into the ditch.

Benedetta stood for a moment in silent wonder; then the quiet of the night was broken by the sound of two shots fired in rapid succession on the plain below. Benedetta rushed to the earth-works and leaned over, seeking in vain to pierce the darkness. "O'Flynn! O'Flynn!" she wailed in a strange voice, for she now was beginning to know the truth.

XXV

GENERAL LUITPRAND VAN DRONK was seated very comfortably in the spacious room which he had chosen for his headquarters at Knockmore on the evening of the day on which the O'Flynn had made bold to entertain the vice-reine and her ladies. This room immediately overlooked the steep cliff of rock which made one side of Knockmore so untakable, and it was Van Dronk's delight in the daytime to look out from the window that overhung the precipice and survey his enemies, employing their futile preparations below; but on the fall of evening, General Van Dronk found better amusement in sampling the contents of the splendid cellars of which he had been at such pains to secure the castle.

Although the weather was summer, the great room was far from warm and General Van Dronk enjoyed the cheerful blaze of the fire that sparkled on the hearth. He sat with his booted feet extended to the blaze, and on the table by his side bottles and glasses were ranged in comfortable abundance, and a single candle shed a faint light.

His great military cloak and hat were cast upon a chair and he was sheltered from the draught which the insufficiency of the window permitted by a great wooden screen which snugly enclosed him and his table, and so made, as it were, a room within a room. Thus settled and drinking Burgundy, General Van Dronk was as happy as a Dutch gentleman had a right to be. He chuckled with pleasure when drinking, and he toasted his august monarch in cup after cup without turning a hair.

While he was thus enjoying himself his solitude was interrupted by a knock at the door. Van Dronk stirred a little in his seat, finished the glass of Burgundy which he had just lifted to his lips, and turning slightly in his chair, he growled, "Kom binnen."

The great door which led into the room from the main part of the castle opened and a young man entered and saluted the general. This was Lieutenant Trusham, who acted as leader of the few English soldiers under Van Dronk's command, and who took the capture of Knockmore and its defence very seriously indeed. He was a ruddy, sturdy young English officer, whiggish and Williamite through and through, and he had a great respect for the genius and daring of Van Dronk, though he did not share his bibulous qualities.

Van Dronk looked angrily at the new-comer. "Wat belieft U?" he growled; and then remembering Trusham's nationality, was good enough to translate in a thick guttural voice, "What you want?"

Trusham explained: "General, the sentinels have just brought in a man who claims to be a deserter from the enemy. The Jacobites fired on him from their lines."

Van Dronk grinned. "So. I myself asked, why those damn fools fire? What he like, this man?"

"An Irishman, General," Trusham answered; "one of the mad Rapparees. He asks to see you."

"What for?" Van Dronk asked.

VAN DRONK RECEIVES A VISIT

"He says he can give you valuable information," Trusham answered.

Van Dronk filled himself another bumper. "Bring him here," he said; "I'll question him. If he no use I hang him."

Trusham saluted. "Yes, General.". He went to the door from which he had entered, opened and called, "Bring in the deserter."

A moment later the O'Flynn entered the door between two soldiers.

Trusham pointed to him. "This is the man, General."

Flynn made to advance cheerfully toward Van Dronk but was checked by the uplifted hand of the reproving Trusham. "Gooden avond, mijn General," Flynn said in very passable Dutch. "Het verheugt mij U vel te zien."

Trusham looked at him with a suspicion natural to an Englishman who hears a language with which he is unfamiliar. "What are you saying?" he questioned sternly.

But Van Dronk explained the matter, "He just say I look well." Then he addressed himself to the O'Flynn: "So you speak Dutch, do you?"

Flynn smiled apologetically. "Just a word or two, General," he said modestly.

Van Dronk grunted. "Well, there is no need; I perfectly English speak for my needs; I am a man of few words."

"And many deeds, General," Flynn added politely.

Van Dronk took a pinch of snuff and grunted again.

Flynn looked at the general with reproachful eyes and sighed heavily. "I fear," he said, "you do not remember me, General."

THE O'FLYNN

"Waarlijk," Van Dronk assented, "I should not 'Who the devil are you' say, if I remembered you."

Flynn sighed again: "I am not surprised. Heroes forget heroic deeds. You saved my life at Schwartzheim."

Van Dronk stared at him with round-eyed surprise. "The devil I did; so you at Schwartzheim were ?"

"Yes, General," Flynn explained volubly. "I was then a sergeant in Littmold's Reiters. Some twenty or so of the enemy were trying to put an end to my career, when you, seeing my extremity, charged into my assailants and scattered them."

Van Dronk scratched his head under his huge black periwig. "I do not remember. I wonder if you the truth speak." He paused for a moment, and then an idea seemed to strike him. "We shall see," and he went on, "What like was the weather at Schwartzheim ?"

But the O'Flynn was ready for such questions, and he answered glibly, "Devilish mixed weather. It began raw cold with a sleety rain, but by mid-day it mended and the rest of the action was fought in warm sunshine."

Van Dronk nodded approval: "True enough, true enough. So I saved your life—I wonder what for ?"

Flynn volunteered an explanation, eagerly. "That I might have this opportunity of expressing my gratitude. General, allow me to embrace you." He extended his arms as he spoke and made as if to clasp Van Dronk to his breast, but he was again restrained by a menacing gesture from Trusham.

"Bridle your enthusiasm, my good sir," Trusham said, sternly, and then, turning to Van Dronk, he explained: "Don't mind him, General; I understand these Irish, thoroughly. I've lived three months in their island. He only wants to pay his respects."

All that Trusham got for his attempted interpretation of O'Flynn's intentions was a peremptory "Hold your head" from Van Dronk, who then addressed himself to Flynn: "You, sir, why you desert James Stuart?"

Flynn explained, plausibly: "I was forced to serve against my will. I care nothing for James Stuart; I care everything for Luitprand van Dronk, my savior." Again he made as if he would embrace the Dutch general, and again he was checked by the disapproving Trusham. "Pray restrain yourself," Trusham commanded; then he added to Van Dronk, "These Irish are so exuberant."

Van Dronk shrugged his shoulders. "Genuk," he said; then he turned to Flynn, "Mijn vriend, I take a liking to you; I suppose it is because I save your life, though I forget it."

Flynn answered genially, "You save so many lives, General."

"Javol," Van Dronk agreed. "Tell me, do you know good wine when you smell it?" As he spoke he filled one of the cups, that stood on the table, from the bottle by his hand, and extended it toward the stranger. It was one of Van Dronk's rules of life to test a man's merits by his capacity for appreciating good liquor.

Flynn took the cup from the general's fingers and sniffed it. "A true votary of Bacchus," he said, "should be able to tell the vineyard by the smell and the vintage by the taste. This juice was ripened in Upper Burgundy and," draining the cup, "I'll swear that 1660 is its birth-year."

Van Dronk beat the table, approvingly. "Hemel en

aarde, you are a fine fellow; you know good wine and you shall drink good wine. Sit!" And he turned to Trusham. "Lieutenant, you may go," he commanded.

Trusham appeared surprised and reluctant. "And leave you alone, General?" he asked.

Van Dronk shrugged his shoulders, drew a pistol from his belt and laid it on the table close to his hand. "Ah, bah!" he said, "you can come in if you hear a pistol-shot."

When Trusham and the two soldiers had withdrawn, Van Dronk motioned to O'Flynn to seat himself at the table, an order which O'Flynn very willingly obeyed. Van Dronk filled Flynn's glass and his own with the noble Burgundy and then addressed him, "Now, mijn vriend, I suppose you expect to be asked questions?"

"And to answer them, General," Flynn acquiesced, cheerfully.

Van Dronk looked steadily at him. "I am man of few words; if you try to deceive me I hang you."

Flynn, who was in the act of swallowing the contents of the glass of wine, set down the cup on the table and looked reproachfully at his host. "Is it after saving my life for me that you'd be talking like that?" he asked.

Van Dronk took no notice of his remark. "Bah! What is the condition of James Stuart's forces?" he questioned.

"Why, wretched enough," Flynn began; then paused in his narrative to interpolate a remark, "but, General, permit me to observe that you don't drink."

Van Dronk glared at him. "I don't drink! I!!" he thundered. "I am man of few words, but I am man of many bottles: I drink all day, I drink all night."

Flynn shook his head, waggishly. "You Dutch gentlemen are gallant topers, I grant you that gladly, but you can't hold a candle to us Irish in the tossing of pots."

Again Van Dronk.banged on the table with his clenched fist. "That is one lie," he cried; "that is one big damn lie. Never was Irishman yet born been that can me out-drink."

"I was never the contradictious spirit," Flynn observed, mildly, "or I'd be taking the liberty of backing my thirst against yours any day of the week."

Van Dronk derided him. "Nonsense, mijn vriend, nonsense! Why you are part tipsy already."

"I may be half seas over," Flynn admitted, "but I can swim the rest of the ocean so long as it is Burgundy like this."

Van Dronk laughed grimly. "Well, you shall have your chance, mijn vriend," he promised; "for there's plenty bottles to hand, and tons more wine in cellar. Wacht een oogenblick."

Van Dronk rose to his feet with remarkable steadiness, considering the quantity of Burgundy he had been im-bibing, and turning away from O'Flynn toward an oaken cupboard, that stood on the right of the fireplace, he pro-ceeded to extract several bottles. While he was thus occupied, and while his back was turned, O'Flynn swiftly produced from his pocket the phial containing the drowsy syrup he had obtained from the Dublin apothecary and leaning cautiously over the table he poured its contents into Van Dronk's goblet. When, an instant later, Van Dronk returned to the table laden with flagons, he found his companion where he had left him with the same cheerful smile of incipient intoxication upon his face.

Van Dronk opened one of the bottles and filled O'Flynn's

cup and his own. He raised his vessel to his lips, "Your good health, mijn vriend," he said, and drank steadily.

Flynn raising his own cup to his mouth and feigning to drink, watched Van Dronk curiously till the Dutch general set down his empty goblet. "The same to you, General," he said cheerily; then, after a pause he spoke again as if to remind his host of an interrupted conversation, "I think you were doing me the honor to ask me a question."

Van Dronk nodded. "Javol! I ask you what is the condition of James Stuart's forces?"

Flynn looked melancholy. "Mighty bad. French officers that grumble and keep apart; English officers incompetent and bombastic. The ragged levies are valiant enough, but they are ill-armed, ill-fed, ill-shod; men can't fight well on naked feet and empty bellies, General."

Van Dronk yawned prodigiously. "That is just so," he said; "you are sensible fellow, man of few words, like me."

It was plain to the O'Flynn that the Dutch general was beginning to get more and more drowsy. His heavy lids drooped over his fierce eyes, his huge face lowered more and more toward his chest; languor was evidently stealing over his senses and his limbs.

O'Flynn, with ironic sympathy, questioned, "Are you feeling sleepy, General?"

Van Dronk, stung by the epithet, made a desperate attempt to rouse himself from the lethargy that was overwhelming him. "I—sleepy?" he fumed; "certainly not. What the devil put that in your fool-head? Only thirsty—always thirsty; never sleepy."

O'Flynn laughed a little quiet laugh of satisfaction.

VAN DRONK RECEIVES A VISIT

"I'm glad you aren't sleepy, General," he said, "for I have a little story to tell you."

Van Dronk lifted his drooping head with a jerk. "Vat is het?" he asked heavily.

Flynn leaned forward across the table and whispered confidentially, "There is a plot afoot to capture this castle, to take it and you by surprise."

Stirred by these words Van Dronk succeeded in rousing himself for a moment from his growing stupor. "Hemel en aarde," he cried; "they are children, those others; I am never taken by surprise."

"Certainly not, General," O'Flynn cried. "Yet 'tis a pretty plot, too, and ingenious."

Van Dronk's head was nodding helplessly again, but his stubborn spirit struggled against the advancing sleep. "Well, go on," he grunted; "don't fall asleep."

"Listen, General darling," Flynn said coaxingly, "there's a crazy fellow in the camp yonder has the wild scheme in his head for getting inside your walls.

Van Dronk lifted his head with difficulty, propped up his chin with his hand and stared sleepily at Flynn. "Donder en bliksem," he murmured; "he will find it hard to manage." His senses were slipping swiftly away from him in spite of his gallant efforts to resist his drowsiness.

Flynn laughed, "Impossible, perhaps."

Flynn's laughter proved infectious to the waning wits of Van Dronk; he began to laugh heavily. "Quite impossible," he muttered.

"Unless," Flynn suggested, still laughing, "he came as a deserter, like me."

"Zekerlijk," Van Dronk agreed, his head swaying forward; "he might do that."

"And then, sure," Flynn continued, "the fellow might gain your excellency's confidence with a wonderful story of your having saved his life in action"—he paused, watching his victim.

Van Dronk made one last futile effort to collect his senses as the meaning of Flynn's words troubled his dulled brain. "The devil!" he gasped, and struggled ineffectually to rise.

Flynn continued laughing, "And then, while sitting at wine with your excellency—" At this point there was no further need for him to continue; Van Dronk gave a strange sound between a grunt and a groan and lay supine in his chair, wholly overcome by the action of the drug.

XXVI

THE FALL OF KNOCKMORE

O'FLYNN rose to his feet, possessed himself of Van
Dronk's pistol, and studied the sleeping man's face
closely to make sure that he was really as helpless as he
seemed. "Come," he murmured, "that's a good beginning, anyway, as Adam said when he found a name for
the elephant." As he spoke he opened his waistcoat and
produced from a secret pocket in the lining a long coil of
fine silk rope. "It's a thousand pities," he continued
addressing the sleeping Dutchman, "you are so sleepy,
General, or I'd tell you the rest of my tale of capturing
your castle." As he spoke he was about to move toward
the door when he was paralyzed into rigidity by a loud
knocking at the door.

For a moment O'Flynn's warm blood seemed to run
cold and he stood thunderstruck; this was an unexpected
interruption that looked like baffling his plan at the very
moment of apparent success. But the O'Flynn's wit was
never still for long; his quick eyes glanced around the
room and surveyed it strategically while his active mind
worked briskly.

In a moment he had drawn the great screen a little
closer round the table where the sleeping Van Dronk sat,
and resumed his own place opposite the general. The

259

screen was now arranged so that no one entering the room could see the person seated at the table without approaching and looking round its curtain. O'Flynn called out, imitating Van Dronk's voice: "Wat belieft U? What you want?" Instantly he heard the door open and the tread of Trusham as he entered the room; then the voice of Trusham spoke:

"An envoy from the enemy, with a safe-conduct, asks to see you."

O'Flynn now did a daring thing: he carried on the conversation between himself and the unconscious general, parodying Van Dronk's voice very happily. "The devil!" he cried, mimicking the guttural Dutch tone. "Houd op. Wacht een oogenblick. Wait a minute." Then, speaking in his own voice, he entreated: "Oh, General darling, maybe it's somebody come after me; sure, you'll never be after giving me up." Returning to Van Dronk's voice, he continued: "Be not alarmed, mijn vriend, you shall in safety be kept." Raising his voice he called to Trusham: "Wat wilt gij zeggen? Why do you me like this interruption?"

Trusham explained: "Your pardon, General, but the matter seems urgent. This person, who declines to give his name or show his face, knows and uses our secret password."

Flynn, with the Van Dronk's voice upon him, muttered: "The devil! This must important be." He became Irish again as he pleaded: "Oh, General, for the love of Heaven, put me somewhere in safety"; and he answered his own pleading as Van Dronk: "Be easy, mijn vriend, you shall in my bedroom go." Again he called to Trusham in the voice of the Dutch general: "Where is this personage?"

THE FALL OF KNOCKMORE

"He waits at the gate, General," Trusham answered, "pending your decision."

Flynn, still speaking as Van Dronk, commanded: "So. Send him to me at once."

Then, as soon as he knew that Trusham had gone out and closed the door behind him, he muttered to himself, "Now, who the devil can this be, and what the devil am I to do?" He addressed the sleeping Van Dronk reproachfully. "If I'd known you were going to have visitors, General dear, I'd have kept you awake a bit longer. As it is, I must take your place for a while, my boy."

A whimsical idea had occurred to Flynn, born of his recent brief successful attempt to mimic Van Dronk's voice: he would carry on still further an imposture so successfully begun. Swiftly he lifted Van Dronk's enormous black periwig from his head, leaving him to look grotesque enough with his round bald skull shining in the fire-light. Flynn pulled the periwig well over his own fair hair, adjusted it to his face to conceal it as much as possible with the drooping black ringlets; then he put on Van Dronk's great military cloak and huge black hat, pulling the latter well over his face and drawing up the collar of the cloak high above his chin.

Taking hold of the great arm-chair in which Van Dronk sat, he swung it bodily round with its occupant so that there was nothing visible of the sleeping man to any one entering the room. Then he blew out the candle that flickered on the table, leaving the room to be lit only by the fitful flames of the fire. He seated himself by the table and waited for events with one hand firmly clasped on the butt of Van Dronk's pistol.

A moment later there came a knock at the door. "Kom

binnen," Flynn called out, and immediately Trusham entered the room followed by a man heavily enveloped in a military cloak. Flynn was mightily curious to ascertain the identity of Van Dronk's mysterious visitor, but in the dim light he could make nothing of him. Flynn made a gesture of dismissal to Trusham, who immediately left the room, and Flynn was left alone with the stranger.

The stranger advanced to speak, and instantly Flynn, with a pang of horror and a thrill of triumph, recognized the voice of my Lord Sedgemouth.

"General Van Dronk—" Sedgemouth began.

But Flynn lifted his hand, and still speaking with the heavy Dutch speech of Van Dronk, said to him, "Stop. First of all, give the password."

"Nassau," Sedgemouth answered at once.

Flynn thanked him. "So. Excuse. I am a man of few words. Who are you?"

"With your permission," Sedgemouth replied coldly, "I will keep my name to myself. I am properly accredited, as you may believe, from my knowledge of the secret password, and as you will know when you do me the favor to read this."

As he spoke he drew a letter from his breast-pocket and handed it to Flynn, who, taking it, went toward the fireplace and glanced at it by the light of the fire; then he turned to Sedgemouth. "You know the contents of this letter?" he asked.

"I do," Sedgemouth answered.

"Repeat them," Flynn ordered.

Sedgemouth obeyed his wish: "In this letter you are instructed by your august master, King William, to open communication with your enemy's general, offering to surrender this castle into his hands if you and your garrison are allowed to march out with all the honors of war."

Flynn grunted. "A very strange letter," he said thickly.

"But one," Sedgemouth said dryly, "that I presume you are prepared to obey."

"Wacht een oogenblick," Flynn replied; "I am a man of few words. Who are you?"

"That is not necessary—" Sedgemouth began.

But Flynn interrupted, insisting, "It is for me necessary. I suppose I speak with Lord Sedgemouth?"

Sedgemouth shrugged his shoulders. "Suppose what you please."

Flynn continued in his broken English: "This is an astonishing order for me who can this castle for a year hold. There must be good reasons for this so astonishing order."

My Lord Sedgemouth began to grow impatient. "Of course there are good reasons," he said sharply.

"Tell them me," Flynn commanded.

"You have your orders," Sedgemouth responded angrily.

"Which I not understand," Flynn continued. "Perhaps I do not English very well know. I must have some reason why I should this thing do."

My Lord Sedgemouth seemed to think that it were best to humor this troublesome Dutch gentleman. "I can say no more than this, that on your obedience depends a plot to rid King William of King James."

Flynn was pertinacious. "How shall the surrender of this stronghold to the enemy rid King William of King James?"

My lord condescended to explain a little. "The surrender of this castle to Lord Sedgemouth means the

18   263

appointment of Lord Sedgemouth to such a post of confidence about the person of King James as will enable him to facilitate the plot."

"A plot to kill King James?" Flynn said hoarsely.

Sedgemouth put the matter in another way. "A plot to get King James out of the way," he said suavely. "Now, are you satisfied?"

Flynn grunted, "Quite satisfied."

"Then you will surrender the castle to-morrow?" Sedgemouth asked.

Flynn nodded. "To-morrow," he acquiesced.

My Lord Sedgemouth saluted him. "I take my leave," he said.

"Your visit has delighted me," Flynn observed politely. He called out, "Hulloa, Lieutenant," and Trusham entered the room. "Send the gentleman to the gate."

Sedgemouth again saluted him. "Good - night, General."

"Good-night," Flynn responded. He waited until Sedgemouth and Trusham had disappeared and then began to carry out his deferred preparations, talking to himself the while. "Here's a pretty kettle of fish; oh, my dear lord, you're a bigger rogue than I took you for. You mustn't know for a bit how I've fooled you, though." And all this while O'Flynn's Own catching their deaths of cold at the foot of the rock, poor dears."

He took off Van Dronk's periwig as he spoke and replaced it on the round head of the slumbering Dutchman; Van Dronk's cloak and hat he returned to the chair from which he had taken them. Picking up his own hat from the table where it lay, he went to the window and opening it cast the hat circling and whirling into the air. Then he began to pay out the long coil of fine silk rope with which he was provided, murmuring to himself the while as he did so: "Sure this is more ingenious than the taking of Troy. Ulysses with his wooden horse was a joke to O'Flynn with his fishing-tackle."

The rope swung lax from his strong hands, but presently it appeared to tighten. "I think I feel a bite," he murmured; "yes; here they come, the bold heroes." As he felt the restrain on the rope he began slowly and steadily to haul it up until after a little while the grappling-hooks of the rope-ladder came within his reach. He fixed them firmly to the window-sill and waited for what seemed an incalculably long time, though it was really only a matter of a few minutes until he saw the head of the first man mounting up to him through the darkness. He drew aside and in another moment Conamur had scrambled through the window and climbed in. He was rapidly followed by Coin, Gosling, Winshaw, and half-a-dozen others of the O'Flynn's Own. The men ranged themselves noiselessly in the great room obedient to the warning of O'Flynn's uplifted finger.

"Now, boys," Flynn whispered, "it's as quiet as mice you'll be, for though I've muzzled the old cat we aren't out of the trap yet."

"God bless you, Captain darling," Coin muttered approvingly.

"Whist, now," Flynn replied; "you remember what you have got to do?"

"Yes," Conamur answered.

Flynn remembered honest Trusham waiting in the antechamber, and he wished the latter to come to no harm. "There's a lad outside," he whispered, "that I don't want to hurt, but he must be got rid of. Stand there in the darkness."

The men drew back into the darkest corner of the room, silent and motionless, holding their breaths. Flynn went to the door of Van Dronk's bedroom hard by the fireplace, opened it, withdrew the key from the lock inside and placed it in the lock outside; then he went toward the main door and called out in a loud voice, "Lieutenant!" Immediately Trusham entered the room.

Flynn greeted him amiably. "The General wants you," he explained; "he's in his bedroom."

There was nothing surprising in the O'Flynn's statement, nothing to cause Trusham the slightest suspicion of alarm. Instantly, Trusham crossed the floor, and, knocking, entered the general's bedroom; in another instant Flynn had shut the door behind him and locked it. He then turned toward his men who now emerged from the protection of the darkness. "O'Flynn's Own, follow me!" he cried, and left the room rapidly, with his fellows at his heels.

For a moment silence reigned in the great room, a silence speedily broken by the voice of Trusham, who discovered, in the first place, that General Van Dronk was not in his bedroom; and, in the second place, that he, Trusham, was locked into that room. Trusham rattled at the handle of the door angrily: "There is no one here," he shouted. "I say, there is no one here, and the door is locked." He shook the door fiercely, but he was unable to open it. "I can't get out," he repeated; "will you please open the door?"

As no one obeyed his request Trusham began to get

seriously alarmed. "What is the matter?" he again shouted. "Let me out, let me out."

At this moment his fears were increased by the ominous tolling of the castle bell. "General, are you there?" he yelled. "Open the door, or I will blow it open."

He paused for a moment, then, plucking the pistol from his belt, he fired at the lock and shattered it. The door was soon opened, and Trusham, with the smoking pistol in his hand, sprang into the room. As he turned to the fireplace he saw the motionless figure of Van Dronk huddled helplessly before the fire in his chair. Trusham shook him violently by the shoulder, but failed to rouse him. "Good God! General!" he cried, "what is all this? Wake up! Wake up!"

Looking wildly about him, he caught up a bottle of wine, poured some of the contents into a cup and dashed the liquor into Van Dronk's face. The touch of the cool fluid did something to restore Van Dronk to his senses; he opened his eyes and stared stupidly at Trusham.

Outside, the night was now full of noises, the shouting of voices, the discharging of firearms, and the tolling of the great bell.

"What the devil are you making this noise for?" Van Dronk demanded, sleepily.

Trusham shook him violently. "Rouse yourself, General; something has gone wrong."

Van Dronk, aided by Trusham, managed to struggle to his feet. "Heaven and hell," he cried, "I begin to remember. Where is that damned scoundrel?"

"Not the Irishman?" Trusham cried, beginning to understand what had happened.

"Yes, the damned Irishman," Van Dronk grunted. "The castle is betrayed! To arms!"

As he tried with Trusham's aid to cross the floor the great door opened and O'Flynn entered the room followed by a number of O'Flynn's Own.

"The castle is ours, General," Flynn cried, cheerfully, to the stupefied Dutchman and the astonished Englishman. "God save King James! I'll have to trouble you for your sword, General."

Sullenly Van Dronk, who was now fairly restored to consciousness by the shock of the sudden catastrophe, drew his sword from its sheath and handed it to the victorious Irishman.

"Well, General," Flynn went on, "if you didn't save my life at Schwartzheim, you did me a good turn this night by believing my story, and one good turn deserves another." He turned to Conamur: "Lieutenant Conamur, find horses for General Van Dronk and Lieutenant Trusham and send them under escort with the compliments of the O'Flynn to General Schomberg's camp. There you can still serve King William, General."

Conamur evidently questioned the discretion of his chief. "Why do you let them go, sir?" he asked, in a whisper.

And Flynn answered him in another. "I have my reasons for wishing them out of the way just now." He addressed Van Dronk again: "Allow me, General," he said. As he spoke he took from Van Dronk's belt the bunch of keys which symbolized the possession of the castle. "Good-night, General." Then, as Van Dronk and Trusham were removed under escort, to be sent as the O'Flynn had commanded, to General Schomberg's camp, he turned to Conamur with a smile, swinging the keys on his finger, "These," he said, "are for my Lady Benedetta."

XXVII

FEW buildings have undergone more changes under the control of cormorant devouring time than Dublin Castle. The traveller of to-day would seek in vain for any traces of the splendid Presence Chamber which the Duke of Tyrconnel had caused to be renovated and decorated in honor of his royal master. Splendid tapestries adorned the walls whose original covering of pale-oak panelling seemed to need no other adornment than its own natural beauty. The banners of great Irish Houses that loved their king hung from the gilded and painted ceiling, and stately pictures and gleaming armor added to the richness of the magnificent apartment.

On the night that followed the capture of Knockmore the Presence Chamber was a blaze of color in readiness for the entertainment that James was giving in honor of that event. But as yet the Presence Chamber was deserted, save for a few servants that were busy in making the final preparations for the evening's festivities. He that appeared to be the head man among these servants, and who carried a wand in his hand and wore a chain of office about his neck, was a man of uncertain age with a calm impassive face which seemed as if denied by nature the power of expressing any strength or other emotion. This man was now giving orders to the other servants in a quiet even voice, and his orders were obeyed with that alacrity of precision accorded to him that knows how to command whether he be no less than an emperor or no more than a majordomo.

Presently the door at the farther end of the hall opened cautiously and the head of Master Burden showed through the opening. Master Burden and his fellowship of players, united now temporarily at least, after the incursion of the majority of its members into the field of war, had been bidden to the castle to divert the king. In the castle they had been entertained, and were now making their way to the room in which they were to give their performance. Master Burden's white face with its mane of sable locks looked all round the splendid apartment with some degree of uncertainty. Then he caught sight of the chief serving-man, who had just dismissed his subordinates on the completion of their task, and entering the room he advanced majestically toward him. "I seek the Gold Room," he said, with a dignified salute.

The calm-faced man pointed in the direction of the door opposite to that by which Master Burden had entered. "Yonder," he said, briefly, and Master Burden immediately returning to the door by which he had come in opened it and cried, "Come, friends."

Thereupon Mistress Oldmixon, Mistress Fancy Free, and Masters Conamur, Tulpin, and Winshaw entered the Presence Chamber clad in their players' costumes.

Master Burden, about to lead his little company in the direction indicated by the serving-man, suddenly paused as if attracted by something familiar in the serving-man's countenance, clapped his hand to his forehead dramatically and cried, "Surely, I am not deceived; you are our old friend, the drawer of the 'Isle of Cyprus'?"

Hendrigg saluted him gravely with a quiet smile of acquiescence. "Yes, sir," he said; "I am now in the castle service, thanks to my Lord Sedgemouth. Will you take a little refreshment?" As he spoke he pointed with his wand of office to an adjacent table whereon there stood a number of flagons of wine and shapely foreign glasses.

Master Conamur tickled his chin. "We have been well feasted," he said thoughtfully; "but a glass of wine is always—" He paused for a minute, evidently in the hope of saying something effective, but the desired inspiration failing him, he concluded lamely enough, "a glass of wine."

While he had been speaking the rest of the players had gathered round the table and accepted gratefully enough the administrations of Hendrigg, who filled glass after glass for their satisfaction.

Mistress Oldmixon lifting a well-filled goblet, protested, "I could not drink another sip," and drained the vessel to the last drop.

Fancy, with characteristic frankness, declared, "I could," and was as good as her word.

Tulpin, with a morose countenance, sipped furtively at his glass of wine and made a wry face as he sipped. "A poor wine," he ejaculated, "a thin wine," but nobody heeded him, for Master Winshaw was haranguing the company with his richest voice and heaviest manner.

"Oft have I worn crown upon the boards," he was saying, "yet never knew till now how well a king might be provided with drink and victual."

Hendrigg surveyed the players placidly. "You play before his Majesty?" he asked.

Master Burden nodded. "Yes, a trifle of Monsieur Molière's, which our friend, the O'Flynn, has found time to make English."

Tulpin laughed a mocking laugh. "English! Ha! ha!" and turned disdainfully upon his heel.

Mistress Oldmixon protested: "Come, he has a neat wit. I fancy some of my lines, vastly."

Tulpin looked upon her scornfully. "You are easily pleased, madam," he said.

Winshaw declined, "He has an ear, he has an eye, he has a heart."

"You are easily pleased," Tulpin commented.

Conamur put in his word, "He appreciates me."

Tulpin grinned. "He is easily pleased," he said, maliciously.

Master Conamur resented this, and a quarrel might have ensued if at that moment Sir George Mayhew had not entered the Presence Chamber through the door that conducted to the royal apartments. As he entered Hendrigg gave him a respectful salutation and quitted the room.

Sir George addressed the players: "My good friends, his Majesty will rise from table in a few minutes. Let me bring you to the Gold Room."

Master Burden made a magnificent gesture, and enveloped himself in his mantle after the manner of an ancient Roman. "Conduct us, Sir George," he cried; "I shall be glad to run through the words again."

Tulpin put his hand to his forehead with an expression of despair. "More study," he murmured.

Sir George, with a grand air of gallantry, advanced to offer his arm to pretty Mistress Fancy, who was quite prepared to take it, but her intentions were quickly frustrated by Mistress Oldmixon, who glided swanlike between the man and woman and linked herself to Sir George's extended arm.

"You are most polite, Sir George," she simpered, and Sir George, making the best of the mischance, courteously armed his Cleopatra into the Gold Room, where he was followed by Burden and Winshaw.

As Fancy was about to go with the rest Conamur caught her by the wrist and stayed her. "A word with you, Fancy," he said.

Fancy looked at him with a little grimace. "What is it?" she asked. "You have ogled me all day. I like you better since I saw you in a soldier's coat, but 'tis too late for us to play sweethearts."

Conamur looked wise. "I'm not so sure. Is it not time you tired of your flightiness. Let us make a match of it honestly, like a pair of cits."

Fancy laughed softly. "They say a reformed rake makes the best husband. Has the proverb a feminine application?"

"For sure," Conamur agreed. "We should make a most sensible couple."

Fancy began pensively: "Truly, this vagabond life is well enough when a body is young, but youth, God pity us! withers, and then the road is dull. I tell you the sight of our Oldmixon frightens me."

"She seems content," Conamur suggested.

Fancy gave a little shiver. "I would not care for such content. Let me leave the scene with limbs still brisk, lips still kissful, eyes still lively."

Conamur tapped his chest appealingly. "Then marry me."

273

Fancy looked dubious. "I am no poor man's darling—though I would have been so once—and if I marry I must have my ease, which, I fear, you could never give me."

"To that point I tend," Conamur said, gravely. "Though I be a poor player, 'tis in my power to be a rich citizen—my father is a wealthy draper of Bristol—"

Fancy interrupted him with a little shriek of amusement. "Why, you rogue, you always told us you were of noble birth."

Conamur flushed a little as he continued his confession. "He meant me for his trade and his heir, but I hated the shop and loved the buskin, so he disowned me and bade me go to the devil."

"If he saw you now," Fancy suggested, "he would swear you had arrived at your destination."

Conamur continued his story. "He would give his eye-teeth to have me home again; he would make me partner. I should be rich. We could marry and live happy ever after."

"What would the good citizen say to me for a daughter?" Fancy questioned.

"Why," Conamur explained, "we should say nothing about the stage or other matters. We will fake you a parentage; you shall play decorum, simplicity—come, what do you say?"

Fancy looked steadily at the young man. He had always amused her, he was a pleasant companion for all his little vanities. His brief experience of soldiering had given him a manlier carriage that became him well, and if he were really a wealthy man to boot, his proposition was well worth considering. She did not give my Lord

Sedgemouth a thought; that friendship was never meant
to be more than a passing episode in her life. "I'll give
you no answer," she said gravely, "till you come to me
and say that you are sure in your father's friendship—
sure of your fortune."

"You are a damned sensible woman," Conamur cried
enthusiastically. He caught her in his arms and was
about to give her a series of kisses when his intention
and Fancy's attention were diverted by the entry on the
scene of Captain Scully.

The genial soldier made haste to deprecate his ill-timed
arrival. "Don't let me spoil sport, young people," he
entreated.

Conamur looked a little sheepish, but Fancy laughed
gayly. "No sport, but earnest," she asserted.

Even as she spoke Sir George Mayhew returned from
his journey to the Gold Room where he had left the
players. He addressed Fancy in a tone of good-natured
reproach. "Come, young lady, Master Burden is impatient." He hastened to add, "So should I be, if I
waited your coming."

Conamur caught Fancy's hand. "Come, Fancy, come,"
he cried, and the merry pair ran out of the Presence
Chamber like a couple of school-children.

Sir George Mayhew, laughing heartily, went up to
Scully, who said, "Sedgemouth will miss that divine little
devil," and looked after Fancy.

"Must he give her up?" asked Mayhew.

Scully smiled significantly. "Lady Benedetta is peremptory," he declared, and was about to say more when
Lord Fawley entered the apartment. Neither Mayhew
nor Scully had seen Fawley of late, for he had been sent

on service outside Dublin for several days, so they greeted him with much cheerfulness.

"Why, Fawley, where did you spring from ?" Scully cried.

"From Dundalk," Fawley explained; "watching Dutch Billy and his mynheers. Tell me all news."

"Knockmore is taken," Scully began.

"And Van Dronk escaped to William's army," Mayhew continued.

Fawley looked astonished. "Who took the place ?" he asked.

Scully explained, "Why, the magnificent O'Flynn."

Fawley seemed more surprised. "Who the deuce is the 'magnificent O'Flynn' ?" he questioned.

Mayhew reminded him. "The extravagant Rapparee in the Joseph's Coat who pinked Sedgemouth."

My Lord Fawley leaned against the table with an air of extreme surprise. "Damn me black!" he cried, and his words set Scully laughing.

"Do you steal Tyrconnel's oaths ?" he asked.

The sound of an opening door caused him to look up and to observe Sedgemouth, who came into the hall from the king's apartments. "Here comes Sedgemouth, let him tell you the tale," he cried, and as Sedgemouth came near he pointed to the new-comer, "Here is Fawley, ignorant as a fish."

"Welcome back to Dublin," Sedgemouth cried, greeting him.

"Where I hear strange news," Fawley observed; "Knockmore—the O'Flynn—"

Sedgemouth took snuff. "The amazing knave took Knockmore by a trick and filched my laurels."

IN THE PRESENCE CHAMBER

"How was it done?" Fawley inquired.

Sedgemouth explained: "Very simply, he told me himself. He got into the place as a deserter, dropped a rope to a few of his fellows and contrived, with their aid, to lower the drawbridge. Easy enough, once you think of it."

Again Fawley rapped out one of the colored vice-regal oaths: "Paint me purple!"

"The rogue did not rest on his laurels," Sedgemouth went on; "he professes a kind of quixotical devotion to my Benedetta, so he gives her the keys with a flourish and gallops off through the night to Dublin. Tyrconnel told me how our dear king was going to bed when the ambassador from the King of Munster—for so the buffoon styles himself—demanded audience."

"Roast me red!" Fawley commented.

"Now, you may believe," Sedgemouth continued, "that when I learned what happened, I lost no time, weak though I was, in spurring to Dublin. I got there half an hour after the rascal, feeling sullen enough, but his Majesty was all smiles, and I must say the Irishman had acted handsomely. As his only reward he had asked his Majesty to give me the post I now hold, the post of which his officiousness had gone nigh to deprive me."

"Beat me blue!" Fawley gasped, in amazement.

Sedgemouth went on: "Ever since the fellow has been the hero of the hour, and has played the fool gayly. He has made himself Master of the Revels to his Majesty, who, as you know, is not much of a reveller—"

"Gad! no!" Scully cried, emphatically.

"Thus," continued Sedgemouth, "at this moment his Majesty is in that room," and as he spoke he pointed in the direction of the Gold Room, "witnessing some foolery that O'Flynn composed in the trenches, while O'Flynn himself is in that room," and he pointed in the direction of the king's apartments, "teaching Lady Tyrconnel and her ladies to dance Irish jigs and reels for the present delectation of the king. Will you not join his Majesty in the Gold Room?"

"Surely," Mayhew agreed.

"Are you with us?" Scully asked.

"In a moment," Sedgemouth answered; "I keep a tryst here."

Fawley, Mayhew, and Scully betook themselves in company to the Gold Room, and my Lord Sedgemouth was left alone in the great Presence Chamber to his thoughts. They were not pleasing thoughts, it would seem, for as he paced slowly up and down the splendid hall an ugly frown deepened and darkened on his handsome face. His meditations, however, were soon interrupted by the appearance of Hendrigg, who, making sure that he was not observed, addressed my Lord Sedgemouth with quiet familiarity.

"I was waiting for you," he said. "The thing must be done to-night."

"Give me a little longer," Sedgemouth cried, impatiently, but Hendrigg's set face showed no sign of concession.

"Not a day," he said, firmly; "not an hour."

"I'm in a damned quandary," Sedgemouth declared, fretfully. "Lady Benedetta was pledged to wed me after the fall of Knockmore, but because I philandered with Fancy she punishes me by refusing to keep her promise."

"Your matrimonial tangles are nothing to me," Hendrigg said, indifferently. "I have reason to believe that

James Stuart may join his army to-morrow, and our chances go forever. To-night, my lord, to-night."

Sedgemouth looked at him wickedly. "How, if I refuse?" he asked.

Hendrigg took his evil glance with absolute unconcern as he answered him composedly: "You dare not betray King William as you dare betray King James."

Sedgemouth grinned viciously at him. "How if I arrest you?" he asked; "deliver you to the justice of James Stuart?"

Hendrigg was never a laughing man, but he did almost laugh now. "You can prove nothing against me," he said. "My presence here is due to your patronage. Cease to be childish, my lord." He glanced over his shoulder as he spoke, "Here comes the lady."

Benedetta entered the room at the moment, coming from the royal apartments. Hendrigg paused for a moment by the table as if he had been busy there, and then, with a respectful salutation, withdrew from the hall. Benedetta advanced slowly to Lord Sedgemouth, and he moved eagerly toward her. "You sent for me, my lord?" she asked, gravely.

Sedgemouth framed his face to its most winning smile, tuned his voice to its tenderest utterance as he pleaded, "Why do you treat me so unkindly?"

Benedetta shook her head. "I think I have acted very gently by you."

Sedgemouth's voice expressed contrition. "I will not deny that I have acted ill, yet every man of fashion does alike."

"Then I would have my lover out of fashion," Benedetta said steadily. "The true lover should love his lady so

19   279

much that she should seem the rarest gift of God to man, and he should have no thought of another. Is there no such love of man for woman? I think there is; I know there is."

"There is," Sedgemouth protested; "and it reigns in my heart. I have done wrong and I ask pardon for my fault. Give me yourself, and all other women will vanish from my world. Forgive me; seal your forgiveness with the gift of this loved hand to-night."

Benedetta found herself strangely indifferent to Sedgemouth's appeal. "It is impossible," she said resolutely, and wondered at her resolution as she spoke.

"It is possible," Sedgemouth insisted. "The castle chaplain will perform the ceremony this very night; I have his promise—"

Benedetta interrupted him. "You go too fast. You ask forgiveness, and I forgive; but you have hurt me to the heart. A week ago I would have married you with my eyes shut, but now I must be more sure, now I must put you to your probation. Prove faithful and loyal for a year and I will listen to you."

Sedgemouth's chafing temper began to get the better of his simulated amiability. "This is childish," he cried; "I want to marry you at once—now. Who knows what may happen in a year, in a week, in a night?"

Benedetta looked fixedly at her lover. "If you love me truly," she said slowly, "you will be glad to prove your love." She dipped him a courtesy and gave him a melancholy smile; "I must not keep her ladyship waiting any longer." Then she moved slowly out of the Presence Chamber, going toward the royal apartments, and Sedgemouth made no attempt to stay her course. He knew enough of women to understand that when a woman really was resolved, she, as he put it, really was obstinate.

Hendrigg, who had been lurking behind a door, now joined Lord Sedgemouth. "Is the lady complaisant?" he asked.

"I must wait upon her pleasure," Sedgemouth answered, frowning.

"We cannot wait upon her pleasure," Hendrigg said with decision.

Sedgemouth snapped his fingers. "No; that tale is told. I suppose there will be fair heiresses at William's Court."

"Plenty," Hendrigg replied emphatically.

"And no cursed Irishman to dance attendance," Sedgemouth added, sourly. "This damnable O'Flynn has a plaguy knack of interference."

"He will not interfere with us," Hendrigg declared; "since he anticipated your lordship in the taking of Knockmore, he has done nothing but play the fool, drinking with the players and dancing with the fine ladies. Why, he did not recognize me but now, though he looked me full in the face."

"I wish I could father our treason on him," Sedgemouth murmured; "for he airs his service on my lady too gayly."

"Enough of him," Hendrigg said sharply. "What time does the king retire?"

"About midnight," Sedgemouth answered. "I understand that his coucher is a mere formality; he dismisses all that wait on him, and often returns here to muse and pace the floor for hours. Be ready at one o'clock. You have the key of the old tower?"

Hendrigg nodded, "Yes."

"Your men are disposed about the castle ?" Sedgemouth asked.

"Yes," Hendrigg said again. "True Puritans, worthy disciples of the men who killed Charles Stuart."

"There will be no guard in the old tower," Sedgemouth affirmed. "Your way will be quite clear."

Hendrigg looked pleased. "Good," he said.

XXVIII

A LETTER FROM O'ROURKE

THERE was no more to be said, and Hendrigg was about to quit my Lord Sedgemouth's company when the door from which Master Burden had entered the hall some little time before was opened again, and Master Beggles popped in his bird-like head. Seeing Lord Sedgemouth, whom he recognized, Beggles entered the room and advanced toward him, saluting him deferentially. "I crave your lordship's pardon," he began, but Sedgemouth interrupted him rudely:

"Who the devil are you?" he asked.

"My name is Beggles," Beggles explained, and was allowed to explain no more, for my Lord Sedgemouth interrupted him again:

"Go to the devil, Beggles," and with that my lord turned on his heel and quitted the hall.

Master Beggles turned appealingly and apologetically to Hendrigg. "I did but wish," he declared, "to learn where I shall find the O'Flynn."

Hendrigg, with the faintest of smiles flitting over his set face, took Master Beggles by the arm and conducted him up the length of the great chamber to the doors that led to the dancing-hall. He pointed to these doors and spoke, "He's yonder, with the vice-reine and her ladies, teaching them Irish dances."

"How can I get at him?" Beggles inquired.

Hendrigg looked at him and spoke impassively: "Stick your head through the door and whistle," he advised.

Beggles bowed to him profoundly. "I am much obliged to you."

Hendrigg smiled his grim smile and left him. Master Beggles, believing the advice was given in good truth, and taking it in good faith indeed, made so bold as to open the great doors and thrust his bird-like head through the opening. In the distance in the dancing-room he could see a number of ladies footing it nimbly to brisk music, and the O'Flynn in the midst of them.

"There he is," Beggles murmured, "in the thick of them, jigging like a chicken." He made a desperate but not very successful attempt to whistle, that produced no result. "He doesn't hear me," he wailed; "he doesn't see me."

In his efforts to attract the O'Flynn's attention he now enforced a horrid sound to issue from his lips, which had the desired effect. O'Flynn came dancing down the floor toward Beggles with the Lady Belinda Fanshaw on the one arm and the Lady Barbara Jarmyn on the other; Beggles retreated before his coming, backing into the hall, and Flynn with his fair companions danced after him through the doors, which closed behind them, and stood facing him.

"You thief of the world," Flynn cried, good-humoredly; "why do you stand whistling there?"

Lady Barbara looked at Beggles in amazement. "What do you want, funny man?" she asked.

"I want the O'Flynn," Beggles explained.

Lady Belinda appeared amused at the explanation. "Why, everybody wants the O'Flynn," she said. She turned to her companion, "But we can't spare you, can we, O'Flynn?"

Flynn addressed the fair ladies, apologetically: "Dainty angels," he said, "I crave your patience. I read urgency on yonder solemn countenance: I will be with you directly."

Barbara laid an impressive hand upon his arm. "Mind you are, O'Flynn," she said.

Belinda gave him a commanding smile. "Or we shall be very angry," she promised.

Then the two ladies went back to the dancers and Flynn was left alone with Master Beggles.

Flynn addressed Master Beggles with a certain imperative tone of assertion in his voice. "Why do you come bothering me?" he asked, "when I'm teaching the angels to dance in Irish?"

Master Beggles produced from an inner pocket a letter that was sealed in many places. It was addressed in a large scrawling hand, and was dirty with many finger-marks. "There has come a letter for you, O'Flynn," Beggles said, as he handed the letter to Flynn, "that was carried by a countryman." As Flynn took the letter he continued, "And now, if you will allow me—"

But Flynn, who was studying the document curiously, paid no attention, but read aloud the address, which ran: "'To the O'Flynn, God bless him, at the place of James Stuart in Dublin. Haste, haste, post haste.'" Then he paused and eyed the handwriting again. "Sure," he said, "I've seen that strange hand before."

By this time Beggles had got out his note-book and was holding it tentatively toward O'Flynn, while he murmured, "I have been casting a quiet eye over my accounts, and—"

THE O'FLYNN

But Flynn still continued to pay no heed to his hench-man's remarks. "Well," he said, "the best way to learn is to open it." He tore the letter open and began to read, "'Master darling'—" Then he cried, "Why, by the holy, 'tis from O'Rourke."

Beggles plucked anxiously at his sleeve, "As I was say-ing," he continued, "I've been looking into our affairs and I find—"

Flynn, indifferent to his solicitude, read the letter rapidly through to himself; then he struck an emphatic blow on his thigh. "Well, in all the world," he cried, "Was there ever? Sure it beats Banagher!"

Master Beggles continued his plaintive screed to deaf ears, "That my capital is burning out like a candle-end, and as Midsummer Day is at hand, I suggest that we should journey to your castle to unearth the treasure."

Flynn turned upon him with a beaming face, and a great shout of laughter. "Treasure! Treasure, is it?" he cried. "Man alive, there is a treasure; just listen to this—" He shook the letter for a moment in Beggles' face and then began to read it aloud: " 'Master darling, may all the saints and angels protect you and continue your steady finger on the trigger and your strong head for the drink. This is to tell you what you'll scarce be believing, that I've found the old treasure after all, and where do you think it was all the time? Under the old pigsty where there hasn't been a pig for ages; but I bought a fat pig with part of the money your honor gave me, to make the old castle seem more homelike, and, in tidying up for the poor beast, sure I stuck my spade into the thick of it. Sure there never was so much gold to-gether since the beginning of the world.' "

286

A LETTER FROM O'ROURKE

He turned to Beggles, his voice shaking with laughter, the tears of laughter running from his eyes. "Now, look at that," he shouted; "never say that the age of miracles is past."

Beggles pointed a claw-like finger at him. "But, sir, you seem surprised—" he began.

But Flynn silenced him with another shout, "Well, and wouldn't you be surprised if you found a heap of gold in a pigsty?"

Beggles addressed him in a horrified voice. "You don't mean to tell me that you didn't think there was a treasure?"

Flynn reproved him joyously: "Now, what business would I have to be thinking there wasn't a treasure when the treasure was there all the time? What, am I to be doubting the munificence of Providence? But if ever there was a place on earth that wanted a treasure to enliven it, Castle Famine is that spot."

"Why this hilarity?" Beggles questioned piteously; "and why has the treasure been revealed before the appointed day? I understood that by the terms of the will—"

"Oh, damn the will!" Flynn cried, still shaking with laughter. "Hark ye, Beggles, if you ask no questions, I'll tell you no lies. Sure this is no time for argufying. Dance, man, dance!" As he spoke he clutched his worthy paymaster by the hands and began spinning him wildly round and round the room.

Beggles, gasping for breath, implored him to stop: "Excuse me, I was never a dancing man; I get dizzy—indeed I do."

But Flynn in his boundless celerity persisted in leaping

and capering. "Skip, man! spin, man! jig, man! for
'tis the light heart you ought to have this day. Twenty
per cent. is it? Sure, you shall take thirty now and
welcome, you blundering old money-monger."

But he interrupted his mad dance suddenly as Benedetta
came into the hall from the dancing-room, and looked
in astonishment at the capering pair.

"What is this, O'Flynn?" she asked. "The vice-reine
sends me to bid you finish her lesson, and I find you dancing with this gentleman."

Flynn instantly released Beggles, who reeled heavily
into the nearest seat.

"Your ladyship must excuse me," Flynn said, "and her
ladyship must excuse me, but this is a little dance of joy
on my own account." He turned to Beggles, "Be off with
you," he commanded; "I'll square accounts by-and-by.
Sure, it's the merry man I am this day." And Beggles
with spinning head staggered out of the chamber.

Then Flynn turned to Benedetta, who said to him gravely,
"Do you know, O'Flynn, that you haven't spoken to me
since we parted at Knockmore?"

O'Flynn looked at her wistfully. "I have nothing to
say," he replied.

"But I have something to say," Benedetta went on; "I
have seen Fancy Free; I have spoken with Fancy Free."

"The devil you have," Flynn cried; "saving your
presence."

Benedetta looked at him half sorrowfully, half angrily:
"Well, O'Flynn, what shall we say to each other?" she
asked. "For you told me a lie about Fancy Free, and
I made a fool of myself, and neither of us show very
glorious."

A LETTER FROM O'ROURKE

Flynn sighed, " 'Tis Don Quixote I seem to be, most of the time, trying to do good and putting my foot in it."

Benedetta stretched out her hand to him and he took it for a moment. "Well, I thank you for what you did," she said, "because you did it to spare me pain—and so let me remind you that you are keeping her grace waiting." She turned to go, but Flynn stopped her.

"Wait a moment," he said; "I have something to say to you after all. Since first I got the glad sight of you I have wooed you, in season and out of season, and 'No' has always been your answer. Now, I've laid the strong vow on myself that I won't ask you again, pretty lady, never again; it's yourself will have to do the asking next time, if so be as you come to want me."

"How, if you have to wait till Doomsday?" Benedetta asked.

"I'll wait," Flynn answered, solemnly.

Benedetta looked curiously at him. "How solemn you are," she said.

Flynn nodded: "Maybe I feel solemn for once in a way. We are a fanciful people; we make friends with the fairies; some of us have the second sight. I feel to-night that something might happen to change our lives. Oh! it's only dreaming I am; but, whatever does happen to us in the unknown, I want you to believe that even this soldier of fortune does not always fight for his own hand."

Benedetta looked at him very kindly. "I know," she said, "you will always prove a gallant gentleman. Ah! here comes the king."

XXIX

AN IRISH REEL

KING JAMES entered the Presence Chamber between Tyrconnel and his duchess and followed by a brilliant company of ladies and courtiers. James carried himself with a gravity that approached austerity: he was clad entirely in black, relieved only by his blue ribbon and the lustre of his star. His stern features lighted up as he beheld O'Flynn: he turned to Lady Tyrconnel and said:

"I declare, your Grace, your Irishman is a most diverting table-mate." Then addressing O'Flynn, he asked, "Do you follow the wars with as merry a heart?"

"Yes, sire," Flynn said with a low bow, "and small credit to me. If a soldier cannot wear a cheerful face that follows the finest trade in the world, how shall the poor civilian seem gay that trusts the soldier's breastplate to defend him?"

James's native sternness of demeanor seemed to relax as he spoke with O'Flynn. "Further to urge your argument," he said, with a faint smile, "the people should be the happiest that were ruled by a mirthful sovereign."

"Why, sire," Flynn declared, "when the king laughs his subjects are like to laugh with him; but if he wear a frowning face the people are like to laugh at him."

"Indeed, sir, and why so?" the king asked.

AN IRISH REEL

"Because," Flynn said, frankly, "to my thinking, the man has no right to be a king who is not grateful to God that has given him the chance."

King James sighed. "What God has given, man sometimes takes away; but I think I should be as merry as ever my brother was if I had you by my side." He paused for a moment, and then said, more gayly, "If we keep Christmas in Whitehall, none but you shall be our Lord of Misrule."

Flynn bowed very low. "'Tis the proud man I am to hear your Majesty say so. But your diversions are not ended yet, if I have your Majesty's leave to direct them."

James extended a complacent hand. "Do as you wish, O'Flynn; you are a king's king to-night." He turned to Tyrconnel, "Does he not merit our complaisance, my lord?"

"My liege," the duke declared, with a broad grin, "I call him the damnedest merriest rascal I ever met."

"That's great praise from your lordship," Flynn protested. He turned and addressed the courtiers, "Now, gentlemen, hasten to yonder room and claim your partners, and while you are busy on that sweet business I will divert his Majesty with a merry tale that came near to cracking my ribs when I heard it."

While the gentlemen, in obedience to the behest of O'Flynn, whom they accepted for the evening as their master of ceremonies, were busy in selecting their partners from among the bevy of beautiful women that thronged the hall O'Flynn made bold to draw the king aside out of ear-shot of any present and to address him with a great air of merriment, laughing frequently as he spoke.

"My liege," he began, "I have played the fool all day,

and must wear my cap and bells a little longer; but I have something grave to say to you, sire, and I pray you to take it as if it were the best jest in the world, for there are eyes upon us and I would have those eyes believe us merry. Laugh, sire, laugh."

James looked curiously at O'Flynn. Though he knew but little of the eccentric adventurer, that little had induced him to believe in his courage, his honor, and his fidelity, he obeyed him now in laughing as heartily as if, indeed, he had been listening to the merriest tale. "Go on," he said.

Flynn continued, "Sire, when I brought you the news of the fall of Knockmore I brought you other news in the same bag."

With a smile James spoke, "You told me that my Lord Sedgemouth was a villain, and yet, in the same breath, you begged me to show him favor."

O'Flynn nodded: "Only that we might thereby secure his accomplices. The plot to which Lord Sedgemouth is privy depends upon his holding this post near your person. It has been given out that your Majesty intends to join the army to-morrow, therefore the attempt will be made to-night." He strove to banish the growing anxiety on the king's face, as he communicated his serious tidings. "Laugh, my liege," he urged, "laugh!"

James laughed heartily. "It is a droll story," he said, aloud, though there was no one near enough to hear his words.

Flynn continued still with a face beaming with mirth: "There is a fellow serving here whose face I have seen before once as a drawer in an inn frequented by my Lord Sedgemouth, whose voice I heard once before, when he

played highwayman on the Cork road to rob Lady Benedetta of the jewel your Majesty's consort sent to you.
Laugh, sire, laugh!"

James, still laughing, asked, "What do you wish me to
do?"

"Put yourself in my hands, sire," Flynn requested.
"My men are concealed in the castle, every man as sober
as a judge and sworn to sobriety till the night's work be
done. If your Majesty will but leave the stage to me I
will promise you as pretty a comedy as ever dished a Whig.
Laugh, sire!"

The laughing king laid his hand for a moment on
O'Flynn's shoulder. "We can refuse you nothing,
O'Flynn," he said. "Do what you please, how you
please."

O'Flynn bowed. "Now, is not that a good story, your
Majesty?" he asked in a loud voice, and James, still
smiling, answered:

"I protest I never heard a better. You should
have served my brother: he was a merrier fellow
than I."

"Your Majesty pleases me very well," Flynn answered,
and James, laughing at his frankness as much as he had
feigned to laugh at his narrative, made a gesture which
brought the courtiers about him again.

"I hear," the king said, addressing O'Flynn, "that you
have promised us some Irish dances for to-night; can
you dance a jig, O'Flynn?"

Flynn grinned. "Sure, I was born dancing a jig, your
Majesty," he said. Then, seeing that the company were
ready, he continued: "Now, my liege, for a right Irish
dance in your honor. Strike up, pipers."

THE O'FLYNN

The company of pipers that Flynn had introduced into the castle now struck up the notes of an Irish reel; O'Flynn found himself facing Benedetta in the merry movements of the dance whose brightness and cheerfulness provoked the pensive king to heartily applaud.

XXX

O'FLYNN THE FIRST

SOME hours later the great Presence Chamber was wrapped in obscurity: the last dance had been danced; the dancers had dispersed; the lights had been put out; the servants had disappeared. The room was only lit by the faint glow on the hearth and the light of a single candle that stood on a table near the fireplace. Another table with a chair by it awaited the coming of the king.

By the fireplace my Lord Sedgemouth stood and waited. Presently he heard a faint scratching sound behind the panel, and, going to that part of the room from which the sound proceeded, he touched the woodwork; the panel slipped back and Hendrigg came out of a secret passage and faced him.

"Is all well?" Hendrigg asked.

"I expect the king instantly," Sedgemouth replied. "I am to read to him here, damn him, till he feels sleepy."

Hendrigg smiled sternly. "He may sleep sound enough to-night. But you should not curse him for his whim; it is easier to deal with him here than in his bed-chamber."

"Your men are ready?" Sedgemouth questioned.

Hendrigg nodded, "They wait in the passage."

He made as if to go, but Sedgemouth restrained him for a moment. "You will not kill save at need?" he asked.

"Not here, at least," Hendrigg cried. "I want no king nor king's corpse to be within the castle walls to-morrow. When he has signed we will pinion him and smuggle him out by the secret stair — hush! I hear footsteps. What signal?"

Sedgemouth took up the book from the table. "I will drop this book upon the ground."

Hendrigg nodded again. "Good," he said, and disappeared through the secret passage, closing the panel behind him.

Sedgemouth returned to the fireplace, and in another instant was bowing profoundly as the black-attired figure of the king came through the door of the royal apartments and advanced slowly through the darkness toward the chair. In this he seated himself with a sigh, his chin drooped upon his breast, the heavy locks of his periwig hid his face; he seemed to be in a mood of profound dejection.

"Shall I read to your Majesty?" Sedgemouth asked, softly.

The melancholy figure huddled in the chair nodded his head in sign of agreement.

"Shall I begin where your Majesty has left a mark?" Sedgemouth continued.

The king nodded again.

Sedgemouth opened the book and glanced at the page: " 'How King James I. of Scotland came to his death—'" he paused. "Why, my liege," he protested, "here is melancholy matter to end so merry an evening. Shall I, indeed, continue?"

As the king again inclined his head in sign of agreement

my Lord Sedgemouth began to read in a clear steady voice:
"'Now, while King James sat in the hall, with his queen
and her ladies, there came one pale with fear that told
how the king's enemies had made their way by stealth
into the castle—'" He paused for a moment and glanced
at the king, who remained motionless. My Lord Sedgemouth resumed his reading: "'Now, from the hall wherein
the king sat there was no issue save by the great door
whither the king's enemies now were hurrying. Then the
queen and her women made to shut the great door, but
some traitor had taken the bolt from the sockets so that
the door could by no means be made fast. Then one of
the queen's ladies, Catherine by name, thrust her white
arm through the iron sockets and said that she would keep
the door while the king hid himself.'"

The head of the king seemed to droop lower and lower
upon his breast; his relaxed arms hung listlessly by his
sides; a faint sound of steady breathing suggested that the
slumber which the king sought had been granted to him.

Lord Sedgemouth, still holding the book in his hand
and reading from it as he moved, crossed the floor toward
the king: "'Now the king seeing himself thus trapped,
made shift to lift a stone and dropped himself into the
cellar that lay beneath the hall—'" Sedgemouth lowered
his voice as he read the last words, for he was now satisfied
that the king was, indeed, asleep. Closing the book and
placing it on the table, he advanced to the secret panel and
pushed it back; leaning into the deeper darkness of the
passage thus revealed, he called softly, and Hendrigg instantly answered his summons.

"The king is asleep," he said; "there was no need to
give the signal. Bring in your men."

THE O'FLYNN

As he spoke, Sedgemouth returned to the centre of the great room: Hendrigg came after him, followed from the secret passage by five men that had drawn swords in their hands; Hendrigg, too, carried a drawn sword. The conspirators ranged themselves in a circle around the sleeping king with their weapons directed against him.

Sedgemouth struck with his hand the king's table and the sleeping figure awoke with a start.

The point of Hendrigg's sword touched the king's breast just above the star. "If you speak one word, you die, James Stuart," he said savagely, and the king in apparent agony of fear did as he was told.

My Lord Sedgemouth, with a mocking laugh, addressed the king: "I trust your liege will forgive me for introducing these gentlemen to your presence. But indeed they have very pressing business with your Majesty, for they wish you to sign this paper." As he spoke he took a paper from Hendrigg's hand and opened it. "This is an act of abdication, James Stuart, which you must either now sign and live, or not sign and die. Will you sign, great King of England, France and Ireland, will you sign, Defender of the Faith ?" The king seemed to shake his head in feeble protest as Sedgemouth continued: "Shall I read it to your Majesty ? My voice will not send you to sleep now." With a cruel clearness he read: "'I, James Stuart, hitherto known of men as James the Second of England, and Seventh of Scotland, being now very sure that it is the will of Heaven and of my people that I should no longer reign over my kingdom, do hereby solemnly surrender my crown to my dear son-in-law William. Given this day of June, 1690, at our Castle of Dublin.'" He paused and looked down scornfully at the huddled

298

figure in black. "Do you now like it, sire? Is it not
well penned? The sight of this to-morrow on every wall
in Dublin will gladden the many that hate you, and
shake the few that love you. Sign, James Stuart,
sign!"

Hendrigg, with his sword still directed toward James's
heart, cried fiercely, "Sign—or die!"

Sedgemouth dipped a pen into the ink and held it forward; the king extended a shaking hand and Sedgemouth
pushed the pen into the trembling fingers. With little
groans of fear the victim hurriedly scrawled a name at the
foot of the paper, and then buried his face in his hands as
Hendrigg caught the paper up triumphantly.

"Good!" he cried, and moved toward the fireplace to
read the signature by the light of the fire. Instantly his
mood of triumph changed. "Damnation!" he screamed.

Sedgemouth was by his side in a moment. "What is
it?" he asked. He caught the paper from Hendrigg's
fingers and read in his turn—"O'Flynn the First!"

Even as he read, the crouching figure in the chair
suddenly stiffened and straightened, and stood up and
the doors leading to the Presence Chamber were flung
open, men carrying torches flooded the room with unexpected light, and the soldiers of O'Flynn's Own crowding
into the room from every entrance, overpowered the conspirators. The seeming king plucked off his hat and periwig, revealing the laughing, excited face of the O'Flynn.
At the same moment King James himself came quietly
through the line of soldiers and advanced to where my
Lord Sedgemouth was standing in the centre of the room,
very pale and motionless.

Hendrigg, standing by him, folded his arms resignedly,

his face as expressionless as ever, "Check-mate," he murmured and said no more.

James advanced to Sedgemouth. "Sedgemouth," he said; "in my time I have become acquainted with many traitors, but never with such a traitor as yourself."

Sedgemouth's face worked convulsively; then he spoke with an air of disdain, weaving the final web for his enemy: "Your Majesty overpraises me," he declared. "There is a better traitor here." He turned and pointed at the O'Flynn. "The Irishman, who has betrayed us and who will betray you. He was our paid creature; it was by us that he took Knockmore. His boasted story is a cloak for the truth. Knockmore surrendered to a paper we gave him, an order from King William, commanding the general to surrender."

James said nothing, but only watched Sedgemouth with a mixture of scorn and dislike on his stern face.

But O'Flynn, still smiling, answered Sedgemouth, and he answered him in the voice of Van Dronk: "Vaarlik, mein vriend. I am a man of few words, but we have met before under like conditions; only then I was General Van Dronk, and you gave me this paper."

As he spoke he took a paper from his pocket and handed it to Sedgemouth, who clutched at it, opened it, and saw that it was the paper which he had given to Van Dronk as he believed, and had signed, as he believed, in obedience to Van Dronk's whim. He looked about him furiously. Hendrigg was standing near in the guard of two soldiers who had disarmed their captive, and one of the soldiers was holding Hendrigg's sword carelessly in his hand. Sedgemouth sprang toward him and wrenched the weapon from his fingers. He turned in fury toward the O'Flynn.

O'FLYNN THE FIRST

"Damn you!" he screamed; "I'll settle you." He made to strike at his enemy, but before he could reach Flynn, Conamur, who was standing near his chief, levelled a pistol he was carrying and fired. My Lord Sedgemouth flung up his arms, dropped the sword, gave a great groan and fell in a heap on the floor.

"So end all traitors," James said, sternly.

Now, by this time, the news that something untoward was going on had began to spread through the castle; there was a hubbub of women's voices, and, as Lord Sedgemouth fell, the Duchess of Tyrconnel, with dishevelled hair and disordered attire, came rushing into the room.

"What is the matter?" she screamed. "Is the king safe?" Then, seeing the king where he stood, she gave a great cry of joy.

James spoke to her gravely: "A wicked plot has been foiled, thanks to O'Flynn. Lord Sedgemouth is dead."

By this time many other courtiers and ladies, roused by rumors and startled by the pistol-shot, were thronging into the room. The words, "Lord Sedgemouth is dead," were repeated from lip to lip. Through the bewildered crowd Lady Benedetta pushed her way, half-dressed, with a large cloak about her; she looked around her with haggard eyes.

"Lord Sedgemouth!" she cried; "where is Lord Sedgemouth?" She caught sight of the body and screamed aloud as she flung herself by the side of the dead man. "Oh! he is dead! He is dead! How did he die?"

The king made as if to speak, but Flynn stayed him with an appealing gesture, as he answered, gravely, "He died—for his king."

XXXI

CASTLE FAMINE AGAIN

SOME weeks later the O'Flynn was sitting again in the front of his hearth at Castle Famine. This time a bright fire blazed in the great chimney, and this time larder and cellar were alike provisioned, but otherwise there was no change in the place, and the place's master, soberly clad in a travelling-suit, sat smoking and seemingly drowned in thought.

Many things had happened since that evening of early summer when he had left that hall with the merry players to seek his fortune in Dublin. The cause of the king was lost and James back in France. The Lady Benedetta, after the death of Lord Sedgemouth, had lain for a while dangerously ill and had been taken to France by her father as soon as she showed signs of recovery, and the secret of Lord Sedgmouth's treason had been kept sedulously from her.

So much Flynn knew, and knew no more of the lady of his dreams. For himself, he had seen to the safety of his treasure, which proved to be large enough to insure him a comfortable fortune, and he was now preparing to take farewell of his ancestral ruin and to follow the war again. The little King of Munster came into the room decently clad now, and looking even more whimsical than before in his new habiliments. He looked wistfully at his master and at last broke the silence.

"Sure, O'Flynn darling, what's the good of sitting daundering there, with never a word to say but only smoke, and your face that sad that it sends me heart to me heels to look at you?"

Flynn blew a cloud of smoke into the air, and turned to him. "You are right, your majesty—you must allow me to call you so, my boy, for since King James has blown back to France, you're the only king with whom I'm on speaking terms—you're right, your majesty, there isn't a ha'pworth of good in it from A to Z, but it's the things that aren't any good to do that are often the sweetest in the doing."

"Arrah, then," O'Rourke asked; "where's the sweetness of sitting there all day drinking smoke like a mummy?"

Flynn answered: "Because while I sit and drink smoke I see sights, your majesty—sights that are good for sore eyes. I see a girl as fair as Queen Mab stand in the gap of a ruined wall and I see an ould soldier that ought to know better trying to whisper the heart out of her young body. You'll be laughing at me, your majesty, for the way I take on."

O'Rourke looked at his master reproachfully. "Oh! master, master, do you think I was born the ould fellow I stand here? Do you think I never had a girl's arm about my neck in all my days?"

"I beg your majesty's pardon," Flynn said contritely; "I'm sure you had a way with you in the days of your juvenility. But the girl I'm thinking of never put her arm about my neck, though I swore like a fool that I'd make her love me."

O'Rourke made an angry gesture; "Sure she wasn't worth the wooing, if she didn't leap into your arms like a live fish."

Flynn held up a warning finger. "Hush! you unnatural ould heathen. What was I—what am I—what shall I ever be to deserve such a darling?"

O'Rourke flicked his hand across his face. "It brings the wet to my eyes," he said, "to hear you so down-hearted. What are you, is it? What harm but you are the O'Flynn, no less, and the equal of any sultan, or Cæsar, or emperor of the far countries, and you were that when you hadn't a shilling, and now aren't you as rich as Crazies?"

Flynn laughed a little bitterly. "The treasure — the treasure—was I forgetting the treasure? Lord, what a cheerful man Master Beggles was when we packed his bags with gold pieces. King James was a ruined exile and Boyne River running red with the blood of brave men, but Master Beggles was happy enough."

"Why shouldn't he be happy?" O'Rourke questioned. "Sure, it's well to be him or a cousin of his with all the money he took off you."

"He gave me good value for it," Flynn said thoughtfully; "and it's little he'd have got if it hadn't been for that blessed pig of yours. Now it's all safe, the treasure is, all shipped to France, and it's a wealthy gentleman your humble servant may call himself for the first time in all his born days. But I'd give all the treasure—aye, and think it little, for—"

"For what then would you be acting so foolish?" O'Rourke asked, with a disapproving frown.

Flynn sighed, "For the jewel that lies at the root of the

rainbow, for the rose that grows east of the Sun, west of the Moon, for the lady that lives in the Land of Youth, for the kisses of the Fairy Queen that make a man think himself immortal—until he dies."

O'Rourke lifted up his hands appealingly to heaven. "Heaven help you, master, if you go on like that; for the kisses of the fairies raise blisters and the rainbow gems are no better than pebbles. Count your guineas while you can, and spend them while you may—and there's the only wisdom."

Flynn shook his fist at him playfully, "Your majesty will never make a poet."

"God forbid," O'Rourke said fervently.

Flynn laughed again: "Maybe you are in the right of it. Well, tell Coin and Gosling to be ready to start at sunset. The ship waits in the bay, and with this wind we should see France to-morrow."

"Why, why will you be going away," O'Rourke asked, wringing his hands. "Why don't you stop here and build up the old place in the way of its ancient grandness? Didn't you tell me yourself that King William—devil take him—doesn't bear you a grudge?"

Flynn smiled. It had been made plain to him in the dangerous days that followed on the Boyne fight that the new king would be willing to accept the O'Flynn's services.

"Dutch Billy would let me stay here if I wanted to stay," he admitted. "But I don't want to stay; I'm afraid of the ghosts."

O'Rourke shook his head. "Sure, the ghosts have all gone with the finding of the treasure."

"Not my ghosts," Flynn said, sadly. "No treasure will

exorcise them; the ghost of a girl in a green gown, the ghost of a man in a shabby white uniform—"

"Don't be taking so," O'Rourke cried, impatiently. "Restore the old place, that will lay the ghosts for certain, and live on the fat of the land like the gentleman you are."

"No, no," Flynn insisted; "let the old place stand as it stands, for so it stood when first she saw it. Do you mind how she came just there, through the gap in the wall, parting the leaves with her fingers, debonair as a flower . . ."

It has always been the tradition in the annals of the O'Flynns that the things which are about to be recorded happened just then, at that very precise moment of time, in order to prove the affection and the esteem in which the good saints of paradise held their soldier of fortune.

The more cautious, the less credulous, may prefer to believe that what happened a little later; that the kind of miracle vouchsafed to the O'Flynn came to pass a little less miraculously; that the reward of his hopes and the satisfaction of his dreams did not follow immediately upon the evocation of an excited memory.

All that is as it may be. It is not for us, however, to quarrel with the chronicles and the credences of an illustrious house, but to retell the tale as it has been told through the generations by the descendants of the O'Flynn of O'Flynn and of Conachor LII., King of Munster.

According to the story then, even as he spoke, the vision he conjured up became reality. Benedetta stood where she had stood before, parting the leaves now and smiling upon the lord of Castle Famine.

"Oh! master, master," O'Rourke cried, with clasped hands; "is it a ghost or a fairy?"

CASTLE FAMINE AGAIN

O'Flynn, without speaking, gave a gesture of dismissal, and O'Rourke silently crept from the room. Then Flynn turned to the girl, who advanced toward him.

"Benedetta!" he cried.

And she called back to him, "O'Flynn!"

"I thought you were in France," he marvelled.

"I was in France," the girl answered, "but the seas are short between France and Ireland, and the wind was kind to my impatience."

"God bless the wind that blew you here," Flynn cried, passionately; "but what have you to do in Ireland now?"

"I have to do justice," the girl answered, gravely.

"Justice!" Flynn echoed.

Benedetta looked grave and spoke very gravely: "Flynn, I have learned a secret thing, and you must answer me honest if what I have been told is true or untrue."

"What have you been told?" Flynn asked.

"I have been told," Benedetta answered, "that the man I loved was a traitor, false to his honor, his sovereign, and his God; and that he was killed while attempting to betray King James to his enemies."

"Who told you this tale?" Flynn questioned.

"Fancy Free," Benedetta answered.

And Flynn repeated the name in astonishment, "Fancy Free!"

"Yes," Benedetta went on; "Fancy Free is married to Conamur—to Conamur who shot my Lord Sedgemouth when he tried to kill you after the failure of his plot to snare King James. A good husband has no secrets from his wife, and what Conamur told Fancy Fancy told me that I might not waste my life in weeping over a dishonored grave. You alone can confirm her story—is the tale true?"

Flynn shook his head, "I have nothing to say."

"You are an honorable gentleman," Benedetta said, softly; "you will not take advantage of the dead. But I have more than the girl's story to go on, for Conamur gave Fancy a paper and Fancy gave the paper to me."

"What paper?" Flynn asked, with a start.

Benedetta answered him slowly: "A paper that you let fall when Lord Sedgemouth attacked you, and that Conamur picked up and concealed. It was an order from William of Orange commanding General Van Dronk to surrender Knockmore to the bearer. That order was indorsed with the signature of the bearer — with the signature of my Lord Sedgemouth. What have you to say?"

Flynn shook his head. "Just nothing," he said, quietly, and there was a moment's pause between the pair.

Then Benedetta spoke again: "Then I must say something. When you and I met I thought I was in love with the man who is dead; I thought that a fair face must be the sign of a fair soul. You saved me from danger—I was grateful—no more. You wooed me and I smiled at your wooing, for my faith was another's. Little by little, as I came to know your worth, that faith was shaken, though I tried to think my idol still worthy of idolatry; tried to deny you the place you were taking in my heart. My love for that other died before his death; yet, when he gave his life, as I believed, for his king I thought it my duty to dedicate myself to his memory, and, if I could, to forget you. When I knew the truth my spirit turned instantly to you. The last time we spoke together you told me that you would woo me no longer—that you would wait till I came to you—"

CASTLE FAMINE AGAIN

"Sure, 'twas the fool talk I was talking," Flynn said, apologetically.

Benedetta advanced toward him holding out her hands: "Flynn, I have come to you. Flynn, do you forgive me? Flynn, do you love me still?"

Flynn gave a great cry of exultation: "Glory be to God that has given me ears this day to hear you, and eyes this day to see you, and hands this day to hold you if you are willing to come to my arms!"

"Will they welcome me?" Benedetta asked.

Flynn stretched out his arms. "Try!" he said, and clasped her in his embrace.

Benedetta released herself a little and looked earnestly into her lover's eyes. "What were you going to do?" she asked.

"Follow the wars," Flynn answered, simply.

"But now?" Benedetta questioned.

Flynn looked at her lovingly. "Sure, it's not for me to say," he declared, "for I've entered the service of a lovely lady, and 'tis she, and she alone, who gives me my marching orders."

"Let us live in France, Flynn," Benedetta whispered, "near to our lonely king."

Flynn cried, cheerfully, "We will live in France near to our king."

Benedetta drew a little closer to him. "Dear lover, God is good to me. Do you recall how I stood at the head of the stairs, and you sang me down them?"

O'Flynn caught her hand and kissed it, kneeling as he did so; then he began to repeat his rhyme of the "Isle of Cyprus":

THE O'FLYNN

"Sure the king has his ribbons, the king has his stars,
To give to the faithful that serve in his wars;
But I'd change all the gifts that the king can command,
For one smile of your eyes, for one touch of your hand."

THE END